HOT-BITES

VOLUME ONE

JORDAN MARIE
JENIKA SNOW

Hot-Bites: Volume One

By Jenika Snow and Jordan Marie

www.JordanMarieRomance.com

support@jordanmarieromance.com

www.JenikaSnow.com

Jenika_Snow@yahoo.com

Books included are:

Book 1: Bought and Pair For
Book 2: Ride My Beard
Book 3: Planting His Seed
Book 4: Jingle My Balls
Book 5: Pitch His Tent

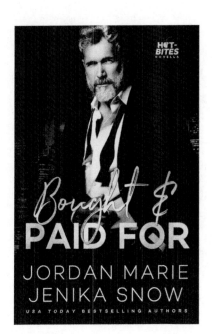

Bought &
PAID FOR
JORDAN MARIE
JENIKA SNOW
USA TODAY BESTSELLING AUTHORS

BOUGHT AND PAID FOR (Hot-Bites Novella)

By Jordan Marie and Jenika Snow

www.JordanMarieRomance.com

support@jordanmarieromance.com

www.JenikaSnow.com

Jenika_Snow@yahoo.com

Copyright © July 2017 by Jordan Marie and Jenika Snow

First E-book Publication: July 2017

Photographer: Juliana Andrade

Cover model: Wander Aguiar

Photo provided by: Wander Book Club

Editors: Kasi Alexander

He wanted my virginity.
He wanted to own me.
I just wanted to be his.

Jackson

I wanted Megan from the moment I first saw her, and nothing would keep me from her.

I could have been called a bastard for knowing her father would fail in paying me for a mutual business agreement, for knowing I would take Megan as payment.

But she was mine and in my world, when I wanted something, I took it. And I wanted her.

She was bought and paid for, collateral damage when her father failed to uphold his end of the deal.

They all think it's only for a week. They're wrong.

I'm keeping her.

Megan

My father couldn't fulfill a debt to Jackson King, but Jackson didn't seem to mind, not when he got me as his payment.

Having been attracted to the brutal businessman for years, I couldn't help but feel arousal and trepidation at what he had planned. He wanted me for a week, to do with as he pleased.

He wanted my virginity.

But I knew this was more than just repaying a debt. This was about

Jackson wanting to own me, not just my body, but every part of who I was.

And the depraved part about it all was the fact that I wanted to give everything to him.

I *wanted* to be his.

WARNING: This is fast and hard ride, featuring an over-the-top Alpha who fights dirty and plays dirtier. It's a safe read, but it's short, filthy and so hot you might need a nice, big, long, cool... drink to get you through to the happy ending.

1

Megan

My heart was thundering, my palms sweating. I looked between my father and the man who was claiming he now owned me. I stared at my father, pissed that he would get himself into the situation, that he always seemed to fuck up on the most monumental levels.

He wouldn't even look at me and I knew it was because he realized how bad the situation really was. With his head downcast, his gaze refusing to meet mine, I could do nothing but want to lash out at him, hurt him in the way he was hurting me right now.

I knew in that moment that he would let Jackson King take me, own my body... fuck me.

"I'm not some piece of fucking property," I almost screamed out. Tears of anger raced down my cheeks, and I felt my face heat.

And then, looking calm, collected, and like he had all the time in the world, Jackson King stared directly into my eyes and smiled. His grin had a chill racing up my spine, this cold sweat covering me, and I knew I should've been afraid instead of aroused.

Jackson King was older, hell, no doubt two decades older than my own twenty-one years, with a headful of short silver and grey hair, and a beard that screamed all man. His body was big, strong, muscular, and despite the situation, he made me feel very feminine.

"Your father owes a debt, and without any funds or any collateral to make up the loss, you're what I'll be taking as his payment." He said those words as if the deal was already done, as if I had no choice in the matter.

I didn't know what my father had done, or why this was happening, but I knew I'd find out eventually.

Forget the fact that I'd wanted Jackson King for longer than I could remember. I didn't "know" him, but he'd been doing business with my father for years, and I knew enough about him through the media that it was like he'd always been in my life.

I could have snorted at the fact that I would assume to know who Jackson King was.

Ever since my father started doing business with him, I'd been fascinated by the man behind the three-piece suits and the billion dollar company. I knew he was ruthless in his endeavors, and that what he wanted, he took.

I just didn't think I would be the object of his taking.

I clenched my teeth together, my anger rising, my annoyance taking over. I stared right in his eyes, not about to back down no matter how intimidating he was.

"You can't make me go with you." I felt pride over actually saying the words and knowing I had power too. "I'm not some piece of property you can own." But the smirk he gave me, that arrogant, all-knowing expression, had this cold feeling rushing over me.

He took a step closer but I held my ground, refusing to back down. He might be powerful in the boardroom, maybe even dominate and dictate to everyone around him, but in this instance I would not bend.

I would not submit.

And when he reached out and tipped my head back with his finger under my chin, I knew there was something inherently wrong with me. The feeling of his flesh on mine, even that small touch, had me instantly wet. I felt my nipples beading, and my inner muscles clenching painfully.

He smiled wider, flashing straight white teeth, but it was more of a predatory expression, one that told me he knew he would get exactly what he wanted no matter what.

"That's where you're wrong, Megan." He ran his thumb along my jawline, eliciting a shiver along my arms. "You'll give me what I want because you love your father, you don't want to see him desolate and broken, and also because..." He leaned in closer so our faces were only inches apart. The scent of his cologne was addicting, and filled my head, making me dizzy, drunk from it all. "You'll come with me because you want me as much as I want you."

And just like that, after he spoke those words— those very *true* words—I knew I would do whatever he said.

Megan

I LEFT with Jackson just an hour ago, my father's words before I left playing through my head.

"Jackson, we can work this out as men. My daughter does not need to be involved in this." He sounded so sincere, *so frightened over everything.*

"It's okay, Dad." I knew he had nothing to offer Jackson as payment. Although I just now realized that. Before Jackson came here demanding payment I just assumed my

father had been stable, that he had money. Apparently I'd been dead wrong.

If I had been able to handle this with paying the debt off myself—sans using my body—I would have, obviously. But I'd barely finished my third year of college, and the jobs I usually worked at were minimum wage, and just for the summer.

As we sat in the back of his limo, the privacy screen up, the air too thick for me to breathe comfortably, all I could do was stare at the man who claimed I was now his.

I forced myself to look away, out the tinted window of the limousine, seeing a grand house come into view. My heart sped up. The car stopped in front of a massive wrought-iron gate, and after a moment the doors swung open and we were ascending this long driveway.

I don't know what I expected, maybe Jackson taking me to his office to deflower me there, showing me that he really did own me. Another chill raced up my spine and I rubbed my arms together. I glanced at Jackson again, and saw he already watched me, his dark eyes locked on mine, this knowing expression on his face.

I was a virgin, and this man, this very attractive, powerful man, who was worldly, and so experienced, would most likely expect me to be the same. What would he do? Did he have any idea that I'd never had sex?

Once the car pulled up to the front doors and the engine was cut, I swear I could feel my heart beating so loudly it filled the back of the vehicle. My throat was so tight, my mouth so dry. I didn't know what to expect, but I had agreed to be Jackson's. I'd agreed to fulfill my father's debt, because even if it wasn't my responsibility to handle his affairs, I did love him and he was all that I had left in the world.

If being with Jackson for this week made things right, then so be it.

I just hoped I could keep my emotions in check. As twisted as it all seemed, I could see myself falling for this intimidating, arrogant man very easily.

2

Jackson

I'm a bastard. You could practically smell the fear that rolled off of Megan in waves. It didn't stop me. Fuck, if it did anything it turned me on. I was rock hard just watching the way her pupils dilated and her breathing picked up the moment we pulled into the drive.

The satisfaction that ran through me at finally having Megan could not be described. I'd envisioned this moment from the first time I saw her.

Her father had just approached me with a business deal, asking for my backing. I knew going in there was no way the venture would pan out. Phillip Beaumont was big on dreams and short on results. Everyone in our circle knew that. Beaumont had taken over his brother Clay's shipping company when Clay died. He had been piloting his own plane, heading toward his private vineyard in Rome when he suffered engine failure. It was a hell of a loss. There were few men I respected, but Clay Beaumont was one of them—his brother, not so much.

Still, he'd approached me at one of the endless charity functions I was obligated to attend. I was bored out of my mind. I just wanted out of there and Phillip Beaumont was keeping me from doing just that. And then it happened. I looked across the room and there she was. She was a vision of innocence in a room full of people who had become hardened by life and jaded by experience.

Long blonde hair, brushed until it was smooth and glittered in the light, framed a pixy-like face with full lips the color of cherries. She was wearing a white gown, simple—almost plain, but it hugged her body like a second skin. It curved around small, upturned breasts, came high up on her neck, but the back dropped down. I could see the line of her spine, that delicate indentation. I instantly dreamt of running my tongue against the skin.

It stopped way too soon.

I wanted it to drop further, revealing the indentation of her ass. Suddenly, I had trouble controlling myself. Me, a man who made billions in a business that demanded complete control of my emotions, wanted to walk over there and rip the dress farther down, pin her against the wall and fuck her right there, in front of everyone. When Beaumont followed my line of sight, that's when I found out who the woman was. *Megan Beaumont.*

In that moment, a decision was made. I would give Beaumont the money he wanted. I would invest in his stupid scheme, because ultimately it would get me the one thing I craved—his daughter.

Even then I knew he'd fuck up... knew she'd be mine.

I was a bastard, but I never claimed to be anything else.

Now, three years later, Megan had become mine.

"Now what?" she asked, after she turned to face me.

"My chauffeur will show you inside and the maid will take you to your room. You will wait there for me."

"You're not coming inside?" she whispered. Her face became so pink in those passing moments that it was hard to miss what she was thinking. Her words taunted and teased me. I definitely planned on coming inside of her. Megan thought I was only keeping her for a week.

But it had taken me years to get her, and I was not about to let her go.

First, I'd train her body and make it crave what only I could give her, and finally I would bind her to me by planting my child inside of her. Every night I was haunted by the picture of her stomach stretched tight and my child growing inside of her. Before this week was through, I would make that dream a reality.

"Not yet. I have business to attend to. I will return for dinner. The maid will show you the clothes I expect you to wear tonight," I instructed her. My fingers tangled in the ends of her blonde curls. Her hair was so bright it was almost white in color. Touching it was like touching the sun, so bright and shiny. The texture of it somehow seeped beneath my fingertips and entered my bloodstream, causing my body to flush with heat and need. I shouldn't have been surprised when I felt a tremor of need move through me, but I was.

"Is this what our time together is going to be like, Jackson? You order what you want and I give it to you?"

"And if it is?"

"I am not a toy for you to dress and pose. I have my own mind. I'm an independent woman." She refused to meet my gaze, but she stood up to me. I was almost impressed. Very few even attempted to do that anymore.

"For the next week, you are anything I say you are,

Megan. You're mine." I felt she needed the reminder. A storm gathered in her blue eyes and they momentarily entranced me. I leaned down, holding her eyes prisoner with my own. She tried to pull her face away, but I held onto her chin firmly, not allowing her to escape.

"You're a monster," she whispered, anger thick in her voice, but underneath that I heard what she was trying to hide. *Desire.* I heard it because I felt the same. Her tongue moved between her two lush lips, for just a moment—moistening the cherry beauties and tempting me beyond reason.

I claimed her mouth then. I wasn't gentle. I was fierce. I bruised her lips with the force of mine, punishing her for trying to deny me what I wanted most.

Her obedience.

I pushed between her lips with my tongue, ravaging her mouth, drinking in her taste and losing myself in her. She'd done her best to remain stiff in my arms, but slowly she softened, melting into me. The sweetest of purrs escaped her lips and her hands slid under my jacket to rest against my chest. I felt each finger uncurl and clench into my skin. Her nails bit into my flesh almost to the point of pain—and I wanted more. Again, just with something as simple as giving me her mouth, my control had neared its edge.

I forced myself to break the kiss, instantly missing

her lips, regretting my decision. I pulled away slowly, knowing only a moment of joy when she tried to follow. In reward I gave her one last, soft kiss. She froze there, her eyes still closed, her lips bruised and swollen from my pillaging and her breathing so ragged that I could virtually see her heart beating against her chest. I couldn't resist letting my thumb brush against the hard nub of her nipple that was pressing against her dress. At first touch her body shook.

"I didn't think you wanted our first time to be while the chauffeur was watching, but that could be arranged." I goaded her further by loosening my tie. Her eyes, already wide, seemed to grow larger. Her body wobbled—at first drawing closer to me, before finally stiffening and pulling away. Embarrassment and anger warred on her face and something about that made my dick get impossibly harder, stretching against the fabric of my suit. She looked up at Carl, the chauffeur, and without one glance back at me slid from the car. She started to walk away, but before she could I called out. "I'll expect you to be waiting for me and wearing the dress I chose when I return, Megan." She stumbled as my words reached her, but she did stop walking. I expected her to turn around. She didn't. Instead she jerked her head back with the dignity of a queen and kept walking.

I found myself smiling as Carl closed the door. He hurried to walk her up the white stone steps that led to the front entrance of my home and even then I could not stop watching.

I could not stop smiling.

3

Megan

Once in the house I was immediately ushered up this grand staircase. The older woman who took me to the room I'd be staying in wore typical wait staff attire, and didn't speak to me. She seemed overly stiff in general.

But I guess when you worked for a man like Jackson King you had to know your place.

The bedroom door was shut behind me and I stood there, looking around, knowing right away that this wasn't *my* personal room, but what I'd be sharing with Jackson. It smelled like him: this intense, woodsy aroma that instantly had my heart racing.

Out of curiosity I went over to what I assumed was

the closet. I pulled open the double doors and saw Jackson's suits lined up.

This was *his* room. Like, his everyday, personal room. Although I didn't know why, I was surprised that he wanted me to stay here. I was to be here for a week, and I assumed he wanted easy access to me.

I explored the room more. There was an armoire across from the bed, and when I opened it I could see clothes lined up. The clothes *he* wanted *me* to wear for him.

I ran my hands along the soft, silky material. I pulled one of the dresses off the hanger and held it out to look at it. It was definitely expensive, formfitting, and exquisitely beautiful.

Heels were on the floor, all lined up, all looking so expensive.

After putting the dress away I turned and faced the bed. It was massive, and I had no doubt about the intimacy that would happen on it—the raw and filthy things Jackson would do to me.

A flush stole over me at those images. I was a virgin, and had absolutely no experience in that department. Would he be disappointed? Or would he be the type of man who would teach me what he liked, what he wanted me to do to him?

It was then that I saw the box on the bed. I'd been so enamored by everything else that I hadn't even noticed it. I moved closer to it, opened the box, and stared at the dress inside.

I felt my heart beat faster. The dress was gorgeous, but it was the fact that I was dressing *for* Jackson that made me so nervous. He'd specifically picked out this outfit for me, probably envisioned what I'd look like in it... and out of it.

The heels that sat beside the dress were stilettos—ankle-breaking heels.

I picked one of them up, ran my finger along the smooth white arch, and turned it around to see the red underside. They were gorgeous, and something I'd never actually worn before. Hell, I didn't even think I could walk in these.

They were fuck-me shoes, definitely.

I set the heel down and picked up the dress, the material feeling heavy in my hands. The detailing was delicate, the beadwork along the bodice and hemline feminine. The white material was sheer. I knew the slip underneath wouldn't hide much.

Chills moved along my arms. I had no doubt that tonight he'd take the dress off my body, tear my panties and bra from me, and devour every inch of me.

I lifted my hand and touched my lips, my mouth still tingling from the kiss he'd given me in the limo. He'd been so brutal, so forceful. And I'd gotten so wet because of it.

I wanted him that way, wanted that intensity, that masculinity that I knew only he could give me.

I might not know what was in store, or had any clue what I was supposed to do tonight, or for the next week. But what I did know was that I wasn't as opposed to the idea of being with Jackson as I thought I should be.

I anticipated all he would do to me, because I knew once it was said and done I wouldn't be the same woman.

I took the items to the bathroom, which was attached to the bedroom, and looked at myself in the mirror. I had to ask myself what in the hell I was thinking. Although truth be told, it wasn't like I had much of a choice.

If I hadn't agreed to go with Jackson I would have been throwing my father under the bus. And if I did that, who knew what the hell would've happened to him in the long run? I didn't know what lengths Jackson would go to make his point, but I didn't want to find out.

I didn't want to tempt him or test his power.

So instead I just took this experience with a grain of salt. I hoped like hell I didn't lose my heart in the process.

I told myself that in a week this would all be over with.

But it was that part of me, buried deep down inside, the one I didn't want to acknowledge, that whispered it didn't know how I felt about those seven days ending. Because I had a feeling once I was really with Jackson there was no turning back.

I knew there would be no mending my heart once it was given to him.

4

Jackson

"The first time I saw you, you were wearing white." I watched as the words I said hit her. Even across the large dining room an audible gasp could be heard from her. When I walked in at first, I just stood and watched her. She was standing by the window, looking out over the grounds and the vision was so reminiscent of the first time I saw her, I had to tell her. The only difference was that night I'd gone home alone, to an empty bed and my hand. Tonight Megan would be in my bed and I would be so far inside of her she would feel me for days.

My words made confusion come across her face and

once I walked closer I could see those blue eyes cloud with the same uncertainty. I saw more than just that, however. I saw the way her nipples instantly swelled, jutting against the delicate fabric.

"I was?" she asked.

"Governor Hasting's black and white gala," I informed her and then I waited while that news sunk in. I occupied the moments it took by letting my hand slide down her shoulders and farther down her back. I trailed my fingers over the indentation of her spine as if I were playing a delicate concerto on a piano—only stopping when my fingertips hit her ass, the dress protecting her from me—*for now.*

I lied. Another thing different about then were the dresses. Back then she wore an obviously secondhand dress, which revealed none of her body, and yet made her look ethereal and untouchable. The dress I chose for her tonight fit her like a second skin. It clung so tightly to her that I literally saw the outline of her breasts. This made me happy. I'd left her a note asking her to wear only one thing under the dress. I had to wonder if she'd followed my instructions and my cock jerked with the need to find out. When she let out a small gasp of surprise, I brought my attention back to her.

"He hasn't been governor for—"

"Over three years," I confirmed. "I'm well aware,

Megan," I added. The scent of her hit me. She reminded me of the honeysuckle that vined uncontrollably on my estate. Wild, sweet and addicting. That was Megan.

And she was mine.

Her long blonde hair was worn loose. It fell in waves down her back. I curled my hand into it so that it pulled her head back just enough to expose her throat. I leaned in close, unable to resist her scent. She trembled against me and my cock pushed hard against the fabric of my suit. I was surprised when the material didn't tear. Her effect on me was that strong.

I brought my head down and let the tip of my nose run along the fine tendon on the side of her neck, inhaling deeply. I could hear how her heartbeat sped and her breathing became ragged and I fucking enjoyed it. I was a predator and she was my prey. Soon, I would devour her.

"Jackson." My name left her lips like a broken plea. I knew she was pure. I had been watching and wanting her for far too long to let another man slide in and take her from me. Whenever one showed the slightest bit of interest in her, I found a way to have him removed from the picture. The last man cost me two hundred grand. He thought he'd won the lottery. *The idiot.* I would have paid more. "Jackson." She exhaled my name out like a question. *Does she know that I'm the answer? Does she know that soon I will be everything to her?*

I brought my lips to her skin and kissed the jumping pulse that hammered against her neck and then— because I could—because after all this time she was finally mine, I pulled her body into me and let her feel the hard outline of my cock pressed against her stomach.

"Your nipples are hard for me, Megan. Is that sweet pussy of yours just as wet?" I growled, my voice so low and guttural. It sounded exactly how I felt—an animal held too long in captivity, finally free to savagely fuck his mate and conquer her.

"I... Jackson, we shouldn't..."

"Answer me and don't lie, Megan. I own you now," I reminded her. She might have been a virgin, but I would not allow her to shy away from me. *From us.*

"I am yours," she admitted quietly, like a dirty little secret she shouldn't reveal.

My hand in her hair tightened and I growled in her ear, "Say it. Give it all to me," I commanded.

"I'm..." She gasped the word, whether from need, fear or pain from the hold I had on her, I didn't know, nor did I care. I needed this from her. "I'm wet for you, Jackson," she called out. Her words were stronger this time, soothing the beast inside of me.

"There's my good girl." I let go of her then, after placing a gentle kiss against her ear.

It took a Herculean effort on my part, but I reined in the hunger once again. My hand nearly trembled with the energy that took. I hadn't had a woman since the moment I laid eyes on Megan. I hadn't wanted anyone but her. Some might call that insane; I didn't care. I was well past the age where getting my dick wet was the sole reason for fucking a woman. I wanted more. The moment I saw Megan I knew she was it. The woman I would claim, the woman I would plant my seed in—the one. It was that simple. It was that complicated.

I regretfully released her hair and let my hand drop to the base of her back. My fingers found that sexy line of her ass and rubbed against it. Soon I would let my tongue follow the same path.

"What are we doing?" Megan asked, clearly flustered, as I walked her to the table.

"We're eating," I informed her and I couldn't help the smile that broke from my lips when she stumbled. It was refreshing to have a woman who did not know how to hide her reaction to me. Megan would never pretend with me. I wouldn't allow it. Everything between us must always be completely real—completely open.

That thought brought me satisfaction as I found my seat at the head of the table and waited for the cook to serve us. There was some distance between us. She was at the opposite end of the long table. I'd planned it that way. Now when I observed the distance between us I had but one vision in my mind.

Megan crawling across the table toward me and then lying on it nude, with her legs splayed out, waiting to be devoured.

Suddenly I knew exactly what I wanted for dessert.

5

Megan

I stared at the plate of food in front of me, my appetite nonexistent. How did Jackson expect me to eat after what he'd told me, after how he'd touched me? I fell so easily to his soft whispers, his hard body against mine. Even now I could still feel his hard cock pressed against my stomach, a testament to what would come, to what he would have deep inside of me.

"You should eat something." He stared at me from across the table, his gaze seeming so dark, so intense.

I felt like he was touching me just by the way he looked at me. This shiver raced along my body and although I was chilled, I also felt flushed, overheated.

This was like nothing I'd ever experienced, and I knew being with Jackson would only make it ten times worse... or maybe better.

"I'm not all that hungry." I was being honest, but it didn't have to do with the fact I was full from earlier, but from the fact that my emotions were so turbulent, so consuming that they filled me.

He'd already finished his meal and pushed the plate away. Someone came and took the dishes, walked over to me, and removed mine as well. The glass of wine beside me sat untouched. I was thirsty, so damn thirsty, but I was afraid that drinking alcohol would only intensify my emotions, my arousal.

"Maybe you'd have an appetite for something sweeter?"

His voice was so dark and commanding that all I wanted to do was melt into it, let it consume every single part of me. It was the way he said those words, the way he asked me, that told me he wasn't just thinking about dessert.

Or maybe he was and I was said dessert.

I reached for my glass of wine, not caring if the alcohol did make my arousal worse. I took several long drinks from it, the red wine sliding down my throat, the sweetness covering my tongue, the flavors exploding over my palate.

When I set it down I glanced up at Jackson. He

watched me with that commanding expression, that dominating persona. I felt the alcohol move through my veins swiftly and I knew intoxication was inevitable if I kept this up.

A second later another tray was brought out to the table. A plate was set in front of me with strawberries, chocolate, and whipped cream all arranged in this delicate, fantastical way.

"You always did have a sweet tooth," Jackson said and my heart started beating faster.

I thought back to three years ago, to that first time I'd met Jackson, that first time he'd seen me. I'd been an eighteen-year-old girl, so vulnerable and innocent, so naïve. I'd let the world around me consume me.

The party that my father had taken me to was unlike anything I'd ever experienced or seen before. I was swept away in the Cinderellaesque moment, taking in the wealth and beauty that surrounded me.

I remembered trying all the delicate little sweets. The treats had been set up on silver trays, the colors vibrant, beautiful. Was that the moment Jackson was referring to right now? Was that the sweet tooth he was speaking about?

"Come here, Megan." The way he said that was so dominant, so commanding that I actually found myself standing on instinct.

I wanted to obey him, to do what he said. Not just

because he wanted me to and probably derived pleasure from it, but because *I* wanted to go to *him*.

I walked over to him and when I stood right before him, my heart beating faster, I couldn't help but look down and see the stiffness of the erection that pushed against his slacks. He was huge, thick and long, but then again I'd felt that pressed against my stomach earlier. What would that feel like thrusting into me, taking my virginity, claiming it as his own?

He pushed the chair back, spread his legs, and gestured me forward. I stumbled slightly, my nerves taking over, this experience totally new for me. I wanted to be with him desperately though, wanted to be his in every way possible. I should hate this man, loathe him and everything he represented. He was using me because of my father... making me the payment.

And the truth—my dirty little secret—was the fact I was soaking wet for him at that knowledge. The fact he wanted me, had for the last three years, and would clearly do anything to make that possible. It made me drunk from it all.

Before I knew it was happening Jackson had his hand on my knee, his thumb slowly moving in circles around my skin. I was tense, I could feel it in every part of me, but I didn't want this to stop. In fact, I wanted it to go further.

I was breathing so hard, my breasts pressing against my dress, my nipples so tight I wouldn't be surprised if they tore right through the material. And then he started moving his hand up, curling his fingers along my inner thigh, making me shiver from the inside out.

He had his hand so close to my pussy, so close to the part that I wanted him to touch the most. But he didn't. Instead he leaned in close, our mouths only inches apart. I stared into his eyes for long seconds, wondering if I should be the one to make the move, to kiss him.

But before I could act on that, he had his mouth on mine—this brutal, possessive intensity coming from him. I braced my hands behind me, the table the only support I had at the moment.

While he continued to kiss me, I felt him move his fingers underneath the minuscule panties I wore. I found them under the dress after I'd fully pulled it out of the box. The scrap of lace and silk barely covered me, but made me feel so sexy, so desirable.

He was mouth fucking me. There was no other way for me to describe what he was doing. He pulled away far too soon, gripped my chin with his forefinger and thumb, and looked into my eyes. He didn't speak as he pushed the edge of my panties aside and stroked my soaked folds.

He started kissing me again as he teased his finger

over my clit. I gasped against his mouth, the pleasure rising inside of me. I was wet, embarrassingly so, but the grunts he made and the way he kept teasing my pussy told me he liked it.

When he pulled back, I couldn't breathe. My lips felt bruised but in a good way. He pulled his hand out from under my dress, brought the glistening fingers up to show me, and started sucking the cream off. He hummed low in his throat, and I watched as his pupils dilated.

"I knew you'd taste so fucking good." He gripped my chin again, tilted my head back, and claimed my mouth once more. He shoved his tongue into my mouth and made me taste myself on him, a sweet and musky flavor that invaded my senses. "Tell me how you feel," he said against my lips.

"Breathless," I responded honestly.

He tipped my head to the side and ran his tongue up the column of my neck, stopping at the pulse point beneath my ear and licking the skin roughly. "When I'm done with you, breathing will be the least of your problems." He moved his mouth to my ear, his warm breath tickling the shell. "When I'm done with you, Megan, you won't be able to walk straight or sit comfortably, and all you'll be able to think about is how my big cock claimed your virgin pussy."

I gasped at the brutality of his words, the crass nature in which he spoke.

"But most of all," he whispered, "you'll be mine irrevocably because I'm not letting you fucking go."

6

Jackson

Megan was so young and naïve. I doubt she had any idea that with those words I laid all my cards on the table. It was not something I made a practice of doing. Yet, what did a man do when the one thing he has wanted for three years becomes his? Apparently he loses his fucking mind.

Tonight I had a plan. I was taking things slow. I was planning on teasing her, making her body crave what only I could give it—train her to need me, and keep her on the edge for days, all before I finally gave her relief.

Instead, I didn't even make it through dinner before I told her I planned on keeping her. I was the one supposed to have all of the control here. Yet when I felt how wet she was for me, I lost it.

The first rule in business is to never lose control, but then Megan was not business. She was my woman, and her virginity my greatest prize.

I cleared the table behind her, shoving my plate so hard it flew across the slick surface, almost making it to the other side before ending up short and falling onto the marble tile with a loud crashing noise. The glass of wine by my plate had fallen over and the deep red liquid seeped onto the glass and then dropped down on the expensive white marble. I could only stare at it a moment. It reminded me that soon my cock would be covered in the innocence of Megan. My balls tightened at just the thought of it.

My hand was still on Megan's thigh and her body trembled, jumping at the noise. If I wasn't holding her, I wouldn't have been surprised if she had fled the room. I needed to control myself—but that was impossible.

"Sir?" the maid cried, coming through the door, the crash of my plate obviously having alerted her.

I already had Megan pushed back on the table, with her dress shoved all the way to her hips. The last thing I wanted or needed was to be interrupted.

"Leave!" I snarled the command. Megan's eyes dilated, and grew impossibly large, but she never took her gaze off of me.

"Jackson," she gasped as she quaked with fear. Maybe I should have held back, but when I moved my hand back to her pussy, she was even wetter than before. I let my finger skim against the lips of her pussy and groaned at the sticky sweet cream I found there. *She wants this.* She wanted to be owned by a man —*by me.*

"Spread your legs for me, Megan," I ordered gruffly.

"Maybe we should wait. Or we could go to the bedroom or something," she whispered to me and the nerves were thick in her voice. I should have slowed down and given her what she wanted, but the taste of her was on my lips, the scent of her excitement filled my lungs, and her pussy was promising me a heaven I'd never thought I would find.

I pulled her legs apart as I stood. I put pressure on her legs so that she had no choice other than to fall back against the table. She braced herself on her elbows, not letting her gaze leave me.

"I'm not waiting, Megan. I've waited too fucking long already. It's time I start taking what is mine—and you are fucking mine. You need to resign yourself to that." I growled the words like an animal, because by that time, common sense was gone. Her gasp, when I ripped the thin lace of her panties from her body, served as music to my ears.

I positioned Megan's body exactly where I wanted

her and when she seemed too in shock to move, I pulled her leg up and tossed her fuck-me heels to the floor. Eventually I might actually fuck her while she was wearing those. The feel of them digging into my back while I drove into her was definitely something I would like to explore. Not today, however. Now, I needed nothing but her, naked and at my mercy.

I bent her knee so that the heel of her delicate foot was braced on the edge of the table. I then repeated the action with her other leg and stepped back to look at my handiwork. Standing there like I was, she was completely open to me. I could see the lips of her glistening pussy, all shiny and pink. It begged for attention. I could see the rosette opening of her ass and my focus was glued to it, watching as her juices trickled down the swollen lips of her pussy into the dark valley of her ass.

Unable to stop myself, I bent down, drew my mouth across her inner thighs, kissing while sucking the tender flesh into my mouth. I rose back up to look at her, suddenly angry at the dress that blocked her body from me. Her breasts strained against the sheer fabric, begging for a touch.

"Jackson?" she questioned, her voice raspy because her breathing was so erratic.

Instead of responding, I bent down, flattened my tongue against her pussy and followed that trail that led to her ass.

I licked her until my lips and tongue were numb, until I was about to come in my fucking slacks. I couldn't stop though, didn't want to pull away from the sweet nectar of her pussy cream that covered my tongue and slid down the back of my throat.

I could have eaten her out all night, made her see with my lips and tongue that she was mine, that I claimed her without even being inside of her.

I placed my hand on her flat belly and forcefully pushed her back, making her sprawl out on the table, making her my feast to devour. I couldn't help myself, couldn't stop myself from mouth fucking her... or from thinking about what I'd be doing between her sweet virginal thighs tonight.

And with that primal, feral thought, I gave her pussy one long lick right through her slit, stood, and lifted her into my arms. I slammed my mouth on hers, forcing her to taste the sweet musk of her cream on my lips and tongue, letting her know what it tasted like to be marked, claimed and owned.

7

Megan

Before I realized what was happening, Jackson
had me in his arms and was striding up the
stairs. I knew he was going to his room, into
the room I was forced to share with him. But I'd be
lying if I didn't admit I anticipated this, that I wanted
this desperately.

And then we were in the room, the door shut with a
hard shove from his foot, the air chilly, my heart racing.
He had me on the bed before I could comprehend what
was happening, before I could even say anything in
response.

But what could I have said? What would I have
admitted to? He knew I wanted this, that I was wet and

primed for him, aroused beyond belief. I was sprawled out, my body bouncing slightly, my heart thundering. My legs were slightly parted, my pussy on display. I knew he could see the secret parts of me, the parts I had let no other man see, the most intimate section of my body.

"So pink and wet." He looked up at me, the shadows playing across his face. He came forward, and then was on his knees before me, his hands on my inner thighs. He leaned forward, and I held my breath. "I didn't get enough downstairs." He ran his tongue up my slit, moving the muscle along my clit.

I gasped in pleasure.

He ran his tongue up and down my pussy, lapping up my arousal, making this deep noise in the back of his throat. He gave my pussy one last lick, causing me to shiver before he rose, taking a step back.

He had his hands on my waist, and in a second he had me flipped over, my belly on the mattress, my ass in the air. My head spun. My pulse raced.

The feeling of his warm breath on my ass had me glancing over, seeing him kneeling behind me, his gaze transfixed on my bottom. He pulled my ass cheeks apart and stared at what he revealed.

Jackson placed his hands on my ass and squeezed the flesh. "You're so fucking ready for me. I could fuck you right now, Megan, and you need me so bad that you'd cry for more." He growled the words low in his throat.

He moved his lips over the top of my ass and took hold of each of my cheeks in his big hands. He just held his hands there, not doing much but kissing my flesh, running his teeth along the mounds.

Jackson smoothed his hands over my waist, digging his fingers into me, forcing me to be still, holding me in place—when I had the strongest urge to thrust into him.

"Oh God, yes, Jackson."

He ran his teeth along my flesh, and a violent shiver worked its way through me. "My need for you knows no bounds, Megan. You've become an obsession." He placed a finger at my opening, teasing my pussy with a bit of pressure. He pulled the digit out, never fully penetrating me, just staying right there at the cusp, at my opening.

I was lost in the sensations, in the feeling of him running that finger up and down me, teasing the hole, gently prodding it. He made me take it, made me want it.

"Spread for me." His voice was low, demanding, take-no-prisoners controlling. It made me hotter, wetter. It made me want him even though I was nervous, and more than a little scared of what was to come.

I watched as he pulled back and started undressing. He went for his belt, then the button of his slacks. He pushed the material off, standing before me like a god. Like someone who could destroy me with one touch.

He can. He will.

"Fucking spread for me," he demanded again.

But before I could move he was grabbing my knees and wrenching them outward, making me spread for him once more.

"When I say spread, that means open fucking wide."

I couldn't breathe, couldn't even think straight.

"I want to see all of you. I want to see your virgin cunt." All he did was stare at me, look right at my pussy, seeming to memorize every part of me. Jackson placed his hands on either side of my pussy, framing it, staring at it and making me feel more exposed than I ever had before. He made this low sound in the back of his throat.

I licked my lips, pulling the sheets between my hands.

He pulled the lips of my pussy apart, and the chilled air moved along my inner folds, teasing me, making me shiver with desire. I was transfixed, frozen in place by the desire I saw reflected my way.

"Turn around; present your ass to me."

"Oh. God." The words were low, uttered out of nervousness. Once I was in position I looked over my shoulder and watched as he stepped closer. I had no time to react, to process any of this because he started spanking me, bringing his palm down on my ass, making the flesh shake, sting, and *burn*.

"That's it. So fucking good."

Hot tears of pleasure fell from my eyes. He got off on this, on seeing the tears leaving me, witnessing my desire and pain.

"Spread even wider," he ordered, and I obeyed. I anticipated this, looked forward to how much further it would go.

"You're even better than I fucking imagined, Megan." I closed my eyes and breathed out heavily. "And I imagined a hell of a lot. I used to lie awake in bed at night, my hard cock in my hand, fucking myself over and over, all while imagining your pussy squeezing me," he confessed. I heard the sound of shuffling, right before the weight of him suddenly covered my back, the hard length of his dick settling right between my folds. He was naked, having removed his clothing before I even realized it.

I was breathing so hard, the air leaving me, making the sheets humid, hot. The thick, long length between his thighs, nestled right at my pussy, was intimidating. He'd stretch me, make me take all of him.

He'd make me feel good.

8

Jackson

I held my cock in my hand and slid it between the lips of her hot little cunt, her pussy so slick. The head of my cock rubbed against her clit and her body quaked. My fingers bit into her hip with bruising force. I wanted her body marked—*everywhere*. When she got out of bed tomorrow, I wanted her to instantly miss my dick stretching her tight pussy. I wanted her craving my cum slipping from the tight, hot depths. I wanted her begging me for more.

"Jackson," she gasped, her ass slightly lifting toward me. Megan ground that perfect ass against me, begging for more. She was so receptive and all mine. I would train her to want my cock... *only* my cock. A wave of possessiveness flooded through my system, one like I had never felt before. One word chanted over and over in my head. *Mine.*

"Tell me what you want, Megan. Tell me."

"I... please, Jackson," she whimpered.

"Tell me," I urged her as I brought my dick through her sweet, slick juices again. I positioned the head of my shaft at her opening, feeling that thin barrier that kept her innocent—*that kept her from me.* "Tell me what you want, Megan. I never want you to keep anything from me. There will be no secrets between us."

"You, Jackson. I want...*you.*"

That was exactly what I needed to hear. I pulled away from her, nearly moaning out loud. It was physically painful to leave the tight walls of her pussy. I wanted to plunge deeper, but when I did that, I wanted to see her face. I wanted to be able to see her eyes at the exact moment I claimed her virginity. *The exact moment she becomes mine completely.*

"No, please," she cried when I left her body. She needn't worry. I would never leave her. I would never do without her again.

"Hush, Megan, I just want to see you when I make you mine," I told her, a foreign feeling of tenderness coming over me.

I maneuvered her body so that she was lying on her back. Her eyes were on me—glowing with need. Her breasts were large and round, the nipples hard and swollen. They were straining toward me—as if they, too, knew who they belonged to. I bent down to suck one of the large distended nipples into my mouth. I curled my tongue around it and then captured it between my teeth. I bit down until I felt her body quake underneath mine and I heard her surprised intake of breath. I slowly released it and then kissed the spot I had marked.

"You're perfect, Megan," I praised her. Her gaze moved over my body like a tender touch—a loving caress. It was a completely alien moment for me, but something I was going to want permanently. She froze when she saw my cock, her eyes round with shock and maybe a little bit of fear.

"You're so big," she whispered. Her face was flushed with a fine sheen of moisture on her skin, and her blonde hair was strewn across the pillowcase. *She's beautiful.* "Jackson... what if you don't fit?" she asked, and her flushed skin darkened further with her question.

"You were made for me, Megan. I will fit. I will be so deep inside of you that you will feel me for weeks. Do you see how my cock is so wet? Do you see your juices covering me? Your little cunt weeps for what only I can give it."

I stroked my cock while she watched me. "Fuck,

yeah," I groaned out as my hand slid through her cream. "I'm going to fuck you so good," I promised her. I moved my hand to her pussy and without giving a warning, I slid my fingers against her clit, the swollen button so hungry it pulsated against my fingers.

"Jackson, please," she begged and having her beg for me made a large drop of cum slide off the head of my cock and run slowly down my shaft. I squeezed my dick tight and focused my mind, trying to hold off my climax. I wasn't coming until I was inside of her so I could fill her so full, her womb would be bathed with my cum.

"I'll give you what you want, Megan. I'll give you what we both want, what we both need," I reassured her.

"Please. I want it, Jackson. I want to belong to you," she whispered so softly I had to strain to hear it.

"This will hurt," I warned her. I might be a bastard, but this was my woman and I needed to make sure she was prepared. If I was a good man, I'd have used my fingers to stretch her and make her initiation easier. I wasn't. My cock was going to be the only thing to claim her innocence. I wanted her virgin blood on my shaft. I wanted it soaked into my skin, so that she marked me as deeply as I planned to mark her. I positioned my cock at her entrance and then looked down at her. "Look at me, Megan," I demanded.

She slowly brought her gaze up to me, her teeth biting into her bottom lip, betraying her nervousness. "Don't take your eyes off of me. I want to watch you as you become mine," I ordered. When she said nothing, I insisted she answer me again. "Do you understand?"

"I'll keep my eyes on you," she said and it felt like a vow. I felt it deep inside and it caused my balls to tighten with the load of cum that waited to be released.

"It will hurt," I warned her again, "but I will make you feel good before we're through. I'll make you feel so fucking good you will be begging for more."

"I know," she promised, and her hand reached out to touch mine. "Take me, Jackson," she said, giving me her consent.

I don't know if it was the words, or the soft touch that ran through me that caused it, but it was in that moment that I lost control. I plowed inside of her, my cock thrusting hard inside her tight little cunt and tearing through the barrier as Megan finally became mine. I didn't stop until my cock was pushing against her womb and once I got there I held myself still. I enjoyed the feel of her, the tight fit of her pussy walls squeezing against my cock—milking it, and the sound of her voice as she cried out my name.

"Jackson!"

In that moment, I felt like a fucking conqueror and Megan was definitely my greatest treasure.

9

Megan

I was in this trance, this dream-like state as Jackson fucked me, claimed me as his, made me take all his thick, long inches. He stretched me in two, split me open in the best of ways. I was wet from my arousal, but from my virgin blood, as well.

He placed both hands beside my head as he continued to make me take his dick. Sweat bloomed along my body and, as if it was a temptation for Jackson, he lowered his head and ran his tongue along the valley between my breasts, licking away the salty remnants of my desire.

He pulled out slowly and pushed back. Over and

over, tormenting me, making me weep with how much more I wanted. I clutched at the sheets, drawing them close to my side, wanting something harder, firmer to hold on to. In that moment I was his, the same as he was mine.

I'm Jackson's, irrevocably.

That discomfort and pain slowly started to diminish. My virginity was gone, my virtue, innocence, in the hands of this man.

And then he started thrusting into me like a madman. He slammed into me so forcefully my body was shoved up the bed, my cries carrying high and loud. He gripped my waist, keeping me in place, making me the vessel for his pleasure. I was full, so damn full of his cock I couldn't think straight.

He was focused on where he was lodged in my body, on where he was claiming me. His frantic thrusting slowed, and in its place was this lazy, prolonged swing of his hips against me, pushing his dick farther into me, making me take all of him.

"God, fucking yes, baby."

"You want me to give you so much more you can't even breathe, can't even fucking walk straight come morning?" He never stopped moving in and out of me.

"Yes," I screamed out. He was the only person who could make me feel like this.

"I want so much more from you." He uttered those words low, sharp, like a blade over my skin.

Jackson was thrusting in and out of me ferociously now, his skin slapping against mine, forcing his way into my body. He pounded, tunneling those long, thick inches into my willing body, making me take it all.

I closed my eyes, opened myself up, and allowed myself to just absorb the sensations. I felt myself go over the edge, felt myself come for the man I cared about more than I'd ever admitted to anyone, maybe even myself.

"Fucking take it all, Megan. Stretch for me, cry out for more." His motions were hard, powerful. "Tell me you're mine," Jackson demanded, ordered.

"I'm yours," I cried out, the words spilling from me as if they were their own entity, wanting out. I wanted to scream those words over and over again, tell him that I'd be—do—whatever he wanted.

Jackson kept slamming his cock in and out of me, and all I could do was hold onto him, digging my nails into his biceps, and just let him fuck me. I could only feel.

He made this low, dangerous sound, and I felt him swell even thicker inside of me.

"You're fucking mine," he said, and then I felt him come, felt him fill me up, bathe me in his seed. He was an animal and I was his conquest, his prize.

He held me down, made me take it all, accept what he had to give me. And I was more than willing to give it to him. And when he gave one last grunt, one final, brutal thrust into my body, he exhaled and rested his body on mine. He was covered in sweat, the same as mine, but it felt good having him this close.

Our breathing was rough, hard, and I felt my body start to shake, felt the aftereffects of what he'd done to me, of what I'd accepted.

I'd given Jackson every part of me, gave him my virginity, my innocence. I was his now, and there was no going back. There was no turning back.

But I didn't want to leave, didn't want to run away. I wanted to be his in every way imaginable, and I didn't know if that made me fucked up or not.

And when he pulled out of me I couldn't breathe, the absence of his body on mine, in me, was this loss I didn't want. He rolled off of me but immediately pulled me in close, his hand between my legs. He teased my now sensitive pussy opening, pushing his thick digit into me.

"My cum belongs in you," he said gruffly, pushing the seed that had started to slip from my body back inside, marking me. He pulled his finger out and brought the tip between my lips, forcing me to lick it clean. I tasted both of us, his saltiness and my sweet musk. I was drunk off of it.

He removed his finger and smoothed the slick digit over my bottom lip.

I sighed, feeling so tried, but exactly where I was supposed to be.

10

Jackson

"Can't you give me a hint as to where we are going?" Megan asked again. She had been asking me relatively the same question since I had the maid help her pack a bag this morning. She looked up at me and there was no mistaking the sincere happiness on her face.

It had been two days since I had claimed her virginity. *Two very long days and nights*—because I had yet to make love to her again. I had used my mouth on her during that time, but I'd somehow resisted taking her again. She needed time to heal and I'd tried my best to give her that time. I knew that our original agreement, at least the duration agreed on, was coming to an end.

Yet, what she'd soon find out was that I couldn't let her go.

I would take her again—*soon*. I wasn't accustomed to denying myself anything, especially if it belonged to me, and Megan definitely did. She was mine. *In. Every. Way.*

"I told you it's a surprise, Meggie." I smiled. I'd never smiled before Megan, but since she moved in with me I found myself smiling more and more.

"I like when you call me that," she whispered and her cheeks bloomed with a deep pink color. "No one ever has before. It's always Megan or Meg. Meggie feels special when you say it." She gave her confession with her head down—clearly embarrassed—and yet she had the courage to tell me. I liked that. I liked it a lot.

I was a jaded bastard. I admitted the fact freely. Yet having Megan sitting on my private jet, wearing a white silk pantsuit, her blonde hair brushed until it shone, and clamped at the back of her neck, she seemed every inch a woman of the world—confident and in control, but somehow she still managed to ooze innocence. The fact that she did all of this, despite no longer being a virgin, amazed me. She had a lightness about her, a clean, untouched beauty that was unique in my world. *Unique and unheard of.*

"Everything about you is special, Meggie," I told her, giving her complete honesty.

"But I mean... special to you," she answered softly, and her blush deepened. I was unable to look away, as her perfect white teeth bit into her bottom lip, worrying it. I wanted her teeth on me again—*soon.*

"Come here, Meggie," I ordered. My voice dropped down and I knew it betrayed my arousal. I watched as an almost imperceptible shiver moved through her body. She pushed herself up from the thick, beige arms of the custom-made reclining seat and came to stand in front of me.

I grabbed her hip and pulled her down onto my lap, helping her to straddle me so that she sat facing me, with a knee against each of my thighs. I loved the way the pantsuit complemented her complexion. Yet, it was the white color that reminded me of her innocence that had me originally purchasing them. Right then, everything about the clothes annoyed me. I wanted her naked, with nothing hiding her body from my view.

I moved my hand away from her hip and had wrapped it around the side of her neck before I even realized it. The warm, delicate curve of her throat felt soft against my palm. I felt her pulse quicken under my touch. It was a simple thing, but the truth inside that fact made my dick almost as hard as the way her soft ass felt pressed into my lap—almost.

I excited her; she wanted me.

"Why would you doubt that?" I asked, my thumb

sliding back and forth against her skin as I waited for her answer. "After the last few days, how could you doubt it?"

"I mean..." she whispered, and then her courage fled. Her gaze left my face after a fleeting glimpse and then she looked down at her hands. I watched as she clasped them together, fidgeting with them nervously. "You haven't—we haven't done that... *again,* not since that night and I thought maybe I... that you were disappointed." She finished her ramblings with a deep breath and her face practically glowed.

"Does this feel like I was disappointed? Does it feel like I'm not dying to have you again, Meggie?" I asked her. I leaned up to kiss along the side of her throat and let my beard graze against her skin. She jumped at first and then her body relaxed in my arms. She tipped her head back, her neck arching backwards, as she silently pled for more. I flexed my hips and even a naïve woman would have known what it meant when the hard ridge of my shaft pushed against her warm center. "My dick is dying to get back inside of you, little one. Even now cum is running down my shaft, weeping to feel the way you ride me. Trust me, I've thought of little else but sliding back inside that greedy little cunt of yours again."

Her fingers bit into my back, scoring the skin even through my shirt. Her body moved against me as she tried to ride me. Her hips were swaying as if she was in a saddle mounted on a stallion. Christ, she was so fucking perfect.

"Then why haven't we... haven't you...?" she asked, lifting her face to mine. Her eyes were expressive, wide and filled with heat.

"Claimed you again?" I questioned. My hand slid along the side of her body. I wanted to fuck her right then—to give her what both of us wanted.

"Yes," she whimpered. My fingers traveled under the jacket of her pantsuit, dived under the camisole, and continued to move up the tender skin on her stomach. Her intake of breath encouraged me to go further, and I didn't stop until I cupped her breast. In that moment, I hated the silky material that separated me from her.

"You needed time to heal. It was your first sexual experience, and I wasn't delicate with you. It would have hurt you to take you again so soon."

"Will I be... *healed* soon, you think?" she asked, her breathing ragged and the nipple of her breast pushing into my hand.

"Very soon," I responded.

My plan was to take her to my private island in Greece and lose myself inside of her. I'd rearranged my entire work schedule for a woman—something I would have never done before Megan. But then, she was no ordinary woman. I doubt she would understand the

gravity of my decision, or how hard it was to push business aside. For once in my life, something was more
important than work. No, not *something*. Someone...

Megan.

"What if I said I didn't care if it hurt me—as long as
I had you loving me again?" she asked.

In that moment I began to wonder which of us was
really in control here.

11

Megan

I couldn't breathe, let alone think. I felt so nervous around Jackson right now, like he was this wild animal and I was his last meal, a morsel to sate his starvation.

"I'm going to make you see how much I want you, how much you mean to me." He said the words low, filled with heat, passion, possession.

He helped me off of him, and before I knew what he was doing he had me turned around and bent at the waist. My hands were outstretched, my palms resting on the smooth leather of the seat in front of me. I was stretched for him, the position making me feel exposed, despite the fact I was completely dressed.

I looked over my shoulder, feeling my cheeks heat, knowing they were red. I was nervous, but anticipated this. And then he was reaching for the zipper at the back of my outfit, and slowly pulled it down. And when the silky material slid off my hips and pooled at my feet, I felt this chill move over me, despite the fact I was burning up.

"So perfect," Jackson said, almost seeming to murmur to himself. He had his hands on my ass, his palms so big, so masculine they covered the mounds.

The panties I had on were just this simple scrap of fabric, the delicate string attached to some lacy material that covered my pussy but left my ass bared.

I couldn't breathe, and the lack of oxygen was starting to make me feel dizzy. Or maybe it was my arousal working overtime.

Before I could contemplate what was about to happen, Jackson had my ass cheeks spread, the chilled air touching the sensitive part of me. Goose bumps popped out along my flesh, and I shivered.

"Hush now," he said, his mouth so close to me I felt the gentle current of his warm breath along my pussy folds and ass.

He ran his tongue up my pussy, starting at my clit and dragging it all the way up until he was teasing the muscle along my pussy opening. I shivered again, but he didn't eat me out anymore. Instead he helped me to stand, turned me around, and held onto my waist.

"So fucking sweet."

He lifted my leg and placed my foot on the armrest, positioning me for his pleasure. The cool air once again caressed the exposed skin of my inner thigh. I was so wet I could feel my juices sliding against the lips of my pussy. I was ready for him and I couldn't wait to be touched, teased, and tormented. I was close to begging him for it, but before I uttered a sound, he was back to licking at my pussy, dragging his tongue through my soaked lips, making me moan, beg for more.

I lifted my arms, placing my hands on his shoulders to steady myself, and just let go. He had his hands on my ass, squeezing the mounds almost painfully as he devoured me, made me his slave to desire.

With one more lick through my pussy he pulled away, his mouth glossy from my arousal, his breathing haggard.

"I'm so fucking hard for you," he said and reached down, rubbing his hand over the monstrous bulge displayed through his slacks. "*Christ.*"

I was panting from how worked up he had me, and I could see just how feral he was right now. I was so naïve when it came to things like this, but I wanted to be bold, to express what I wanted in the most brutal way possible.

Before I could be bold and wanton, Jackson was feasting on me once more. He had his thumbs on the lips of my pussy, pulling them apart, licking and sucking at them like he couldn't get enough. It was like he was dying for me, like he was so turned on that it didn't matter how high in the sky we were, or that his flight staff could walk through the door that separated us and see the filthy, good, depraved things he did to me.

He ate me out until my legs started to shake, until I was on the verge of coming for him, just screaming out his name and begging him to shove his thick cock in me. He moved his mouth over my clit, sucking at the hard little bud, making me cry for more, needing it all.

"You taste so damn good, so sweet, so... *mine.*"

He licked and sucked, tormented me and pleasured me. And just like that I came for him, crying out and digging my nails into my palms. He grunted and renewed his efforts on me.

And when I couldn't handle the sensitivity anymore —when the pleasure was so much it was almost painful —I pushed him away gently, and only then did he rise up and embrace me. He moved his hands up and down my back, soothing me, making me feel like melted butter.

I watched in rapt awe as he went for the button of his slacks, popped it free, and pulled out his thick, hard cock. Jackson stroked himself over and over again, just watching me, making me feel so exposed in more ways than just being naked.

"Fuck me." I don't know what got into me. I felt like this fiend, this addict that needed what only Jackson could give me. I heard the harsh groan spill from him right before his fingers dug into my flesh and his hold became rough and out of control.

I knew then that this was it, that he'd finally take me again.

Jackson pushed my legs open brutally, a kick of his foot to mine, making me open like a flower. And then I felt the tip of his dick at my entrance, a thick intrusion I couldn't wait for.

"I hope you're ready for this, because I'm going to give you everything you wanted, Meggie." And in one powerful thrust he buried himself deep in my body.

I gasped at the intrusion, at the way he stretched me. I couldn't think straight, and could only feel him deep inside of me. He groaned behind me, his face pressed between my shoulder blades, his breathing harsh.

I couldn't help the fact my pussy kept clenching around him, contracting, trying to draw him up inside me, deeper, higher.

"You're mine and I'm not letting you go."

And despite the fact I knew this, had known this from the very beginning, hearing him say it was music to my ears. It was the sweetest surrender for me, and I wanted nothing more than to give myself over to him irrevocably.

12

Megan

"I love it here, Jackson. I wish we never had to leave," I confessed to him.

We were lying on a quilt on Jackson's private beach overlooking the ocean. The warm sun shone down upon us and I never wanted to move again. I was okay with that. Jackson had taken me to his private villa just outside of Kissamos, Greece. We had been here for two days and I was having the time of my life.

Jackson took me through the streets of Kissamos to see the culture. We'd enjoyed boat tours, visited museums and shopped specialty stores. We had even traveled to the ancient city of Polyrinia. That was perhaps my favorite. Jackson had held my hand as we walked through the village and patiently told me about each place. You could literally feel the history in the air.

With everything we had experienced, the greatest thing about all of it was being with Jackson. He held my hand, kissed me, talked to me and made me feel... important... almost... *loved*. I'd never been so happy.

He also made love to me relentlessly. My body had achieved a golden tan—*all over*—because of the number of times he took me passionately on the beach, in the heated Grecian sun. Jackson refused to give me the option to be shy. One touch from him and I was gone. I lost myself in the things he did to my body and all I could think about was getting more of him.

"I have to go back to work tomorrow, little one. But I will bring you here again, I promise," he assured me. "We will come back often."

His fingers sifted through my hair as I curled deeper against him. I had my head on his chest and was lying on my side. Jackson was lying on his back and from my position the sound of his heart beating thrummed in my ear. It was steady—reassuring.

I hated the idea of leaving, but his answer brought up something we hadn't really discussed—except during sex in the heat of the moment—something that weighed heavily on my mind.

"My father will be expecting me back home when we return to the States, Jackson."

"It doesn't matter what he expects. You're not his concern anymore."

"He's already called several times and left messages on my phone."

"Did you speak to him?" Jackson practically barked the question. I sat up, worried about where the conversation would go and looked out once again over the waves of the Mediterranean and contemplated my future. I was afraid to look at Jackson just then. I wasn't sure if he would see the fear in my eyes. I was scared of even thinking about leaving Jackson. What would happen if I did? Would he replace me? The idea of Jackson with another woman was one of my biggest fears and it left a bitter feeling in its wake.

"No. I should have, but I didn't know what to say to him, so I ignored it."

"You should have told him the truth," Jackson growled. He must have sat up behind me because he pulled my body back against his chest, cradled his chin against my neck, and wrapped his arms around me, holding me close. The wind blew around us, leaving the smell of the salty air. It was almost as soothing as Jackson's hold on me.

"What is the truth?" I questioned, driven to know.

"That you belong to me now. That I'm never giving you up," he announced, while placing a kiss along the side of my neck.

"Is that practical? We don't know much about each other."

"I know everything I need to know about you, Meggie," he whispered and in that moment I almost believed him. "I know you love exploring new things. I know that you're comfortable in casual clothes and hate dressing up. You despise parties because they make you nervous, but you love spending time in crowded shops and talking to complete strangers. I know you love wild-flowers more than bouquets from a flower shop."

"Jackson—"

"I know the sound you make in the back of your throat right before you come all over my cock, and the hungry look you get in your eyes when I touch you."

His words sent shivers of awareness down my spine. I should have known a man like Jackson King would pay attention to everything, but the fact that he knew so much about me was astounding. I didn't know how to begin to process it. I just knew that it meant... *something special.*

"Wow," I whispered, because I had no idea what else to say to that revelation.

"Ask me what else I know, little one."

"What else do you know?" I asked, my breath lodged in my chest because it felt like this was important.

"I know that what we have begun isn't over. That it

will never be over, Meggie. And do you know why?"

"Why?" I asked, unable to stop myself.

"Because even now you could be pregnant with my child." His words slowly filled me, the truth in them warming me so deeply it was almost as if they marked my soul. Involuntarily, my hands moved to my stomach.

"I could be pregnant." I murmured the words. They were laced with disbelief, because until that moment it had never occurred to me that I could be carrying Jackson King's child. Jackson's hand came down to my stomach and overlapped mine.

"I'll tell you something else. If you aren't pregnant yet, I won't stop until you are," he vowed. His words were like a caress that slowly swept through me.

He moved to the side and slowly drew me down on the blanket.

"Jackson..."

"You like that idea too, don't you, my sweet Meggie." It wasn't stated like a question. "You want my baby growing inside of you. You want us linked together forever," he whispered right before his lips came down on mine.

I didn't answer him with words. There was no need. My answer was in my kiss.

I wanted all that Jackson said—and more. I wanted him...

Forever.

13

Megan

We'd been back in the states for several days now, and although I was due back at home, with my father, and my things, I hadn't been able to find myself leaving Jackson.

I didn't want to.

He made me feel like I could be anyone I wanted. I didn't feel afraid of being myself, of looking outside of the box and seeing that there was an entire world that I could learn about.

But most of all, I didn't want to leave Jackson because I loved him.

Even now I had my hand on my belly, wondering if I carried his child.

I glanced at the ornate clock on the wall, waiting for my father, whom I'd agreed to have dinner with to tell him how things were going. I knew he worried about me—despite everything. In his way, he loved me and was concerned over the fact I was still with Jackson despite the agreed-upon ending time.

But I'd clear the air now, let him know what I wanted in my life, and that Jackson was here to stay for me.

I hadn't even told Jackson I was seeing my father tonight, not because he'd disapprove, but because he didn't think my father had any right to know what was going on, seeing as he'd agreed to hand me over. But the truth was *I'd* agreed to be with him to help my father.

I hadn't realized just how much I'd grow to care for the brutal CEO.

I saw my father enter the restaurant, and instantly felt guilty. He looked like he'd aged a decade in this short time. He was in front of me and helping me out of the seat before I had time to do that myself. He embraced me, his body seeming so frail.

"You're okay," he said softly.

"Of course," I responded. He pulled me back and eyed me, looking me over as if he expected to see battle wounds covering me.

"You're ... glowing," he said, his brows furrowing, this look of almost disbelief crossing his face.

"I feel great, Dad," I answered, not about to sneak around. It was one of the reasons I'd wanted to have dinner tonight. It wasn't just about seeing him and making sure he was okay, but because I was going to tell him I was staying with Jackson.

I loved my father. He was a good man, just had bad habits. It was those said habits that had gotten me into this situation, that had gotten him into the position he was in as well. But in this short time something in me had changed. I felt more alive, freer than I ever had before. I didn't want that to go, not ever.

Once we were seated across from each other I took a stuttering breath. I didn't want to prolong this, and by the expression on my father's face I knew he suspected something was up.

"I have a feeling this dinner wasn't about you telling me you wanted to come back home."

I shook my head. "No, because I don't want to. I'm happy with Jackson. He makes me feel alive." I was surprised the words came out like they had, so truthfully, instant, genuine. He didn't answer me for long seconds, but did glance down and finally shake his head.

"I guess I don't understand this." He looked up at me once more. "How can you stand to be with a man who used you as collateral, who wanted you because of my mistake?"

This wasn't what I wanted to do, wasn't how I wanted this to go. I didn't want to argue about this or what I wanted. I'd asked him here to tell him the truth. "I can't really explain it, and even if I could I don't think I could properly make you understand." I started picking at my napkin, feeling nervous, afraid he'd make this huge scene. "I'm an adult, and don't expect you to accept any of this right away, if at all..."

"You're happy? He treats you well?"

I stared into my father's eyes, feeling happier than I ever had before. "I am," I said and smiled. "I love him."

And just like that I saw the genuine acceptance on my father's face. He'd worried about me, and wondered if my life would be the same, no doubt. But the truth was I hadn't known what living was until spending time with Jackson.

I hadn't known what truly being happy was until I broke through the mold that held me down for so long. Being with Jackson was swift, frightening at first, but it had been real, true. I loved him, and it was time I let myself be happy.

It was time that I thought about myself.

EPILOGUE ONE

Jackson

Two years later

"Did they finally fall asleep?" Megan asked me from the bed. I stood there for a moment and drank the vision in. Next week Megan and I would have been married for two years. In that time, I had only fallen more and more under my wife's spell. All those years ago when I saw her standing at that party I thought she was the most beautiful woman I had ever seen. Now, over five years later, I couldn't believe the beauty I held in my hands.

She lay in our bed, her blonde hair spilled against

the crisp white sheets, the blanket pulled up to her breasts. Somehow even after two years of marriage and three kids, she still looked innocent.

"Tabitha has been out for hours, but our boys fought it until they couldn't anymore," I confirmed. Tabitha was our oldest child. We found out Megan was pregnant a couple of months after coming back from Greece, and to celebrate we flew back and got married on the same beach we'd created our daughter on.

Megan got out of bed and walked to me, and just like always took my breath. She wore a white silk gown that clung to her curves. You would have never guessed that this woman gave birth to twin boys just two months ago.

When she stopped in front of me, I slid my hand along her hip and let my gaze take all of her in. I knew that she'd chosen the color for me, because that is how I saw her—how I have *always* seen her. Megan was pure and untouched from the harshness of my life and my business. She was mine to care for, to protect, and to provide for. *Mine to love.*

"Have I told you how much I love you, Jackson King? There are times that I cannot believe this is my life."

"It's our life, little one. *Ours*," I corrected her just before I claimed her mouth. She tasted like heaven.

Which is more than fitting, because she is my angel and maybe that's the true reason I like to see her in white.

Whatever the reason, I'm grateful that she chose to love a cold, selfish bastard like me.

EPILOGUE TWO

Megan

Ten months later

"We spoil these boys," I said with happiness thick in my voice. I looked around at the disarray of the house, the twin's first birthday party a hit, especially with the kids.

I glanced at Jackson, who was already watching me with this smile on his face. God, he looked so good, and every day I fell in love with him even more. He pulled me over and onto his lap, and I snuggled deeper into his chest, loving that he cradled me, kept us safe, made me the happiest woman on the planet.

My heart started beating a little harder, because

what I was about to tell him was nerve wracking. "Do you ever think about having more children?" I asked and sat up, wrapping my arms around his neck.

"I do," he said, smiling at me. He pulled me forward so my chest was pressed to his. He had his mouth at my neck, sucking at my flesh. I tipped my head back and moaned, the feeling of his lips on my throat, and his beard scratching at my skin making me feel content and safe.

"That's good, because I'm pregnant."

I felt him tense against me a second before he pulled back. He stared into my eyes, realization settling in.

I cupped his cheeks, his beard soft under my palms.

He pressed his mouth to mine and kissed me so passionately I lost my breath for a moment.

"God, you make me so fucking happy."

"I love you," I said between kisses.

"I love you too, Meggie. It'll only ever be you for me." He leaned in and kissed me softly. "You're the only woman I'll ever want."

Every day I fell more in love with this man, and I knew he felt the same for me.

The End

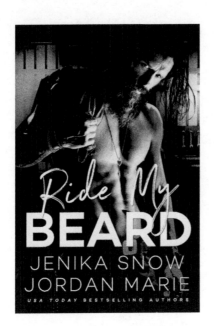

RIDE MY BEARD

By Jordan Marie and Jenika Snow

www.JordanMarieRomance.com

support@jordanmarieromance.com

www.JenikaSnow.com

Jenika_Snow@yahoo.com

Copyright © September 2017 by Jordan Marie and Jenika Snow

First E-book Publication: September 2017

Photographer: Wander Aguiar

Cover model: Victorio Piva

Photo provided by: Wander Book Club

Cover Design: Letitia Hasser

Editor: Kasi Alexander

Ride My BEARD

JENIKA SNOW
JORDAN MARIE

USA TODAY BESTSELLING AUTHORS

Lola

My entire life I have been in love with one man.

Ryker Stone.

It doesn't matter that he is more than double my age.

I don't care about the whispers that say he's too wild to ever be tamed.

I like that he's reckless.

He makes me feel like I can be uninhibited.

Truth is I saved myself for him.

I belong to him.

Ryker

I've had my eye on Lola for more years than I should admit.

Her beauty drew me in, but it was her innocence that trapped me.

I shouldn't want to claim her, but she's all I desire. So I stay close and make damn sure no one else touches her.

I'm all wrong for her, but too damn stupid and hard up to stay away.

She can run, but I'll follow.

By the time it's all said and done she'll be riding my beard.

Warning: This is a short and over-the-top dirty novella that will have you searching out your very own dirty mechanic. It's to the point and leaves nothing to the imagination, but then again, doesn't everyone like it that way? *wink*

1

Lola

I grab two beers and set them on my tray, turn, and walk toward the table, moving around horny, drunken guys as they try to grab my ass. But this is the norm at the bar where I work.

The Bottom of the Barrel, which name is pretty accurate for the customers who show up here, is busy as usual. If I didn't need the money, and wasn't always guaranteed a handful of tips at the end of the night—mainly because the guys think I'm sleazy and roll that way—I'd walk away from this place and never look back.

But as it is, the shitty town I live in doesn't have very many options of employment, especially for an eighteen-year-old with a family that has made sure everyone views her as trailer-park trash.

A mother who has a steady number of random men rolling between her sheets and a father who only sees me as a one-night-stand mistake. This is the life that has always been my constant.

The music is loud, the jukebox in the corner older than I am. It's got buttons missing and a few songs skip constantly. But for the crowd that comes into the bar it's good enough.

The only thing they care about is slinging back cheap drinks, getting lap dances from the loose women who hang around town, and asking me for fifty-dollar blowjobs after my shift like I'll finally give in and do it one of these nights.

I take another order and go back to the bar, waiting until Slim makes his way toward me.

"A Jack and Coke and two Millers."

He doesn't say anything as he fills the order, but it's busy as hell tonight and we're both running on steam. My feet ache, and my shorts are a bit too small, but then again it's what gets me those killer tips.

I might dress so I show off a bit of skin, but I'm not easy. And if any of these assholes knew I was a virgin, that I've never even been felt up because I chose that, because I wanted it as a consenting adult, they would probably become even more disgusting than they already are.

I turn and look at the bar, the crowd thick, the air hot and heavy. This place is such a dump, with half the customers missing teeth, their guts hanging over their too-big belt buckles, and the stains on their shirts as prominent as the watermarks that line the ceiling.

I'm about to turn around and grab the orders that Slim put on my tray when I notice the front door swing open. Despite how hot I am, the beads of sweat between my breasts trickling down, I freeze. Chills race along my spine, move over my arms, and I swear it's as if this icy touch has a hold on me.

There, walking in like he owns the damn place—which holy hell, does he ever—is Ryker Stone.

His pants have that worn appearance, and God, does he look good in them. The silver chain that hangs from his pocket and down across his thigh catches the light briefly. He's wearing a t-shirt, that, although it fits him perfectly, also tells of the power he wields.

He's not a huge guy, not muscular like a body-builder. But he is tall, toned, ripped in every aspect of the word. He's lean with cuts of muscle that tell a person he'll kick their ass and not have any trouble doing it.

My throat is so dry, my tongue suddenly feeling too

thick. He's older than me, by a couple decades, in fact. But I don't care about any of that.

I have wanted him since I was sixteen years old and saw him working under the hood of a car. Grease had covered him in the best of ways. And his hands—God, his hands—are so big, with veins that are roped up his muscular forearms. Every time I see them my legs get weak, I grow wet between my legs, and my breathing becomes ragged as I think of all the things he could do to me with those hands. I might be a virgin, but it's purely by choice. I'm not shy about the things I want... It's just I want those things with Ryker Stone. He makes me think filthy thoughts.

I look into his face and take in his beard, one I image pressed between my thighs as he eats me out...

"Order up," Slim shouts over the music so I can hear.

I force myself to turn around, grab the tray, and deliver the drinks. But even though I'm not looking at Ryker I can feel his gaze on me. I swear it's like he's taking my clothes off, just tearing the material from my body so he can get to the good parts.

And God, do I want him to get to the good parts.

2

Ryker

I feel her gaze on me the minute I walk into the bar, and my dick hardens slowly against the inside of my thigh. I go to my usual table in the corner. I hate this fucking bar. There's nothing here to like, except for one thing. Lola Webb.

She's the only reason I've been coming here for over a year. I don't touch her. She's not mine. She's too fucking young and the kind of woman a man could lose his head over. So I stay away, as much as I can.

Still, I'm so fucking pussy-whipped that I've been coming to this bar, eating their shitty food, and drinking their watered-down beers for a year, not because I want to be here, but because I know I'll see her. Up until six months ago she only worked in the kitchen—because she wasn't old enough to serve alcohol. I hate that she slings drinks to the assholes here, but I'm not claiming her, and the she-bitch-cunt-from-hell she calls a mother sure doesn't support her. So, Lola's always earned her own way. I admire that, even if I don't like the way she does it.

Lola has a spirit about her that I like. She's free, self-sufficient and she refuses to take shit off of anyone. It's the kind of spirit a man—a real man—nurtures. Fuck. The truth is, I like everything about the little spitfire. *Every. Fucking. Thing—save one.*

I've forced myself to stay away from her because of her age. Even now she's barely legal at just eighteen. She's much too innocent for a hardened, filthy asshole like me to touch and she deserves a hell of a lot better than an old, broken-down grease monkey. So I stay here, watching her. Sitting just one table over from the tables that she takes care of. All that is on purpose.

If I had my fucking way I'd throw her over my shoulder, take her back to my place, and she would never leave. I'd probably tie her to my fucking bed.

An image of Lola bound to my bed and completely naked springs to my mind. My dick jerks at the image. She'd have to depend on me for everything. I'd be the one to feed her, bathe her...brush her hair. She would be completely at my mercy—forced to ask me for whatever she wanted or needed. *Maybe even beg.*

I could have groaned at that image, and the filthy fucking thoughts slamming into my head.

The idea alone is so potent it goes to my head like a fucking drug. One of the nameless waitresses brings my usual bottle of bourbon over and a glass. She tries to make small talk, but I ignore her. I'm only here for one reason and it's not her.

My gaze is glued to Lola's ass, round, tight, and fucking delicious, molded against those denim cut-off shorts she definitely had to be poured into. I throw back my first drink, so pissed my hand literally shakes. Her fucking ass cheeks are hanging out of the back of her shorts. I can literally see the curve that leads to the promise land—which means every fucker in here can see it too.

The view gets even better when she turns around. The tight black tank she wears hugs those tits of hers like a second skin. Every time she takes a step they sway and do this seductive dance that draws a man's eyes. There's no fucking way she's wearing a bra. My heart rate speeds and my fucking breathing goes ragged as I wonder if I could see her damn nipples if she were closer. I bet I could and I bet they'd be small and get so fucking hard for me. The kind of nipples a man could wrap his tongue around and suck hard, turning them bright red before biting into them and letting the thrill of pain explode over her body.

I force myself to take another drink and count backwards from fifty. I remind myself of all the reasons I shouldn't touch Lola Webb. I do all this while my body is reminding me that I haven't fucked a woman in over a year, because the only woman my dick seems to want is the one woman I'm trying to deny myself.

Fucking hell...

3

Lola

Why I thought tonight would be any different I don't know. Ryker spends the entire evening nursing a bottle of bourbon, staring at me but doing nothing. It's enough to drive a girl insane.

"Damn it, Lo, watch where you're going!" Tina, the other waitress working with me, yells. I look up just in time to avoid crashing into her.

"Sorry, Tina. I was...distracted."

"You were eye-fucking Mr. Hot, broody, and a whole lot of trouble over there," she mutters. I'd try to deny it, but there's not much I can say.

"I should just give up," I whine, feeling completely

out of my comfort zone and frustrated. The man sets my body on fire just with a look. I can tell he wants me. *Why won't he do anything about it?*

"You should, but only because he's too damn old for you," Tina answers. "You need to leave men like Ryker to women like me. He'd scare you to death. Cut your teeth on boys your age before you try to wrangle a man like that between your sheets. Fuck, Ryker would probably have you running away the moment he whipped his cock out."

I have to literally pull myself back from snarling at her.

If she knew how in love with Ryker I was, she'd think I was insane. Hell, maybe I am. I've loved that man since I was sixteen and I've been praying and praying he'd notice me. I can still remember the day. I had just turned sixteen and my mother's shitty car needed some repair work. She pulled it into Ryker's garage and got him to fix her brakes. She tried to pay him for fixing her car—and in Mom's world that didn't include money. I can still remember how stunned I was when he turned her down.

"I didn't fix the fucking brakes for you. Your girl should be safe and have someone looking out for her," he shrugged, ignoring her. But his dark, almost black eyes stared straight at me. It felt as if his gaze was marking me, branding me from the inside.

Until that moment no one had really given a shit about me. My life consisted of finding a job and working all the hours I could, trying to finish school, and trying to stay out of the reach of the horny losers Etta Mae—my mother—brought home.

"What do you mean, '*scare me to death*'?" I ask Tina, shaking my memories of the past away.

"Word on the street is that man is a freak in the bedroom and packs a huge cock."

I didn't even comment on the dick part. "A freak how?"

"See? That right there is proof you're not made for a man like him. The talk is he's into public sex, whips and ropes, and any of the other kinky shit a man can get in his head," she says.

I feel my eyes go round as I imagine what Tina just said. I immediately get a picture of Ryker taking control of my body. I look out across the crowd. My gaze zeros in on his table. He's staring right at me—*that can't be my imagination*.

I picture myself walking over to him and taking my clothes off, demanding he take me right there with everyone watching us. I'd never do it, but the fantasy of it makes me flush all over with a heat I can't explain. I can feel the insides of my thighs coat in my excitement. *What would he do? Would he fuck me right here in front of everyone? Would he finally claim me in all the ways I've dreamed of over the years?*

"Oh," I whisper lamely, my body so excited that getting through the rest of my shift may be a problem.

"Get him out of your mind, little girl. You're in over your head." She snorts and then laughs, leaving me to feel like an idiot.

If only it were that simple.

4

Ryker

I must have been sitting here for hours, just watching Lola, envisioning all the dirty fucking things I want to do to her. I've been milking the bourbon, and with the bottle half empty I have a good buzz going on. I know I should leave before I do something I might regret.

As it is, I am harder than fucking steel, my cock pressed against the zipper of my jeans, wanting to be out and buried deep inside Lola's tight pussy. I bet she will be hot, and so damn pink. I bet she's a virgin too.

Fuck.

Just thinking that she never had a man between her thighs, that she still has her cherry intact, has me gripping the edge of the table so hard I won't be surprised if the wood cracks.

I watch Lola come out of the back room, a couple of fresh bottles of Jack in her grasp. She bends over to put the bottles on the lower shelf and her jean shorts rise up. Damn, just a small piece of denim covering the sweet spot I want to bury my face in.

But because I don't want to be a dirty bastard I toss a few bills on the table and leave. I need some fresh air, maybe even a smoke to calm this raging arousal rushing through me. I pull out a cigarette and place it between my lips. I grab the lighter and light the end before inhaling deeply. I need to quit this shit, but the nicotine hits right to the problem areas and soothes the shit out of it.

The bar door swings open and a couple of rowdy guys stumble out. It is clear they are drunk by the way they slur their words, but I ignore them. I have other things on my mind, things that include getting Lola naked in my bed, screaming my name as she comes.

You dirty fucking bastard.

I stay out here for half an hour or more, trying to resist the urge to go back inside. I know the minute I do, my dick will come alive at the mere sight of Lola. The damn thing is still semi hard, but manageable, less noticeable.

It's a mistake, but I just need one more look at her

before I go home and jack off to my hand. I snub out my cigarette, about to head back inside, when I hear the shattering of bottles.

Maybe I should have minded my own damn business, but I find myself walking around the corner and stepping into the alley. One of the parking lot lights is on, the muted yellow glow casting shadows over the twin dumpsters.

At first I can't make out what is going on. I can only see the two drunks I noticed earlier standing by the dumpsters. But then I see her small form between them, the trash bag she clearly had been taking outside now sitting by her feet.

I don't know what in the hell is going on, but the two assholes are crowding her. It has this rage burning brightly inside of me. I find myself stalking closer to them, my hands curled into tight fists at my side, my focus solely on the two pricks who will soon be on the asphalt.

And then I hear the foul, disgusting things that they are saying to Lola. I growl low and reach one of the guys, gripping the nape of his neck and yanking him backward. He falls to his ass on the ground, and I immediately go for his buddy.

I have the front of his shirt twisted in my hold, and lift him easily off the ground. I toss him away and hear his body slam into the brick wall. I face both of the pricks then and watch as they pick their sorry asses up off the ground. Maybe it's the anger coming off of me in violent waves, or maybe they're not as stupid as I think, but they both hightail it out of there.

I turn to face Lola and see her staring at me wide-eyed. I want to take her in my arms and just hold her in that moment, let her know that everything will be okay, that I'll never let anyone hurt her. And because I have all these insane emotions running through me, I do just that.

I pull her in close, her small body forming perfectly to mine. She smells good, like sweet vanilla, and that makes me even more intoxicated. I cup the back of her head but she pulls back slightly and looks up at me. Because I'm a dumb motherfucker I know what I want to do in that moment.

I want to kiss her.

I want to fuck her.

I want to make her know she's mine.

5

Lola

He's going to kiss me. He's going to kiss me. The thought repeats in my mind over and over. I run the tip of my tongue over my lips and fight down my nerves. My heart is thundering in my chest like a herd of wild elephants. Ryker has to be able to hear it. I stand up on my tiptoes, leaning into him, begging him silently to kiss me.

I inhale deeply, and the air I suck in is thick with the very essence of him. Sandalwood, old leather and a tinge of motor oil are scents that I always associate with Ryker. Some women might curl their nose at it, but not me. It makes me feel...alive.

His hands are at the small of my back and I feel his

fingers just barely brushing the hem of my shirt. They are rough from hours of working on cars. The harshness of them tickles against my sensitive skin and sends a wave of goosebumps up my spine and on the back of my neck. My entire body has excitement running through it that leaves me breathless.

I put my hands on his chest, my knees suddenly weak. He lets out a low rumble that I first feel vibrate under my hands and then hear from his gruff voice.

"You shouldn't be out here by yourself," he says and takes a step from me, his hands moving to my hips as he roughly pushes me away. He keeps his hands on me until I steady myself. I immediately miss the warmth of his body, his masculine scent and the feeling of being safe in his arms. I mourn the loss of him silently for a moment while I gather my thoughts.

"I was only doing my job," I defend quietly, wondering what he would do if I ran my fingers through his long hair and pushed it off of his face.

"You nearly got yourself raped," he says, his lips almost curling in distaste and I hate that he is looking at me like that.

"I didn't, though. You saved me," I tell him, trying to hold onto my pride.

"Only by chance. Another five minutes and I wouldn't have been here. If you're going to hold down a job like this, little girl, you can't be stupid," he growls at me again and his condescending words and tone spur my anger.

"I'm fine," I mumble, feeling foolish for thinking he was planning on kissing me. Clearly he wasn't. *I was delusional.*

"You need a fucking keeper," he growls, raking his hands through his hair in frustration.

"Well, I don't have one. I never have and unless you're planning on taking the job, I better get back to work," I huff.

I go to step around him so I can go back inside the bar. I take about three steps before he reaches out and grabs my arm, pulling me close to him.

"I don't know what kind of boys you are used to, but you need to take care how you talk to a man, little one," he warns, his voice dropping down into a deep timbre that sends shivers of awareness all through me.

"Ryker—"

"Before one teaches you exactly what to do with that mouth," he interrupts, his voice almost a growl. His thumb traces over the bottom of my lip. I can't stop myself from opening my mouth enough so that the tip of his thumb is right there. I'm dying to suck that digit into my mouth. *What would he do?*

Instead, I let the tip of my tongue lick against it, tasting his skin. We're standing so close that I can imagine it, and the deep hue in his eyes seems to deepen in color. I could get lost in the inky black depths. His pupils dilate, and I might be a novice but I can hear the change in his breathing. He's excited. *I'm exciting him.*

"Are you volunteering for the job?" I ask him, my heart pounding, my voice sounding as breathless as I feel.

He stares at me a moment. Mentally I'm screaming at him to say yes, to do something, anything to relieve this ache inside of me. For a moment I really think he's going to. I envision him pushing me up against the side of the building and fucking me raw. My legs tremble from the very thought of it. And then...

"You don't know what you're inviting. Run back inside before you get yourself into trouble, Lola. You're not ready for what I would do to you."

His words make me ache; they make my heart clench painfully. I want to argue with him. I almost do, because I can see the interest in his eyes and I see the hard outline of his dick against his jeans. I'm close to asking him to show me what he'd do—begging him to make me his. Then Tina's words come back to me and I feel fear.

What if she's right? What if he's right? I'm a virgin. I might know what a man and woman do with each other, I might even dream of doing that with Ryker, but when it came down to it, would I panic? Would I disappoint him? What if I wasn't enough for him?

"Lola, you okay out here?" my boss yells from the door, interrupting us. My gaze stays locked on Ryker.

"Yeah, I'm fine. The damn trash bag ripped open." I lie easily, not wanting to admit what just happened.

"Leave it. I'll have one of the guys pick it up. Get back in here where you're safe. I don't like you being out here alone too long."

"You better go," Ryker says, and I nod my head in agreement. Disappointment curls in my stomach and I think I see it flashing in Ryker's eyes too.

"Maybe if you explained what you expected from me first, I wouldn't be scared at all, Ryker. I really don't think I would be—but only if it was you," I whisper, feeling a little out of my depth. Handling drunks and warding off men is one thing. Admitting to the one man I've always loved that I want him—even if I am clueless—is quite another.

I walk back to the bar and step inside, carefully closing the door. My mind is too consumed with doubts and fears. It makes it hard to breathe. I don't look at Ryker. I'm afraid of what I'll see on his face. Or worse, what he would say about my admission.

I hope I see him tomorrow. I hope I didn't push him away forever. I don't think I could handle it if I did. I need him to be here in the bar tomorrow. I need him to talk to me. Because the only thing I'm sure of in my whole, messed-up life is that I want Ryker Stone to be the man to take my virginity. I want him to be my first, to show me everything he knows about sex, because I'm tired of being a virgin.

And maybe, just maybe if I learn enough to please him, he might want me back. If I please him, maybe he'll keep me. Because Ryker Stone is the only man I want to touch me...*ever.*

6

Ryker

I toss my keys on the table and go to the fridge to grab a beer. Truth is, I don't need more alcohol, but after the interaction I had with Lola earlier tonight, I need something to take the edge off.

I pop the cap and drink half the beer before setting it on the counter and exhaling. My dick is hard, and the blood rushes through my body. I want to go back to the bar and take Lola right then and there, just press her to the fucking dumpster, push down her shorts and panties, and push my hard dick into her sweet pussy.

I moan at the thought.

I have no doubt she'll be tight as hell, sucking at my cock, milking the cum from me. I groan at the thoughts that slam into my head, the images that are so filthy I could get off right in my jeans. I am a dirty bastard, and I make no claims that I'm not.

Lola deserves sweet and gentle, a man who will worship her body in a delicate way. I am rough and hardened, and used to raw fucking sex.

All I can think about are those assholes trying to touch her, trying to have her. She is mine. I know that with everything in me. I tried to warn her off tonight, even though I know that trying to pretend I can walk away and let her be with some other prick is unrealistic. I've known that I wanted her since it was legal, since I allowed myself to see her as a woman.

I was trying to give her a choice. I really was. I wasn't prepared for her soft voice to pull me in further. I can still hear her words ringing in my ears.

"Maybe if you explained what you expected from me first, I wouldn't be scared at all, Ryker. I really don't think I would be—but only if it was you."

How can a man fight that? I can't. It doesn't matter that the things I want to do to her are fucking dirty, maybe even depraved. She as much as offered herself to me and I can't walk away. It's not possible. No other woman could take her place, because it's not just about having my cock buried deep in her pussy. It's not just about filling her up with my cum and marking her as mine. It's also about keeping her close. It's about keeping her safe. I can do that better than any other man alive. I was born to do that. *She's mine.*

I know the shitty life she's had, that her mom is a whore who doesn't even care about her. I know that she's all alone, just trying to make a place for herself, just trying to survive.

I'm older than her, more experienced, and I can show her what she needs, what she's never had.

I can show Lola that she doesn't have to be alone. I'll fuck up anyone who tries to hurt her, who tries to stand in my way from claiming her as mine. Even if the best thing for her is for me to walk away, for me to not get involved, that's a dead end.

Going to the bar every night has proven that over and over again.

No, I know what I want and that's Lola as mine, and I won't try and fucking hide it or deny it any longer.

She invited me into her life; now it's time to claim her. *No more waiting.*

I go into the bathroom and crank the shower, making sure the temperature is cold enough that it might get my arousal under control.

I strip out of my clothing and climb in, the initial shock of the frigid droplets on my flesh dimming the hunger that consumes me. My dick is rock hard, my need for her going strong.

Because I am done fighting Lola's pull. I give in.

I reach down and grab my cock, stroking myself from root to tip. My forearm flexes, and I place my other hand on the tile in front of me. Hanging my head, I close my eyes and really start to work my palm over my shaft, faster and harder, thinking only of Lola.

I squeeze my eyes tight, picturing Lola on my bed, her legs spread, her pink virgin pussy on display. I imagine myself between her thighs, my mouth right by her sweet cunt, my warm breath bathing her pussy lips. I'd devour her, lick and suck her until she screamed my name, until she begged me to stop...pleaded for more, and her sweet pussy dripped on my beard.

My balls draw up tight to my body, my breathing becoming ragged. I'm going to come so fucking hard and it's all from thinking about Lola.

Fuck, I want her so damn badly, even if I know that it is wrong, even if I know she deserves better. And as much as I should stay away, give her space, let her find someone who will be gentle with her, I know I can't.

I won't.

I can't walk away from her. I can't let some other fucker touch her. She's mine, and nothing will ever change that. No one will take her from me.

I come then, my seed spraying out of my cock and landing on the tile before me. I groan and grit my teeth, letting the pleasure wash over me, letting it consume me.

I want to make Lola feel good, have her wrapped up in everything that is me. I want her smelling like me, feeling my body.

I want my cock in her pussy. I want my seed filling up her womb.

What I need is Lola as my woman, my wife...the mother of my children.

When I'm drained dry I let go of my dick and place both hands on the tiled wall. I breathe harshly, my eyes still closed, my thoughts still on Lola. No, I am not going to walk away from her.

I am going to make her mine.

7

Lola

"Order up, Lola!" Slim yells and I do my best to give him a smile. The truth is I don't feel like smiling. My head hurts, my feet ache, my back is tight—and that's just the beginning of my ailments. My chief complaint is that I'm almost through my entire shift and Ryker hasn't shown up. He's always here. *Always.*

I feel so stupid. *Why did I have to sound so pathetic? Why couldn't I have just played it cool?* If Tina had been in my shoes she would have just attacked Ryker and been in his bed that night. I had to act like a stupid, terrified virgin. *How do I ever expect someone like Ryker Stone to take me serious if I can't even act like an adult around him?*

I put the round of beers a group of customers ordered down on the table. I'll be glad when these idiots go home. There are four of them here for a bachelor party. Hell, they were shitfaced when they got here, and their comments are getting more lewd with each round. I'm doing my best to avoid the grabbing hands. One of the men thinks to get smart and trips me. Because of these damn heels I wear, I can't keep my balance and fall straight into the lap of the loudest drunk of them all. He's also the one that is supposed to be getting married.

He latches a hand painfully onto my breast. I cry out in shock and hurt. I'm trying to calm my panic, getting ready to bring my serving tray back against the man's face when suddenly the hand is gone.

"You think you can touch what's mine?" Ryker growls in a voice so cold and so deadly it feels like everyone and everything in the bar comes to a complete standstill.

"Hey, man, we're just trying to have a little fun. Dressed like she is, she's asking for it. Don't worry, we'll treat her good," the idiot says, obviously not seeing how dangerous the situation is. Everyone else can sense the violence coming from Ryker, including his friends, because they've gone quiet.

"Lola, get up," Ryker commands—and it is most definitely a command. Until that moment, I was so intent on watching Ryker that I didn't realize I was still sitting in the man's lap. I quickly get up, nervously moving aside.

"Ryker—" I start, but one look from him stops the rest of the words in my throat. He's pissed. He was mad last night, but that pales in comparison to the fury coming off of him right now.

"Slim," he calls out.

"Yeah, man?"

"Unlock your office," he says, but his gaze is glued to the man who grabbed my breast. He's still holding the asshole's hand and it's an intense grip. It's the type of hold that I know will leave a bruise. Maybe the guy is starting to sober up too, because he's not trying to fight with Ryker, or even get away from him. He's barely breathing—almost as if he's afraid resisting too much will unleash the anger Ryker is carrying. The man is obviously smarter than I gave him credit for.

"Buddy, listen. We don't want any problem. I didn't know she was yours. No harm, no foul here. What do you say?"

"Lola, go to Slim's office and wait for me," he says and his voice drops down. It's much quieter now, almost deadly.

"Ryk—"

"I'm barely hanging on right now, Lola. Do it and do not argue," he all but growls out.

I should be terrified. The anger and force behind Ryker's words should chill me. The look in his eyes as he's staring down at the drunken asshole who hurt me should make me run away. Instead, I'm excited. I won't lie; I'm nervous as hell. But Ryker Stone just called me his in front of everyone in the bar. *His.*

"Okay, Ryker," I say softly, touching his shoulder as I walk around him. He takes his gaze away from the other man—just briefly.

"When I get back there, Lola, you better have your ass bared and bent over the table."

"What? Ryker, I..." I cannot believe he is saying these things, let alone in front of everyone.

"I told you to protect yourself and to be careful. You weren't. It's time you find out what happens when you jeopardize what's mine."

"Now, listen here. I know—"

"You offered yourself to me last night, do you remember, Lola?" he prompts.

God, I should be humiliated he's saying these things, but the truth is I'm excited, aroused.

"Jesus. You're all fucking crazy," the drunk slurs out. He's jerking his hand away now, but it's useless. Ryker's not about to let him go. All he manages to accomplish is making Ryker angrier. Ryker shifts and maneuvers so the man is now standing up. Ryker spins him around so he's facing him, then drives his elbow into the man's side, causing him to bend in half, crying out in pain.

"Lola?" Ryker prompts again.

"I remember." I swallow, wondering now if it is nerves or excitement making me feel more than a little dizzy.

"You told me to tell you what I wanted first. So I'm telling you. When I get back there you better be in the position I want you, the way I want you, and ready for your punishment. Do you understand?"

"Ye...yes," I stutter, wondering why my nipples pebble at his instructions. I can feel how wet I am now, my panties soaked clean through. His crass words and demanding tone should turn me off, but it doesn't. At the very least, I should be embarrassed that the entire bar is listening and knows what Ryker will be doing to me soon.

I'm not—not really.

I hold my head up all the way to the back of the building where the office is. Out of the corner of my eye I see Tina and I know she's looking at me with envy. I can't resist smiling.

8

Ryker

I have the fucker's shirt wrapped tightly around my fist as I haul him out of the bar. When we are outside, I toss him away from me and he lands on his ass in the parking lot. He looks up at me, maybe wanting to retaliate, maybe thinking he can go up against me.

I want him to try because right now I am feeling pretty pissed. He put his hands on what is mine and I want the fucker to pay for it.

He picks himself up off the ground and we stare at each other for a few seconds. "Come on, motherfucker, come after me and let me beat your ass."

I can hear the door to the bar opening behind me,

and have to assume his friends have come out. Maybe they're smarter than him and will take his ass home.

Finally he just shakes his head and runs a hand across his face. His friends move around me and it's clear they are smarter than I've given them credit for. They walk away from me and head to their car, but I still feel pretty pissed off.

I run my hand across my jaw and exhale roughly. Part of me is angry at Lola, mainly because I hate that she's in this situation constantly. I don't want her working at this bar, don't want bastards looking at her, touching her...thinking they have a chance with her.

I turn and look at the bar, knowing she's waiting for me in the back room. I curl my hands into tight fists at my sides and grin. What I'm about to show her, do to her, will make it abundantly clear that she is mine.

I ignore everybody and everything as I head back into the bar, toward Slim's office. I don't bother knocking before I swing the door open. I stare at her, her body so much smaller than mine, so innocent and vulnerable...so feminine.

My arousal is strong, like this fucking beast inside of me. I kick the door shut behind me with my foot and reach around to lock it. No one is going to interrupt this.

I could ease her into things, give her some sweet-talking and be gentle. But I know she wants me the same way I want her, and going slow is more than I can offer her right now.

"Take off those tiny as fuck shorts, pull your panties down, turn around and bend over the desk," I order her, leaving no room for argument—heaven help her if she tries.

She hesitates for just a moment, but then I lower my gaze and watch as she unbuttons her shorts and pulls the zipper down. My heart starts thundering then, and I feel my cock jerk violently. The fucker gets hard in that instant, pressing against the fly of my jeans and demanding freedom.

When her shorts and panties are pushed down to her ankles, I can't help but growl at the sight of the trimmed thatch of hair that covers her pussy. She turns around and bends over like a good girl. With her back toward me now, her ass in the air, I reach down and palm my dick through my jeans. I groan at the pleasure that shoots up my spine.

I walk over to Lola and don't stop myself from reaching out and cupping one smooth, peach-colored cheek. I want to smack the flesh, spank her good and hard until my handprint is covering her pale flesh.

"Baby, I'm about to show you that working here, being around these motherfuckers, has consequences." She looks over her shoulder at me, her eyes wide, her mouth parted.

"But it's not my fault there are a bunch of assholes who come here," she defends and if I wasn't so fucking hard and ready to go off, I would smile.

No, it wasn't her fault, but I need an excuse to touch her in the way I want to, in the way I need to. I also need her to understand that when it comes to her, to her safety—fuck, anything to do with her, I'm not about to be reasonable.

"Tell me you want my hands on you, want me to smack this perfect ass until the pleasure and pain melt into one, until my mark is on your body and you know that you're mine."

She still looks at me over her shoulder, her eyes so wide, her pretty, pink lips still parted.

"Tell me, dammit." My voice is harsh, rough, exactly how I'm going to be with her. I won't be satisfied until she is screaming out for more.

"Yes," she says softly and I can hear the need in her voice. Her hands are stretched out in front of her, her fingers curled around the edge of the desk.

I take a step back and put my foot between her legs to kick her feet apart. I look down at her ass, her legs spread wide enough that I can see her pussy lips. They are pink and glossy, and slightly swollen from her arousal. My mouth waters and my balls draw up tight to my body.

I want to reach down and unzip my jeans, pull my

dick out, and align it right at the entrance of her pussy hole. I want to shove it deep inside of her, claiming her cherry and making her know she's mine.

But instead of doing that, I bring my hand back and strike her ass. The spanking I deliver is hard enough that my palm stings, and I see her back bow. I know that the pain is there. I do this over and over again, bringing my palm down on the fleshy globes, seeing the skin shake from my actions. I'm careful never to land my hand in the same spot twice. This is about teaching her to need what only I can give her. I'm not going to physically hurt her; she's precious to me. I merely need to teach her that there is pleasure in the pain.

Her ass is a beautiful shade of red, and I can hear her panting, hear the sweet moans of hunger as they leave her mouth. I know it hurts, but I also know it feels good. It's several long minutes before I finally stop spanking her and take a step back. I'm breathing hard, my dick like a steel rod between my legs, and sweat dotting my brow.

Before I can even think about what I'm doing, before I even know what I'm doing, I'm on my knees behind her. My hands are on her ass cheeks, spreading them wide, taking in the pretty pink cunt that I have revealed.

She's so fucking wet for me. Her juices are covering her inner thighs and her clit is engorged and peeking out for my mouth. I lean in and run my tongue from her clit to her pussy hole, lapping up her cream, swallowing the musky sweetness that she produces for me.

Only for me.

Her legs are shaking and I push my way between them, using my shoulders to make sure her thighs are spread good and wide for me. I devour her then, licking and sucking the lips of her pussy, taking her clit into my mouth and drawing circles around it with my tongue.

She's moaning loudly for me now, and I renew my efforts. I dig my fingers into her ass cheeks, holding her in place as I eat her out. But all too soon I pull away, stand up, and help her up off the table. I turn around and she looks up at me with this dazed, almost crazed expression. But I'm not nearly done with her yet.

I walk over to the chair behind the desk and take a seat, wrap my hands around her waist, and lift her up so she is now sitting in front of me.

"Put your feet on the arms of the chair," I demand as I look into her eyes.

When she's in the position I want her in I look at her cunt spread open for me. She's so fucking ready for me, so primed for my cock. But tonight I'm not going to fuck her. There are things I need to discuss with Lola before I take that pretty cherry as my own.

I reach around and grab her ass, pulling her forward so her bottom is right on the edge of the desk.

And then I start devouring her again. I lick and suck, working my way through every part of her pussy until her stomach is heaving up and down and she's begging me for more.

And just when I have gotten started, Lola starts rocking her hips back and forth. She has her arms behind her, bracing herself so she can find more pleasure. She grinds her pussy on my mouth, all over my beard, crying out as she gets closer to exploding. I sit there and let her do her thing, let her ride me until she's crying out and coming all over my mouth.

I lap at the juices that come from her. I use my thumbs to pull her pussy lips apart and lick at every single inch of her. I twirl my tongue around her clit until she's begging me to stop, pleading that she's too sensitive. Only then do I pull away, her cream all over my mouth and beard, her satisfaction filling me.

"You're mine." The words come from me on their own, demanding, and set in stone. Her mouth is open and she's breathing hard, her chest rising and falling, her tits pressed up and out, her nipples rock hard.

"I'm yours."

Yeah, she fucking is.

9

Lola

"Look at me, Lola," Ryker commands.

I'm standing awkwardly by the door— now fully dressed, my head down, and trying to process what just happened. It's everything I've been dreaming about—maybe more, but now that it's over I'm unsure about what comes next, how I'm supposed to act. I don't know what Ryker expects of me. No, I know what he expects...*all of it. All of me.* Which leaves me standing here like a dummy, using all the courage I have just to raise my head and look Ryker in the eye.

The minute I do I see the ownership in his gaze. I see the satisfaction on his face. I also see signs of my arousal on his mustache and beard. I feel my face heat and I know I'm blushing. The harsh lines on Ryker's face soften and he comes closer, hooks his hand around my neck, and pulls me into his body. He's tall and made up of lean muscle, but he encircles me and I feel tiny and feminine next to him. I feel protected and safe. That's it exactly. It's a strange sensation, but I have to acknowledge it. Ryker makes me feel *safe*.

"You're mine." He repeats his earlier words and I can't stop the small smile that spreads on my face, because he sounds kind of like a caveman.

"I know," I acknowledge.

"Are you ashamed?" he asks, his voice all growly. His other hand comes up and he holds my head between them, as if he is preventing me from looking away. There's an emotion on his face I can't name, but it makes me feel like my answer has more weight than I can understand.

"No. Of course not," I murmur. Nothing could make me ashamed of what we just did. I feel like I've wanted it my whole life. There's still a part of me wondering if it's really happened. Maybe I've dreamed it for so long, this is just another fantasy and I'll wake up and none of it will have ever happened.

"Then why are you suddenly so shy, when minutes ago you were riding my face and begging for more?" His question makes me squirm a little from embarrassment, but more because I can feel a fresh wave of excitement roll through me, making me even wetter. My body instantly craves the relief I know only Ryker can give me. He's a forbidden fruit and now that I've had one taste, I just want more.

"Slim," I start, but then stop, unsure of how to explain it.

"Does he have a claim on you, Lola? Has he laid a hand on you?" Ryker growls, his hold growing stronger, losing its tenderness and becoming almost bruising with its force.

"No! I've never thought of any man like that except for you, Ryker. It's just he... They all know what we did in here. It's...embarrassing."

"Nothing we do together will ever embarrass me. It should never embarrass you. You belong to me, Lola. You give your body to me when, how and where I say. Do you understand?" he asks, and his frank words should bother me, but they don't. They make my body flush with heat.

"Yes, Ryker," I answer, unable to say anything else. I'm hypnotized by the dark promises held in his gaze. My answer seems to please him because his hold gentles and he moves his thumb across my cheek.

"Good girl," he says and then, as if he's giving me praise, he kisses my forehead in the sweetest kiss I can ever remember feeling. "We'll come back to just how I want you, Lola, when it's time," he adds and looks positively sinful when he delivers that promise. It's a look that makes my knees weak. "Tell me exactly what you mean when you say you've never thought of giving yourself to anyone but me. Is that true?"

I swallow, nerves assaulting me, but I push through them. Now is not the time to get weak, not when I might be on the verge of having everything I've ever wanted.

"It is. I've always wanted my first to be you," I tell him, calling on courage that I didn't know I possessed.

"Your first? What exactly are you saying, Lola?" he questions, but he knows what I'm saying. The truth is there on his face and I read it plain as day. He wants me to tell him, though, and since I've come this far, I might as well jump in head first.

"I want... I've *always* wanted you to be the man who takes my virginity, Ryker," I tell him and, though my face heats, I keep my gaze directly on him.

"I'm too old for you," he discounts, but I can tell he likes what I've said.

"Then you will know how to make it good for me," I tell him and then, because I can't stop myself, I bring my hand up to hold it against his. "You can make it good for both of us, teach me how to please you."

"You know what kind of man I am, Lola. You've heard the talk in town. I have needs a girl like you might not like," he growls, his body vibrating and I think it might be with desire.

Ryker Stone wants me.

"And I already told you, Ryker. If you took time to show me, nothing you would do to me would scare me."

"How do you know?" he asks, studying me closely and suddenly I know my entire future rests on how I answer this simple question.

"Because it's you and I'm yours. Ryker, I've always been yours. I've just been waiting for you to claim me," I tell him, my breath lodged in my chest as I wait to see how he answers my bold statement.

10

Ryker

I know she is at the shop before I even see her. I swear I can smell her, can see the lines of her curves, taste the flavor of her pussy on my tongue. Hell, I've tasted her since we left that office and I held her close as we faced the bar. Everyone knew what we'd done, what I'd done to her.

Their focus had been on us, the surprise clear on their faces.

I didn't give a fuck. I pulled Lola closer, had my hand right on her luscious ass, and let every bastard know that she was mine.

"Someone's here to see you," Rocco calls out.

I roll out from under the car, my body covered in grease and sweat, my focus on the hot little ass in front of me. Lola stands there in these cutoff shorts, her long legs tanned, creamy, and so fucking smooth. I let my gaze travel up her thighs, over the small patch of denim that covers her delicious, sweet pussy, over her midriff that's shown, and up to her generous breasts.

Fuck, ever since I had my mouth on her cunt, felt her grinding her pussy on my lips, riding me like she was dying to get off, all I can think about is shoving my cock deep in her and tearing through her cherry.

I stand and grab a towel to wipe off the grease and sweat from my face. She's looking so fucking good I can't even think straight at the moment. All I can imagine is having my face buried between her thighs, eating her out until she comes all over my face. I want to do it over and over again, make her sore, sensitive because of my lips and tongue.

"Hey," she says softly, and glances down as if she's embarrassed.

I move closer to her, lift her head up with a finger under her chin, and lean in an inch. "Baby, those pink cheeks aren't necessary. I've had my mouth all over your virgin cunt, tasted your sweet arousal and claimed you as mine already." Her cheeks turn even redder.

I take her hand and lead her back to the office, shutting the door once we are inside. I can see that she's nervous, her pulse beating rapidly right below her ear. I want to run my tongue over it, feel how fast her heart is actually beating, taste her skin and memorize every part of her.

I wait for her to say something, tell me what she desires. I made myself perfectly clear the other night when I had my face between her thighs. Now it's up to Lola to make the next move.

She clears her throat and looks down at the ground, and I watch her cheeks become even pinker. I'm embarrassing her, but I like that. I like that she's on edge, that I make her feel this way.

I step closer and lift her chin up again with my finger, wanting to look in her eyes, wanting to let her know without actually saying anything that I'll give her whatever she wants.

She licks her lips, and I watch her tongue dart out and smooth over the pouty flesh. I want to see that mouth wrapped around my cock, her cheeks hollowed as her head moves up and down along the shaft.

"Tell me what you want, Lola. Tell me and it's yours."

She inhales slightly, and when she exhales, her warm, sweet breath moves along my neck. She looks up at me with this wide, innocent and vulnerable expression.

"I want what we did at the office. I want more of that, want to go further."

I watch as her pupils dilate, the darkness eating up the lighter color. I lean down close so our faces are at the same level. "Do you want me to take you back to my house, strip you naked, and touch every inch of your body?" She nods slowly, her breathing increasing. "Do you want me to spread those pretty thighs of yours, place my big fucking cock at your pussy hole, and push right through that cherry of yours?"

"Oh. God."

She closes her eyes and I move my hand behind her head, steadying her. I feel her relax against me, and pull her impossibly closer to me. Then I move my mouth to her ear and say softly, "I'm going to pick you up tonight, take you back to my house, and fuck you until you can't walk straight." I pull back, waiting for her to open her eyes and look at me.

There's some noise outside the office and she looks over to the side, the worry on her face clear.

"Or we can do it right here. I can push the shit off the table, bend you over, remove these little shorts of yours, and plunge my cock deep in your tight little body."

"You really don't care if anybody hears us, or what we are doing, do you?"

I shake my head slowly. "Lola, when it comes to you

I want the whole fucking world to know that you're mine and what I do with you...*to* you." Then I lean in and kiss her harshly, plunging my tongue between her lips and making her see that my words are a promise. When I break away we are both breathing hard and heavy. "Tonight, Lola. Tonight you'll fully be mine."

11

Lola

I look in the mirror for the hundredth time. I'm so nervous. Ryker called me and told me to dress up because he was taking me out tonight. I was excited and sad at the same time. I didn't envision us leaving the house. I had hoped...

It doesn't matter. If Ryker wants to take me out, then I'll be fine with that. I look at the black dress I'm wearing. It's not really fancy, but it does look flattering on me. It's loose and flowy, falling just below my knees. It has a V-neck that shows off just enough cleavage to be called sexy. It comes up on my arms but has these cut-out sleeves that expose my shoulders. My long hair is piled high on my head in this messy bun that somehow looks kind of classy.

Overall I think I look good, attractive and ready for tonight. But at the same time I don't know if it screams *'sexy, mature woman.'* Will Ryker be disappointed? I'm hoping having my hair up will make me appear older and worldlier—a woman fit to be on the arm of someone like Ryker Stone. I look at my choice of shoes. I should have just gone with the flats. After working all night the evening before, my feet hurt. Still, it's my first night off in forever and I'm going out with the man of my dreams—and hottest fantasies. I'm not about to do half-assed on this date.

With that in mind, I slip on the glossy black heels. I've nicknamed them fuck-me pumps. I've never worn them before, but then again, I've never wanted to be fucked by anyone other than Ryker. Now that this night is actually happening, I'm not taking any chances.

I just finish adjusting the strap on my heel when the knock sounds on my front door. I can almost feel my heart flip inside my chest as my tension cranks higher. I take a deep breath, trying to calm my nerves before I open the door. When I have a hold of the handle and pull it open, Ryker is standing there in his old, faded jeans. The denim fabric hugs his body like a second skin, lovingly clinging to his thighs and stretching in ways that make my knees weak.

He's wearing a black t-shirt that looks soft and comfortable and I wonder how it would feel against my bare skin. I can feel wetness pool against my panties and coat the inside of my thighs. I have no idea how I'm supposed to go out with Ryker tonight when all I can think about is what he will do to me when we get back to his place.

His words play through my head, a promise of the dark, pleasurable things he'll do to me tonight.

I step back to let him inside, running my tongue against my lips because my mouth suddenly feels terribly dry.

"Hi," I murmur, my voice sounding deeper to my own ears. Can he hear how much I want him? Somehow I think a man of Ryker's experience can.

"You look good enough to eat," he says, his hand reaching out to run a finger along the inside of my neck.

His words are dirty and we both know how he means them. Goosebumps pop up on my flesh and I have to bite my lip to keep from begging him to touch me in other places.

"You get all dressed up for me, Lola?" he asks, and I can't find my voice to answer. I nod my reply instead. Worry instantly assaults me when Ryker takes a step back, appraising me. "Turn around," his rough voice commands.

My gaze lifts up to his, startled. I don't think of disobeying him, however. I don't see how any woman could. I turn slowly, wondering if I will meet with his approval, or if he will be disappointed. Will he wish he had picked out someone older? Someone with more experience, someone who can please him in the way he wants? A woman who understands and anticipates all of his desires? I feel completely out of my depth. You would have thought after spending the time in the office where Ryker brought me to orgasm, I'd feel more at ease. It appears the opposite is true.

"Are you wearing anything under that dress, Lola?" he growls as I turn back to face him.

"My..." My words come to a stop when I begin to literally feel the vibration of Ryker's mood. At first I mistake it for anger, but one look at his face tells me that's not it. It's...*hunger.* "My panties," I whisper, suddenly feeling more secure.

"Take them off," he growls, issuing the order.

"I...I thought we were going out?" I question him.

"We are, but I want your pussy bare under that dress."

"Why?" I ask, and it's not that I'm that naïve, but I have this need to hear him tell me exactly why he wants me open to him.

"Because I'm going to fuck you with my fingers while we're at the restaurant," he tells me, crossing his arms at his chest as if daring me to deny him.

"What if... I mean... I might come..."

"Oh, you will definitely come, Lola," he agrees and this time his throaty voice sends shockwaves through me, and they all seem to center in my very wet pussy.

"People around us will hear me, Ryker. They will know."

"And every man there will be grabbing their cocks and wishing they were me. They'll all be wishing they could fuck your sweet little virgin cunt. But they won't, will they, Lola? They'll be nutting off in their hands instead. And do you know why, Lola?" he asks, his dark gaze almost burning me with its intensity.

"Because I belong to you," I tell him, instinctively knowing what he wants from me.

"Damn straight. Now I'm not telling you again. Take off those panties and hand them to me." I move to turn around to go down the hall, but Ryker stops me by reaching out and grabbing my arm. "Where are you going?"

"I was going to my room to take off—"

"You'll take them off right here in front of me," he interrupts. My breath shudders through my body and I feel my excitement slide from my pussy, soaking my panties and dripping along my thighs. I'm so wet it's embarrassing. I can even smell my own arousal. If I go out without panties on, others will too. They'll all know I'm dying to have Ryker's cock inside of me. They'll know and I realize that's exactly what he wants.

I reach under my dress, hooking my fingers in the waistband of the small black lace thong, thanking my maker that I decided to go with the sexy lingerie tonight to please Ryker. My dress covers me, though it rises high on my thighs because of my hands. The cool air hits the wet lips of my pussy and I feel wicked and desirable at the same time. I slide them down my legs while Ryker steadies me. I use one of my hands to brace myself on his arm as I step out of my panties and then straighten back up. I tentatively reach out to slop the material into Ryker's waiting hand. They're soaked. My cream has coated them and I should feel embarrassed, but I don't—especially when Ryker brings them up to his face and pushes them against his nose, breathing in my scent. It turns me on in ways I never expected and I feel a fresh gush of wetness. At this rate he's going to make me come and he hasn't even really touched me.

"That's good, Lola. Really good. I think you deserve a reward," he tells me and it takes everything I have not to beg him to take me right then and put me out of my misery, because really that's the only reward I want.

Instead, he pushes my panties into his pocket. It's then I notice the small white box he is carrying. In my excitement and hunger before, I failed to take notice. He opens it and inside is a leather strap. It's beautiful, slim, and delicate despite the material used to make it. It's shiny black with one single silver pendant in the shape of a heart. Inside the heart is also a gold embossed L, standing proudly among a sea of small, shiny stones I know instantly are diamonds. I run my finger along the strip of leather, fingering the diamond heart, but that's not what has my attention. I move my finger along the hand-tooled engraving that has been etched with clear painstaking care. One side says 'Ryker', and on the other side of the heart is the word 'property'.

The words should turn me off, worry me, or at the very least make me send him away. They do none of those things.

"Is this for me?" I ask, unable to believe it. In answer, he turns me around and I move as if in a trance. He stands behind me then and I feel the leather come around my throat.

"It's definitely yours, Lola," he rumbles against my ear as he secures the collar—because instantly some sixth sense tells me that's what it is—around my neck. The weight of it feels heavy, solid...*significant*. "Ask me how long I've had that made, Lola."

"Ryker..."

"Ask me," he instructs again.

"How long?" I ask, almost afraid to hear the answer just in case I'm wrong.

"Since the moment I first saw you as my woman,

Lola. You were always mine. I just needed to wait on you to get ready for me," he says.

My breath becomes ragged and before I know what's going on I'm in his truck and he's buckling me in the vehicle before I can form a sane thought.

I'm more than ready now.

12

Ryker

We've been at the restaurant for the last hour, our food already eaten, and my blood pumping hard and fast through my veins.

When we first entered the restaurant, Lola sat across from me. I didn't say anything to make her move closer, to have her sit right next to me...even if I want her on my fucking lap.

I let her eat in peace, let her get her bearings and get more comfortable. I can see she is nervous and a little scared about what I have planned for her tonight, what I promised I'd do to her.

But I can also see that she is ready, prepared for me.

I feel the weight of her panties in my pocket, still have the smell of her pussy ingrained in my nose, making me drunk. I pick up my beer bottle and take a long drink from it, watching her the whole time. She has her head downcast slightly, but her eyes are trained right on me, her focus right there with mine.

I set the beer bottle down and lean back against the booth. I requested this table in the back of the restaurant, away from prying eyes, from the general population. It gives us some privacy, especially for what I am planning on doing to her.

"Come here, Lola." I don't expect her to disobey me, but I can see the nervousness on her face. She is looking around, maybe worried that somebody will see or hear us. Good. I want the world to know what I do to her, how I make her feel.

"I..."

I can see she wants to maybe argue, wants to go somewhere private, but I also know that if we do this here and now it will be even more exhilarating for her.

"Come here, Lola."

She slips out of the booth and I let my gaze linger on her long legs. The dress she wears is sexy, but also has this touch of innocence to it. I want to see it off her body, tossed on my floor as she lays naked on my bed.

I get up and let her slide into the booth, and then I sit beside her, blocking her in. She is breathing hard, her breasts rising and falling underneath the thin material of the black garment. Her nipples are hard, these little twin erasers that poke against the fabric and have my mouth watering.

Because I am a dirty bastard and am impatient, I shift my body so my back is to the rest of the restaurant. I move my hand so it's now on her thigh and slide it up, pushing the dress up her leg. She feels tense beneath my touch, but her mouth is open and she is breathing hard. Her pupils are also dilated, and as she watches me I know she wants this.

I know she'll be wet as soon as I touch her between her thighs.

"Lean back for me, baby. Let me work you over real good."

"Someone will see, or hear, Ryker." But even as she whispers those words she spreads her legs for me.

I growl low in my throat, the vibrations moving through my chest. I slide my hand toward her sweet spot, and as soon as my fingers touch her soaked folds I make a deep noise in the back of my throat. She makes a small noise and leans back in the booth, giving me full access to her. I stare into her eyes as I start moving my fingers over her cleft and up to her clit. I move the digit over that tiny bundle of nerves.

I lean in even closer to her, our mouths only inches apart. Her breath smells like the vanilla ice cream and strawberries she had for dessert, and I let my tongue run over her bottom lip, tasting that sweetness for myself.

I can feel her shaking, and I work my finger over her clit faster, harder. "Come for me, Lola. Just let go and don't worry about anybody else."

She closes her eyes and moans again, and just as a waitress walks by, oblivious of what I'm doing right now, I move a finger down and tease Lola's pussy hole.

And just like that she comes for me.

She reaches out and places a hand on my thigh, close to my hard dick. She curls her nails into the denim of my pants but I don't stop touching her, don't stop wringing the orgasm from her. She's making little noises, these moans and groans of pleasure that have my cock jerking behind my zipper.

I could come right now just watching the pleasure morph across her face.

And when she finally relaxes I move my hand out from between her thighs, urge her to open her eyes without actually telling her to do so, and hold the glistening fingers I had just been pleasing her with up so she can see them.

Her eyes widen as I bring those digits to my mouth and lick them clean. The groan that spills from me at the flavor of her sweet muskiness has me feeling like a fucking animal.

"Now it's time to go back to my place so I can really show you how you're mine."

13

Lola

Ryker puts me in the truck. He doesn't speak, touch me unnecessarily, nor does he kiss me. He buckles my seat belt and closes the door with a loud slam. He does it all without much more than looking at me.

This does nothing to ease the questions and nervousness that begin to barrage my brain. I would love to talk to him. I have questions, concerns, things I would like to ask him, but instead I remain silent—just waiting.

The ride to Ryker's place is quiet. The only sound I can hear in his old truck is my own breathing. It sounds abnormally loud. I have to wonder if he can hear it too.

I suppose that should embarrass me, but it doesn't. *Not really.*

I'm pretty sure we will make it to Ryker's place in record time. If I was driving this fast I have no doubt I would get a speeding ticket. We pass several county law vehicles and one state police cruiser. None of them attempt to pull Ryker over. Maybe they know it is him and are afraid to tangle with the town bad boy?

It would be a wise choice for them to steer clear.

He pulls into his drive so quickly that gravel flies out from around the truck tires. I feel us slide in them and then hear the pinging noises they make as they smack against the undercarriage of the truck. He practically slams on the brakes and I lurch forward in the seat, jarred by the sudden stop. The seatbelt keeps me in place, but I brace my hands on the dashboard to keep from getting whiplash.

He's out of the truck and making his way around the front before I can even contemplate what's going on. I start to unbuckle when Ryker opens the passenger side door and pushes my hands out of the way, taking over completely.

He pulls me straight from the truck and into his arms, not allowing me to walk. I wrap my arms around his shoulders, holding tightly, and do the same with my legs around his hips. I like being this close to him, and having him take care of me in all ways.

"Ryker, stop. I'm too heavy," I finally say, because even if I like him carrying me, it is a little embarrassing. I've never had a man carry me quite like this. In response, his hand slaps hard against my ass, making it jiggle with each step. He growls—an animalistic noise that sends off a multitude of butterflies in the pit of my stomach.

He somehow manages to get the door opened, with me still in his arms. I get a quick glance of the main room of his home. It's surprisingly big. His house is attached to his shop, and I didn't think it would be as spacious as it is. The living room is huge, though sparingly decorated, with just a large black leather couch and a television. It's open to a kitchen, which is similar in size and full of cabinets and a table and chairs.

It's out of sight before I can make note of anything else since he's headed down a dark hallway with me still in his arms. We pass a few doors but at the end of the hall there is an open entryway with a light shining from it. He takes me there and I blink to focus my eyesight just as he puts me down so I can stand on my own.

I keep my hands on his biceps to steady myself and look around. There's a king size, four-post bed off to the side, and a large dresser across from that with a television mounted on the wall above it. That's it. There's nothing else in the room except for a high-back chair that sits directly at the foot of the bed. It's leather and looks like a chair a king would sit in as he greets his subjects. My gaze darts back to Ryker and a chill runs down my spine. I can see him as a king—a conqueror of nations...a conqueror of...*me.*

I take a step away from Ryker. I can't resist looking back at the bed. It's turned down as if waiting for me. The sheets are shiny silk and jet black. They look sinful and remind me so much of Ryker's eyes. I look back up at him—anticipating what is to come. He doesn't make me wait long.

"Undress for me, Lola," he says, his voice dark and commanding.

I swallow down my nerves. Now is not the time to let my nervousness from being a virgin or my fear of the unknown get in the way. I am Ryker's. *I belong to Ryker.* On reflex, my hand comes up to touch the soft leather choker he had made for me. A collar really; I might as well call it what it is. Even in my limited experience I realize exactly what it is. *Realize and embrace it.* I let my finger dance over the embossed 'L' in the center of the collar and I hold Ryker's gaze at the same time. He looks at me as if he is daring me to back out. Does he think I will? The thought that he might think I'm that weak in my conviction leads me to turn around, giving him my back.

"Unzip me?" I ask softly and then because it feels

right, feels like something I should give him, I add, "Please, Ryker?"

I'm rewarded by his deep, throaty growl and I know without even having him say anything that I have pleased him. He carefully unzips my dress, but he keeps a hand on my hip, not allowing me to turn back around. Instead, his fingers dance across the small area of skin now exposed. I can feel the hair of his beard gently tickle me and a moment later I feel his gentle kisses. He runs his lips up to the base of my neck. Again his beard tickles the skin and the sensation spreads a fresh wave of goosebumps on my flesh. My eyes close on their own as I feel his teeth rake across the skin, not biting, merely teasing.

Next, I feel his hands in my hair, seeking out the pins I used to pull the strands up. One by one, he begins to release them until my hair is completely down and falling along my shoulders.

"You have beautiful hair, Lola. I want to see it against my sheets. Now, be a good girl and turn around and finish undressing."

I bite my lip to keep from moaning out at how delicious it feels to have Ryker's breath against my skin. I turn around slowly to face him. I take the straps of my dress and slowly lower them, allowing the dress to slide from my body and fall to the floor. I step out of it and force my gaze to lock with Ryker's. It's not easy. I can feel the heat bloom across my skin as I stand before him in nothing but my black lace strapless bra and heels.

"Finish," he commands, his voice hoarse.

Immediately I move my hands up to unhook the clasp between my breasts. My fingers fumble with it, but it releases and I let it fall to the floor. Without thought, I use my arms to cover my breasts. The rest of me is out there. I don't even think to cover my pussy from him, but somehow the cool air against my nipples makes me feel more exposed.

"I..." I start to say something, but the words lodge in my throat when I see the heat in Ryker's gaze. I can almost feel it as if it was a literal touch. His hands come out to capture mine, forcing them away from my body and exposing my breasts completely. I bite back an apology, feeling unsure of myself. I start to bend down to take off my heels, but he stops me.

"Those fucking stay on," he orders. I look up at him, surprised, and watch as he palms his dick through his pants as if he's adjusting himself. The outline of his cock is more than visible against his jeans. I was wet before, feeling my juices painted along my thighs, but seeing the physical effect I have on Ryker just makes me wetter.

"Okay," I murmur, standing back up and suddenly

feeling more in control. He might be calling the shots, but I'm the one feeling powerful here.

"Get on the bed on your hands and knees, Lola," he orders. I get on the bed, but freeze when he puts a finger under my chin and pulls my face up to look at him. "Face the headboard," he says and I nod in under-standing as he steps back. Once I'm in position, I do my best to steady my breathing. I jerk my head around when I feel Ryker's hand wrap around my ankle.

I watch as he pulls out a silver cuff that is attached to a strap coming from the post on the bed. He connects the cuff around me, and the metal feels cold and foreign. He pulls out my other leg and does the same. I can still remain on my knees, but it's harder; I've had to spread my legs out and I know from where he's standing it opens me even more to him.

"What are...what are you doing?" I ask, unsure if it's okay to question him, but doing it anyway. I look over my shoulder as I hear movement behind me. I see Ryker pick up a box from the dresser.

"Eyes to the front, Lola," he commands, his voice sounding as if he is disciplining me for being bad. I immediately respond, not wanting to displease him further. "Good girl," he approves, stroking my lower back. I'm dying to turn around to see what he's doing, but I don't. I want him to be happy with me. Excitement flushes through me, heating me from the inside out. If he can make me feel like this without actually doing much more than touching me...

"Ryker," I exclaim, when without any type of warning I feel the rough pads of his fingers caress the lips of my wet pussy.

"You're so fucking wet," Ryker growls at the exact moment his fingers find my swollen clit and zero in on it. "So primed for me, so responsive," he adds, and he's right. My body is on fire for him. "You're going to like what happens next, my sweet Lola," he says, kissing the cheek of my ass.

That's the only warning I get before he inserts something between my legs. It's warm and soft...almost gel like. It's also long and thick and it slips between the folds of my pussy and puts pressure against my clit. I go completely still, unsure of what will happen next, when it begins vibrating.

"Ryker," I cry out as sensation immediately begins to crash in on me. My hips move of their own volition as I try to ride the wand that he's torturing me with.

"That's it, Lola. You're going to ride this little beauty while I sit in the chair behind you and watch. You'll do everything I tell you to do, because you want to please me. Won't you, Lola?"

"Ye...yes, Ryker."

"Such a good girl. I'm going to be over here stroking my cock while I watch you. If you do exactly what I tell you, I'll make sure I give you all my cum. Will that make you happy, Lola?"

"Yes. God, yes. I want it, Ryker," I tell him, and I'm already panting, trying to squeeze my pussy so my juices aren't obscenely running down the insides of my legs. But honestly I don't care. I want to come. I want to get off while Ryker covers me in his cum. I see the picture in my mind and I feel dirty and sexy at the same time.

I know the moment he walks away and I can hear him grunt. I know he's stroking his big, hard cock. I thrust my ass back even more, hoping to give him exactly what he wants.

Because I know if I do that, he will give me everything I want—and more.

14

Ryker

I sit in the chair, kicking my pants off to the side to join my shoes. I grab my t-shirt and pull it over my head to throw it with the rest. Lola is positioned in a way that she can grind herself on the silicone wand I pushed against her pussy.

She has to really work to get it moving through her cunt with her current position, but seeing her move her hips back and forth, all but fucking the hell out of that vibrator, makes me so damn hard I could bust a nut right here and now.

The binds I attached to her ankles still allow her plenty of movement. I won't tighten them until I flip her over and play with her some more. I don't have the willpower to do that without coming first.

I take my cock in my hand, and, holding it at the base, I squeeze tightly to hold back my orgasm. It's either that or come right then and there as I watch how Lola moves faster on the wand, choking it between that sweet pussy. Damn, will she act the same way with my cock? If so, she might break the fucker in two.

"That's it, baby. Ride the fuck out of it. Show me how bad you need my dick," I growl and she cries out my name, a long shudder rolling through her body. She's already close to the edge.

It's that moment that something happens that never has before—*not until Lola.* Suddenly, I don't need to come as much as I need to make her fly apart. I get up and march over to her, covering the small distance quickly.

I move my fingers against her pussy, her sweet cream instantly drowning my digits, coating them. I push against the vibrator, torturing her clit so much more in the process that she cries out and her legs tug against the restraints. I can't wait until the moment I tighten them further so she can't move.

I wonder if she'll scream loudly for me then. Maybe while I'm thrusting my hard cock through her virgin pussy. I groan at the mental image, promising myself it will happen. Her virgin blood will be all over the shaft of my cock and she will own me then, as much as I own her.

"Ryker, I want to come," she whimpers, riding the wand so hard her body is thrusting back and forth.

"Not yet, Lola," I warn, still dragging my fingers through her juices. I hold her hip, forcing her to be still. She cries out in frustration and tries to fight my hold. In answer I lean down and bite one of the plump, juicy globes of her ass. Her entire body shudders for me. I let my tongue slide against the outline of the bite. Fuck, now I want that mark permanently tattooed on her ass. No other fucker will touch her...ever. I'll just have to make sure I do this often. If the way she's throwing her head back and trying to thrust against me is any sign, she likes it, wants a little of that pain.

I take my fingers that are still coated in her sweet cream and push between her cheeks to find the small rosette opening of her ass. I paint it with her cream, smearing it on until the dark area glistens, beckoning me. After I've claimed her pussy, and fixed it so that it's shaped to fit my dick and mine alone, I will be claiming her ass. There won't be a hole on her body I haven't taken and made my own. *Fuck that.* There won't be a part of *her* that won't have my ownership written across it. Lola is mine and I'll kill the first asshole who says differently.

I use my other hand to smear my fingers along her

pussy again right before dipping back into her cunt, purposely shifting the wand so that it hits her clit at a different angle. Lola lets out a high, keening cry. Maybe she's beyond words at this point, her breathing so loud it sounds like music to my ears as it echoes in the room loudly.

I take my fingers that are soaked in her sweet pussy juice and, without even trying to be gentle, I push them into her ass. It's so fucking tight I have to shove them in almost violently, but nothing will stop me from claiming everything about her. Once I push through the small ring of muscles, I let my fingers separate, widening her opening. I must have been wrong because it's that moment Lola gives me something I didn't even ask for.

She goes down low on her arms, her head touching the mattress. The action pushes her ass out higher in the air and the whole pose is one of surrender. That is fucking hot enough, but then she makes it even better.

"Ryker, Ryker, Ryker..." She repeats my name over and over like a prayer—or as if she's looking for me to save her, to answer her plea.

That's what finally drives me to fuck her ass with my fingers, pushing them in and out, first slow but steady and then faster, as I use my hand to take over her body and dictate her thrusts. She moves on the vibrator like a rodeo queen, fucking herself like she's riding a thoroughbred at the Derby.

Jesus, I can't wait until my cock is inside of her. I can already feel pre-cum running down my cock. We're both too fucking close to the edge. For that reason—and that reason alone—I finally decide to take pity on her. Although if I'm completely honest, I might be doing it because I can't stop myself. Lola destroys my control completely.

I remove the wand from her, shutting it off and tossing it to the other side of the bed.

"No!" she cries out, her entire body fighting against the loss. I shift my position, taking my fingers away and slapping her ass in warning all at the same time. "Ryker!" she cries, drawing out my name. Still, even with the protest, her body stills when I deliver her spanking.

I pull on her thighs, widening her stance, and then slide under her body. With very little encouragement and limited direction using my hold on her, she adjusts until she's sitting on my face. Her clit is throbbing against my lips, hard and engorged. I flick it with my tongue, burying my face in that sweet pussy. I eat her like a man starving, pushing my face into her warm depths. I shove my tongue deep into her sweet spot, licking against her inner walls. My cock, which is already as hard as concrete, grows impossibly thicker. She's so fucking close to getting off she tries to squeeze against my face, riding the ridge of my nose, bathing me in her sweetness.

I hear her crying out above me, and for a moment I wonder if I can keep her like this, torturing her over and over until she comes so hard she loses consciousness. I'd be willing to try it if I wasn't so close to the edge myself. So instead, I slide my fingers back into her ass, pushing the digits deep inside at the same time I capture her clit between my teeth and apply a gentle pressure. In that moment she climaxes, and I lick it all up.

Every. Fucking. Drop.

15

Ryker

"Please," she whispers.

"Please what?" I murmur against her swollen, soaked folds.

"Fuck me."

I groan deeply. Yeah, I'll fuck her all right. "You want me to pop that cherry of yours?"

She nods. "God, yes. Now. Please." And then she moans and thrusts her pussy against my face. I want to fuck her so damn badly, but I keep torturing us. I start rubbing her pussy lips, sliding my fingers toward her center, and run the digits up and down her slit.

She grinds herself on me even harder, more frantic. I know I could get her off again but I want her to come on my cock, with me buried deep inside of her. I work my fingers along her pussy lips, the silky smoothness of her flesh so fucking hot I know I won't last once I'm balls deep in her cunt.

I pull away, regretfully moving from the bed, but only long enough to take the ties off her ankles. I give her ass some hard slaps, growl at the way she cries out, and flip her onto her back. When I move up her body, letting my cock slide along her upper thigh, my pre-cum coating her skin, I envision myself marking her up real good. I start thrusting my dick against her belly, the friction feeling fucking fantastic.

I could come just from the motion alone.

And I want to get off, but I'll be deep in her body when that happens.

"How much do you like it, baby? How much do you want this?"

"God, Ryker, I want it so much."

I move my other hand that wasn't just ass-fucking her between our bodies and find her clit, rubbing my thumb over the bud back and forth, harder and faster.

"I want to be deep inside of you. I want to be so far up in you all you can think about is me." I start licking and nipping at her neck, loving the saltiness that forms because she's starting to sweat from this. I'm giving her a hard workout and this is only the beginning. "I want my cock in your cunt, want to feel your pussy milking me, strangling my dick." I stroke her clit faster, harder, and suck her skin with more force, knowing there will be a mark...needing there to be one.

She starts moving her hips, grinding her pussy on my hand, clearly wanting to get off. And hell, I want her to come.

But I need to be inside of her first.

Removing my hand, I lift it so she can see how glossy my fingers are. "Open your mouth." She does without hesitation, and it makes me so fucking turned on my balls hurt. "Suck on them." She opens her mouth and I push my fingers between her lips, watching as she does what I say.

"You taste good, don't you?"

She nods.

I lift my digits to my mouth and suck on them too, groaning at how good she fucking tastes.

I'm done with the foreplay. I need to have my cock deep in her.

I need to make her mine.

"I'm going to pound my cock so hard into your pussy, so raw, so possessively, you'll feel it tomorrow when you sit down." I am such a filthy fucking bastard, but fuck, she likes it. I know she does. "You'll feel that soreness, that tenderness from having my huge dick in you, and you'll know you're *mine.*"

Yeah, she'll feel every last inch of me tomorrow, hell,

for the next several days. I'll pound my cock deep in her body so there is no doubt in her mind who she belongs to. And any motherfucker who thinks they can challenge me for her, who tries to tell me Lola isn't mine in all ways, will find out swiftly what it is like to get their ass kicked by me.

Lola

I FEEL LIKE ANOTHER PERSON, like this really isn't me participating in this wanton, erotic act. I don't want to be the virgin who doesn't know what is going to happen. I want to be experienced so I can give Ryker exactly what he is about to give me.

Then do it. Jump outside of the preconceived notions that you have to be the shy virgin. Tell him what you want.

"I need you in me," I finally manage to say, forcing myself to be the woman I've always wanted to be with him.

The sound he makes is of a man losing what little control he has left. I'm flipped over onto my belly a second later, the air leaving me.

He parts my ass cheeks, slides his fingers between my thighs, and I gasp at the sensation of his thick fingers moving through my soaked flesh.

"You're so fucking wet for me, so ready for me to break in this virgin pussy, aren't you, baby girl?"

I can only nod.

"I can't wait any longer to tear you up. I have to break this cherry and make it my own. I have to watch as your cunt swallows my dick whole."

A second later I feel the head of his dick press against my entrance.

In one swift move he buries all of his monstrous inches into me. I feel my eyes widen, feel like I'm splitting in two. Tears prick the corner of my eyes, and I suck in a breath. I am stretched fully. The burn is there, the discomfort instant. He slowly pulls out and pushes back in. He is so big and long, so thick and completely consuming me.

I look over my shoulder at him. Every muscle I can see on him is taut, and his face is strained. I feel his hands tighten painfully on my waist, and I know I'll get exactly what I want soon enough.

He doesn't give me time to adjust to his size, doesn't give me a chance to think about what is going on. He starts fucking me then. Ryker pulls out so just the tip is lodged in my pussy, then shoves deep in me. He does it so hard, so fast I feel the air leave me. My inner muscles clench rhythmically around his monstrous cock.

"You feel so fucking good."

He fucks me like this for long seconds, but then

pulls out before we can really get this going. In the next moment he has me turned around so I'm facing him. He runs his hands down my inner thighs, frames my pussy, and for a second just stares at me.

"All mine," he says and grabs his cock. I look down and see my wetness and blood covering the length. The virgin redness is streaked on his impressive cock, and I feel my inner muscles clench.

He aligns his cock with my pussy again, and while holding my gaze, he thrusts in deep once more. As the seconds move, his motions become more frenzied. He is like a madman between my legs, making these grunts and growls that remind me of a wild animal.

All I can do is hold on and let him fuck me.

"You like my big cock between your thighs, my fingers digging into you, don't you, Lola baby?" He slams inside of me, and I gasp.

"God, yes."

He groans. "You're so fucking tight and wet."

"God, yes." I can only repeat the same words. Thinking is beyond me. My words are high-pitched as they spill from me. The sound of his cock moving in and out of my pussy is loud, dirty in a good way.

I am about to come, but he slows and leans forward, licking my breasts, the stiff peaks hardening under his tongue. And all the while he continues to work his dick in and out of me.

"As much as I fucking love watching my cock slide in and out of your cunt, your body craving mine, I want to see the pleasure on your face when you come all over my dick."

God, I get off for him again.

"God, fuck yes," he grunts against my mouth, and starts slamming his dick into me then.

And then somehow I come again, just let go, fall over the edge. I can't even breathe.

"*Christ*, baby girl, you're so fucking hot. You're so damn wet my cock is soaked."

He pulls out slightly and then slams back into me hard. I cry out at how intensely good it feels.

"I'll never get enough," he says, and although this is the first time we've been together, I can't help but believe him. "I want you to ride me until you're bouncing on my cock, until you get so wild you're sore tomorrow."

"Oh. God," I whisper. The next second I am shifted and he is under me. My legs are spread over his hips, my pussy almost aligned with his cock head.

"Fuck me, baby. Put my cock deep in your pussy and ride me."

And I do just that. Once his cock is lodged deep in my body, I start rocking back and forth on him. I rest my hands on his pecs, bracing myself. I start bouncing on him, up and down, harder and faster.

"*Christ.*" His voice is rough, his hold on me fierce.

Everything in me tightens. He stretches me so good, and the burn of the pleasure is still there. I never want it to end. My breath leaves me and my arms shake from holding myself up, but still I ride him.

"You're mine. All fucking mine."

I am his. All his.

I don't want this to ever end.

16

Lola

Three days. That's all it's been since I've been in Ryker's bed, but it feels like forever. It feels like my life has always been this wonderful. Ryker took my virginity three days ago and I'm completely his. Everything is better. Tonight is my first night back to work. Ryker wasn't happy. He doesn't want me working here. I told him no one would dare mess with me now—not when word has gotten out that I belong to him. He still doesn't like it. Somehow I convinced him to let me come to work tonight, but only on the condition that I stay inside the bar, let one of the others take out the garbage and that he brings me and picks me up. Since I really don't want to be without him, I agreed easily.

He dropped me off with a kiss that melted me and left me hungry for more. He had to go back to work at the shop, but he promised to be back before time for me to get off. I'm about an hour from my shift being done and there's still been no sign of him. I miss him; my body misses him. Maybe he was right and I should quit work. If I wasn't working, I could be at his garage right now. He offered me a job in his office. I could do that and see him all the time... maybe even beg him to fuck me on my desk...

For a woman that three days ago had never had sex, it seems to be all I can think about now. I know instinctively it's because it was Ryker. It's because I am his— and he is mine. He's ruined me for other men, and he seems to have no interest in other women either. He tells me I'm the one he's been waiting for and... *I believe him.*

"Lola, we need to talk." I turn around quickly. I hate that voice. *My mother.* When she's around trouble is bound to be close behind.

"I can't talk right now. I'm working."

"Working," she scoffs. "Why do you need to work? Word around town is that you've managed to capture Ryker Stone's attention. Was it all a lie?"

"I... That's none of your business, really, Mother," I

tell her, not liking the idea of my mom spending any time whatsoever thinking about my relationship with Ryker. There are people in this world that are just toxic and my mother is definitely one of those. I don't want her near anything that Ryker and I share.

I'm so lost in my thoughts that I don't see her hand coming toward me. I cry out when it connects with the side of my face, the burning sting of pain following the hit swiftly.

"You don't talk to me like that! I am your mother!" she cries out.

"You touch my woman again, and the only thing you will be is planted in the ground for the worms to devour," Ryker growls out, his voice colder than anything I've ever heard. It chills me and I know without a shadow of a doubt he would never hurt me. "Lola, come here," he orders and I walk to him, still holding my cheek. He pulls my hand down to inspect my face. I can't know what he sees, but I feel the glowing heat from the hit still, and I can tell from the anger vibrating through him, and showing on his stern face, that it's not good. "Slim!" he yells out, his gaze never leaving mine.

"Yeah, Ryker?" my boss answers.

"What the fuck are you doing here? You can't protect my woman one night? First she almost gets gang-raped out back last week and now this. Where the fuck are your bouncers?"

"Man, they've been watching for other men, but well... Shit, man, it's her mom."

"That woman is nothing but a piece of trash to take out," Ryker growls and I don't disagree with him. She's never been a mother. I actually have to wonder why she showed up here.

I shouldn't have worried, though. She makes the reason abundantly clear with her next screeching statement.

"Who the hell do you think you are? Calling me trash like that! I'm her mother! I fed and clothed the ungrateful piece of shit year after year! She owes me!" she hisses and my eyes go big. I started work at sixteen and even before that I mostly ate at one of the neighbors' trailers in the park we lived at. My mother never gave a shit about me.

"What exactly do you think—" I start to respond, but Ryker doesn't let me. He crosses in front of me protectively. My mouth shuts closed, because it's apparent Ryker doesn't want me dealing with her.

"What is it you want from her?" Ryker says, getting to the heart of the matter.

"I think this discussion is better had between me and Lola."

"Lady, you are crazy if you think you are getting

anywhere near my woman again. Now, my patience is wearing thin. I want to take my woman home, make sure she is okay and then get lost deep inside of her and go to sleep. You are keeping me from that. So spit out exactly why you crawled out from under your rock and let's be done with it."

"I would rather speak with Lola," she argues stubbornly.

"And we're done here," Ryker says, turning away from her and back to me.

"I need money!"

"What the fuck?" Ryker mutters. He looks at me and, despite the still burning pain of my cheek, I know the color drains from my face. It's one thing to know your mother is a bitch who could care less about you; it's quite another to let the man you love see it. I want Ryker to see me as someone worthy of love—someone he could be proud of.

What if he thinks because she is my mother that I will end up being just like her?

"Ryker—" I start, but he doesn't let me finish. For a second I'm scared this will cause him to leave me. Then he turns back around to my mother.

"I'm listening," he snarls out.

"I need to get out of town. I'm going to California."

"What does that have to do with Lola?"

"I need some money to get out of here."

"How in the hell is that our problem?"

"It's not yours! But Lola is my daughter and she owes me! She's got a job and now you. Everyone in this godforsaken town knows you're loaded. The least she can do is give me enough money to help me start over!"

"How exactly does she owe you?"

"She stole years of my life! She's the reason Phillip left me!"

"Who the hell is Phillip?" Ryker barks.

"Her last boyfriend," I whisper, feeling sick to my stomach.

"Then he probably left because he couldn't handle waking up to a rack of bones that stays doped up out of her mind," Ryker justifies.

"He left because of Lola!"

"I doubt—"

"He left because I told him the next time he tried to break into my room and climb in my bed I'd have him arrested!" I defend, sick of all of this, and mostly sick that this person is my mother.

"He what?" Ryker asks, his voice deadly.

"You should have just let him. Phillip was good to you. You didn't complain when he put food on the table," my mother claims, like she's tired of talking about it.

"You aren't getting a penny from Lola or from me," Ryker says and this time he's not yelling at my mother.

He's not growling in his normal tone. This time his voice is deadly quiet and has the strength of steel behind it.

"She—"

"We don't really know each other, so I'm going to give you advice now. Lola is mine. She saved herself for me. You just told her she should have given what was mine away. More than that, you just admitted you would have sacrificed your innocent daughter to keep your man happy since you couldn't."

"How dare you!"

"This is the only warning you get, so you better heed my advice, lady, because I'm not giving it twice. You leave this place and you don't even try to contact Lola again. As far as you are concerned she's dead to you."

"You don't have that right."

"I have every right. I'm protecting my woman from a viper like you."

"You have no control over me. I'm not some lapdog like you're trying to turn my daughter into."

"I can see you're not going to listen to my warning. So let me tell you what will happen if you don't leave. That fucking candy store you've been running out of the trunk of your car will be discovered. I'll make sure enough fuckwads come forward to pin your ass to the wall."

"You can't. You don't have the proof to do that."

"It's amazing what money can do, and as you just said... I'm loaded. So try me. I'll make sure they lock you in a federal pen with security so tight you'll never see the light of day."

My mother is watching Ryker closely. I can see the moment she knows she's hit a wall she can't get around. I even see a glimpse of real fear on her face.

I don't know what she would have said next. I don't get the chance to ask.

Ryker spins around and picks me up, throwing me over his shoulder in a fireman's carry so fast my head spins. I cry out and try to steady myself by using my hands on his back.

"Slim?"

"Yeah, Ryker?"

"My woman quits. She's going to work at the garage where I know she's safe and filth can't touch her."

"You got it, man," I hear Slim answer right before the door to the club slams behind us.

Ryker marches over to his old truck like a man with a purpose. He opens the door and then shifts me so I'm standing.

"Do you have a problem with anything that happened in there, Lola?" he asks.

"No," I answer honestly.

"Good. Then I'm taking you back home, I'm fucking

you raw and then after I've calmed down, I'll fuck you soft. You got anything to say to that?"

"Take me home, Ryker," I whisper softly.

He grunts in reply, scoops me up and deposits me in the seat of his truck and buckles me in. He's still vibrating with anger at my mother, but even in his fury he takes the time to kiss my lips. He kisses them softly, too, letting none of his anger bleed through.

With Ryker I know I'll always be safe. It's such a beautiful feeling.

EPILOGUE

Ryker

One year later

For me there is only Lola. There will only ever be Lola.

Until she came into my life I didn't know I could actually be happy, that a bastard like me deserved something so pure and good.

A year has already passed since I staked my claim on her. I made her quit that fucking bar job, and told her whatever she wanted to do I'd support her. And now she is enrolled in some community classes and loving the hell out of it.

I pull into the driveway and cut the engine. I'm out

of the truck and in the house, anxious to see her, in a few minutes flat. She's in the kitchen, the smell of steak filling my nose. My woman might be younger than me, but fuck, does she know how to cook her man a meal.

With her back to me I walk up to her, my dick already hard, my need for her never dimming in this last year. Hell, I fuck her nearly every day simply because I can't get enough of her sweet fucking pussy.

I reach out, wrap my hand around her waist, and spin her around. She gasps and falls into me, and I let out a pleasurable growl as her taut breasts press against my chest. I grind my cock into her belly and she hums in approval. She's always ready for me, her pussy always soaked for my big dick.

Her mom is no longer in the picture. And even though the bitch had started shit was us a year ago, I was glad she wasn't messing with what Lola and I had anymore. She knows better. No fucking way I'll let her fuck things up.

I lower my face to her neck and inhale deeply. "You wet for me, baby girl?"

She sighs her answer. I run the tip of my nose up the side of her throat, loving the smell of her. She makes this sweet little moan and presses closer to me.

"You smell like you've been working all day."

"What, all of a sudden you don't like the smell of a garage on your man?" I tease.

"I love it."

Yeah, she does.

As much as I want to fuck her, I need to get serious.

Really fucking serious.

"You okay?"

"I'll be right back." I leave her alone for a second and head into the bedroom to get the engagement ring box I hid there. Once back to where she is, I drop to one knee, not about to prolong this, and hoping I don't fuck it up.

When I show her the box her eyes widen. "I can make this long as fuck, try and woo you, show you I can be a gentleman, but the truth is you love me for the gruff bastard I am." I cup the side of her face again. "I love you so damn much." I open the box and show her the ring. "You're the only woman I want to spend my life with, to be big and pregnant with my babies." I slip the diamond on her ring finger. "Will you marry me?"

She doesn't say anything for a few seconds, but the happiness is clear on her face. "Yes. Always. Forever."

I pull her into my embrace and hold her tight, never letting go. She's mine, always has been, and always will be.

The End

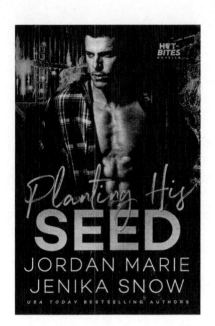

Planting His
SEED

JORDAN MARIE
JENIKA SNOW

USA TODAY BESTSELLING AUTHORS

PLANTING HIS SEED

By Jordan Marie and Jenika Snow

www.JordanMarieRomance.com

support@jordanmarieromance.com

www.JenikaSnow.com

Jenika_Snow@yahoo.com

Copyright © November 2017 by Jordan Marie and Jenika Snow

First E-book Publication: November 2017

Photographer: Wander Aguiar

Cover model: Travis S.

Photo provided by: Wander Book Club

Cover Design: RBA Designs

Editor: Kasi Alexander

Planting His SEED

JORDAN MARIE
JENIKA SNOW

USA TODAY BESTSELLING AUTHORS

Carson

Jenny is too young for me and way too innocent.

I'm older, set in my ways—and her guardian.

Her father was my best friend and when he passed away she became my responsibility.

Our relationship should have stayed just that.

But I love her.

I've loved her for longer than I want to admit and I just can't stay away.

When it's all said and done I'm going to make her mine.

She'll be by my side, be my wife.

And Jenny may not know it yet, but she'll also have my babies.

Warning: If you're looking for a quick, hot ride with an over the top Alpha who has eyes only for his woman and will stop at nothing until he's given her everything—even his babies. Then you've come to the right place.

1

Carson

"When's Virginia's plane due in?" Mavis asks.

I don't turn around to look at her. I'm standing at the large picture window in my study, looking out across the land that has been in my family for generations. Land that has seeped into my bones and oozes out when I bleed. Land that is a part of me. Land I would die without.

Living in Blayton, Wyoming might not be for everyone, but it's all I've ever known—and all I've ever wanted. *Except for one thing.*

Virginia Madison.

I've wanted Jenny for as long as I can remember.

She's been my biggest blessing and my biggest curse. Her father, Luke, was older than me, but he was my best friend and someone I trusted and leaned on. Being a farmer in the heart of ranch country isn't fucking easy. Being a farmer anywhere these days is hell. Luke was a sounding board when I needed it. I depended on him every damn day and I think he did the same with me.

When cancer took him out six years ago it felt like I lost a piece of myself. I had already lost both of my parents and except for Luke and this land I didn't really have anyone. I'd do anything for Luke, and when he asked me to take care of his daughter, I agreed—against my better judgment. What the hell does a thirty-year-old hardened bachelor know about sixteen-year-old girls—other than they're trouble?

And Jenny is definitely that.

She was angry at the world after losing her father. She had no one left either and if anyone knew that feeling, it was me. We settled into a routine. I was never her father, would never try to be. I became her guardian and her friend and that was fine. My housekeeper Mavis was more of a parental role for Jenny.

For the first year, it worked out great. I began to look forward to spending time in the evenings listening to Jenny talk about school and her plans for the future. Hell, I didn't even mind listening to hours and hours of talk about her friends. Slowly that changed. At seventeen, Jenny began dating. Fuck, I might have been thirty-one at the time, but I still remembered what seventeen-year-old boys did and what stayed on their minds. I had to watch Jenny like a hawk. I owed it to Luke to make sure no one took advantage of his little girl. That's all it was.

Until it wasn't.

One night, on the eve of her eighteenth birthday, we were on the front porch watching the stars, reminiscing about her father and the past and that's when it happened.

We kissed.

It wasn't planned or premeditated. It happened from bonding over common grief. I had no business touching her. I'm fourteen years older than her, she was placed in my care by her father, and I am supposed to look out for her. Hell, I'm supposed to protect her from perverts trying to get in her pants—not become one of them.

I've fought it. I've fought it for four years. I found excuses to stay away from her until I could get my libido under control. Then, I made sure she went all the way to Florida for college. That almost killed me, because with just one touch of her lips I became a marked man. There was only one woman I wanted, and one woman I had to have from that moment on.

Over the years I've become an expert at keeping my

body's reactions hidden from Jenny. Every time she came home for the holidays or during breaks, I was both in heaven and in hell. Having her close to me, hugging her and just spending time with her was an exercise...in torture. Jenny, for her part, was and is clueless. She has no idea how much I want her or how much I *need* her. She has no idea about all of the dirty little things I want to do to her body.

I pull my gaze from the window and the landscape outside, to the well-worn photo in my hand. It's a picture of Jenny from last Christmas. Her long brown hair is pulled back on the top of her head in a ponytail, and stops at her lower back. Her sparkling green eyes shine like they have the answers to life's greatest mysteries. She's tall and slim. She's too slim if I'm being honest.

Some damn boyfriend she had convinced her she was too heavy and she ended up going to the gym religiously. That little asshole didn't last long. I had to work to get rid of him. Jenny deserved better than him. Hell, she deserves better than me. But tonight she's coming home. She's done with school, having earned her bachelor's in education.

In three days she turns twenty-two. I'm done waiting and holding back. I've fought with my guilt. I've warred with my conscience, but in the end I don't have a choice. Jenny will be mine.

"She'll be home in a few hours," I tell Mavis. "Make sure everything is ready for her."

"Pfft... Like I wouldn't have the place ready for our girl. Everything is ready, don't you worry. Ole' Mavis is going to make sure everything is perfect for her."

I nod, but I don't answer. I want everything to be perfect. It needs to be. Because I'm claiming her. Jenny doesn't know it yet, but she's my future. She always has been. I was just too blind to see it, to accept it. I'm going to marry her and I'm not even going to let her catch her breath before I claim her body, plant my seed deep inside of her and make sure it takes root. I'll tie her to me in the most elemental way a man can. She'll give me a son to guide this land into the next generation and a beautiful daughter with her mother's glowing green eyes for me to protect. Jenny will give me everything.

I won't stop until she does...

2

Virginia

My heart is thundering and I haven't even gotten off the plane yet. I know Carson will be waiting for me, know he won't have Mavis pick me up.

Although it hasn't been that long since I've been back at the ranch, it feels like an eternity. Truth is, every time I see Carson my feelings for him grow. He is all I think about, all I want. I've foolishly saved myself for a man who probably sees me as nothing more than his ward.

Carson has been my guardian for years, looked after me when my father passed away, and here I am lusting after him when I have no clue if he even reciprocates my feelings.

And truth is, I am too weak, too much of a coward to ever admit how I feel.

I grab my bag and get off the plane, my heart pounding so hard I feel like it's going to burst through my chest. The airport is small, very rural for this area. I had to do a layover before boarding this smaller airplane, and Carson's ranch is still almost an hour away.

But honestly, I've been looking forward to this trip since I was last here. I finally graduated with my degree, put what little possessions I had in storage, and couldn't wait to get back here. But for the last year I've been working on finals, making sure I pass my classes, and trying not to think about seeing the one man who I want more than anything else.

I leave the small airport and am momentarily blinded by the sun. I blink until my vision clears. I see Carson standing there, his back against his old pickup truck, the red color faded, and the rust spots around the wheels telling of age and use.

He's had the truck for as long as I can remember, and damn does he look good with his arms crossed, a faded baseball cap on his head, and a pair of sunglasses covering his eyes. When he's not wearing a cowboy hat while working out in the fields he has on that ball cap, one that I will always associate with him.

The smile he gives me has my heart pounding faster and this warmth seeping through my entire body. I smile in return but I feel like it's a bit shaky, a little bit forced. My feelings for him are so consuming. Even though it has been a while since I've seen him, my love for him has only grown. But I can never admit how I feel for Carson, can't even say it out loud when I'm alone.

He takes the bag out of my hand and puts it in the back of his truck. When he turns around, there's only a second where we stare into each other's eyes before he pulls me into the hardness of his body and embraces me. He's so big and strong, and my head fits perfectly against the center of his chest.

I close my eyes for a second and listen to the beat of his heart. It sounds fast, as if maybe he's a bit nervous too. But no, Carson wouldn't be nervous. He's always so steady and controlled.

When he pulls away, the grin he gives me is genuine. He reaches up and tucks a strand of hair behind my ear. His fingers linger right at my pulse point. Can he feel how hard and fast my heart is beating? Can he see the effect he has on me?

"How was your flight?" he says, his voice gravelly, harsh. He takes a step back and clears his throat. I watch as he lifts his hand and runs it over the back of his head, his bicep bunching underneath the red plaid shirt he wears.

God, he's so big, so muscular. But working on a farm your whole life will bulk you up that way.

I nod and glance away, my cheeks feeling hot. I know I'm blushing, and wonder if he notices I am staring at his body. I clear my throat before looking back at him. "It was good."

"You're probably hungry and tired," he says and I stare into his blue eyes.

So many times I've thought about the dirty, inappropriate things I wanted Carson to do to me. I should feel ashamed, given the fact that he looked after me when my dad died. But the truth is I never saw him as a guardian, never saw him as a parental figure. Even before I knew what attraction and love was I knew there was something more I felt for Carson. I just didn't know what it was until later on in life, until we lived under the same roof and I felt my feelings for him grow to something womanly.

I may have graduated, but I still don't know what the hell I am going to do with my life. I haven't even told Carson that my plane ticket is one way. I no longer live in the dorm, no longer have connections to the university that will keep me there. Sure, I made friends along the way, even went on a few dates, but I have nothing substantial back there.

The only thing I want, the only person I want to spend time with, to be around, stands right in front of me. I just need to know, to understand and realize, that I will never have the courage to admit it to him. I'm too afraid of losing him.

Which brings me to the decision I've made. I promised myself when I came back to the farm that I would finally move on with my life. I've had feelings for Carson forever, but I can't continue to build dreams around a man who more than likely will only see me as his best friend's little girl—his ward...another responsibility in his life.

I have to move on. I have to begin building a life without Carson being the focal point. It's not going to be easy, but I don't really have a choice. I want to keep Carson in my life and if he knew the feelings I have for him, what I want from him, it would ruin our relationship forever.

I can't let that happen.

3

Carson

I t feels so damned good to have Jenny back. Just having her riding in this old truck beside me soothes me in ways nothing else can.

"You look good, Jen," I tell her before I can think better of it. I was supposed to play it cool, but as always with Jen, I react first, think later.

"No one looks good after spending the day flying and catching a layover, Carson," she laughs, her face coloring in either embarrassment or shyness. I can never be sure of which with Jenny, I just love that she still blushes. I've always been a throwback in this world, set in my ways and liking the past much more than the morality and people in the present. I feel like I should have been born in a time when a man claimed his woman and he kept her and devoted everything he did to her. It's not a popular way of thinking now. I get it.

Women want equality and to prove they can do any job a man can do. I'm not saying they can't. Fuck, most of the women I know are capable of doing things better. I'm saying that if a man is any kind of a man, he busts his ass so his woman doesn't have to work, doesn't have to do anything...*but have babies.*

And just like that, my mind has drifts off into dangerous territory. What would Jenny say if she knew that I want her barefoot and pregnant with my children? A better man would probably warn her that I'm bringing her home and making sure she never leaves... And maybe I will tell her—after her stomach is stretched with my child.

That's my plan and it's only cemented since Jenny walked up to me at the airport. The time for waiting is over. All I need is time. That's it. I have to make myself move slowly. I don't want to spook her and have her leave. First I need to make sure she gets settled back into the farm. I want her to relax and realize that this ranch is her home too—*that I'm her home.* The next part of the plan is a little more complicated. I need to make sure she starts seeing me as a man...but not just any man.

I want Jenny to see me as *her* man, because she sure as hell isn't getting another one. It may take some time, but I'm okay with that. I have Jenny home now.

I have nothing but time.

"Did you hear me, Carson?" Jenny's sweet voice asks, and I shake my head free from my thoughts, glancing at her before turning my attention back to the road.

"Sorry, honey, what were you saying?" I ask, the endearment slipping out naturally.

"I was asking if you had plans tonight. Because if you hadn't planned anything, I was thinking of going to stay with Donna for the night."

"Donna? It's your first night home, Jenny. I thought we'd stay in and watch a movie after dinner. Like we used to," I answer, irritation firing inside of me. Jenny hasn't even walked through the front door and she's already planning on leaving? I want her sleeping under my roof tonight.

"I know, Carson, but I haven't seen Donna in months. I'd like to catch up with her and it's planting time on the farm. You won't be in until late. I'm surprised you could tear yourself away to come pick me up," she answers and my fingers tighten against the steering wheel.

"I always put you first, Jenny," I answer, my voice tense. I need to calm my ass down, but I'm having trouble with that, considering Jenny hasn't even been home for five minutes and is making plans. *Plans that do not include me.*

This is not how I envisioned her first night home going.

"You always have, Carson. I know that. I don't want to be a burden to you though."

"You've never been—"

"I don't want to be just another chore you cross off your list, Carson. I may be home now, but I'm not going to get in your way or become a liability."

"A liability?" I ask, dumbfounded and fucking confused. How could she ever think I would view her like that?

"Exactly. I refuse to inconvenience you any longer. You will see. Things will be different now that I have my degree and I'm ready to start my own life. I just need a little bit of time to get my feet under me. That's all."

"You can go to Donna's tonight, but I'll have the corn planted on the east side of the farm done by tomorrow. Tomorrow night is ours. Understand?"

"If you're sure? I mean, I can always—"

"I'm sure," I tell her, interrupting her before she can upset me further.

I didn't see this problem arising. I'm not altering my plan, but I'm starting to realize it might take me a little longer to get Jenny under control, to make her see what plans I have for us.

That's okay. I always did like a challenge.

4

Virginia

The smell and feel of Donna's house brings back memories. I used to come here almost every weekend before my father died. We would watch cheesy romance movies, stuff our faces with popcorn, and even occasionally sneak some of her mom's red wine. But her parents have since moved to Florida and left her the house. Even still, it's like being back in a very good dream.

I hear her banging around in the kitchen and I snuggle deeper into the plush, yet ancient couch. This is the same furniture, same decor as it was all those years ago. The TV has been upgraded to a flat screen instead of the old box model, but aside from that even the seventies themed wallpaper is still in place.

I think about Carson and how he acted in the truck just earlier today. He seemed upset that I had plans with Donna, although I can't understand why. Yeah, maybe I should've given it a day or two and caught up with him and Mavis, but honestly I need to get my head sorted out. I need to figure out what I am going to do. I know I need to move on. I can't waste any more energy or my feelings on something that will never happen.

Donna comes in a few minutes later with a bowl of freshly popped popcorn, two glasses, and a bottle of white wine under her arm. She grins at me and sets everything on the coffee table.

"Brings back memories, doesn't it?" She smiles wider. And right on cue the doorbell rings, signaling our pizza has arrived.

When Donna comes back in with a large pizza box and sets it on the coffee table, my stomach gives a loud growl. We both laugh. For the next twenty minutes we eat and drink our weight in pizza and wine.

Donna leans back and pats her stomach, a contented sigh leaving her. "Man, I haven't eaten pizza and drank wine like that in forever." She glances over at me, this little snort of laughter leaving her. "Remember when you used to come over and spend the night and we'd sneak into the kitchen and do shots of red wine like it was hard liquor or something?" We both start laughing so hard that tears trickle out the corners of our eyes.

"Oh my God," I say between fits of laughter. "I swear I got drunk from like two shots, too." I shake my head at the memories that slam into me. It is good to be home, good to be back.

We watch a little bit of a cheesy romantic movie, just like old times. The silence is comfortable, welcoming. I am exhausted from traveling all day, but I don't want this night to end just yet.

"Oh, I forgot to tell you I ran into Jake a few days ago."

I shift on the couch to look at her. "Jake Anderson? I haven't thought about him in years."

Although Donna is looking at the TV, her grin stretches across her face. "Oh, he's definitely thought about you."

I feel my brows pull down lower in confusion. "What does that mean?"

She turns partially on the couch so she's looking at me as well. "I just told him that you were coming back to town since you graduated and you should've seen the way his face lit up with that information. Dude, the guy has a hard on for you like nobody's business. I swear he's been carrying a torch for you since high school."

"You're insane," I say and laugh a little awkwardly.

Although I knew Jake had a crush on me in high school, she makes it seem like he is still thinking about me, wanting me all these years later. That is a little unbelievable.

She shakes her head. "No, I'm not insane. The guy totally wants you. He even wanted me to give you his phone number so you guys could go out while you're in town." She reaches for her cell and holds her hand out for mine.

I stare at her palm for a long second, wondering if contacting a guy I haven't spoken to in years, who may or may not desire me, is really a good idea.

Take the number. You need to stop lusting after a man who will probably never see you as anything more than that little girl who lost her father.

I close my eyes for a second and exhale. Truth is I'll never fully know if Carson wants me. I will never have the guts to actually ask him, to admit how I feel for him. Because I know as soon as I utter those words, things will change between us. I know lines will be crossed, and that uncomfortable, awkward relationship that I dread having with him will be established.

I hand over my phone and watch as she types in Jake's phone number. Besides, what's the worst thing that can happen? So I call him up and we go out and catch up on old times. It can't hurt, and it would be nice to see someone from back in the day.

But even thinking that, knowing that, I can't help but feel this uncomfortable sensation wash over me at the fact I'm contacting another guy. I've only ever wanted Carson, and even a friendly date with a guy I used to go to school with seems...wrong.

5

Carson

I've worked my ass off today, but it's worth it. Owning a farm isn't exactly a glamorous life. It's a lot of hard work. But I have the cornfields planted in the north pasture, and I have the hay mowed and ready to be turned in a couple of days. That means as of tonight, I am free to enjoy the evening and all day tomorrow and tomorrow night with Jenny. She's been a little distant since she came back from her friend's. I made an effort to come in for lunch to see her, but she was in her room. Mavis said she had a migraine, so as much as it hurt me not to—I didn't bother her.

Now, though, I'm dying to see her, to smell that familiar scent of vanilla when she's in the room, to hear her laugh and to feel her head lie against my chest, while seeing the smile on her lips that haunts me every day. I throw on clean clothes, and run a quick comb through my damp hair, anxious as hell to get to her.

I expected to see her on the couch, watching one of those damn television shows she loves. I only keep cable because she likes it. I rarely get time to turn a television on. Hell, when she's gone, I never touch it. Then again, when Jenny is not here I can't bring myself to go in the living room. I stay in my office. The house feels empty without her. *I* feel empty without her.

I head into the living room, but to my disappointment the room is empty.

"Mavis!" I yell out, staring at the empty couch like a mad man—as if that will make her appear out of thin air.

"Yeah?" Mavis answers, doing a half walk, half jog from the kitchen.

"Where's Jenny?"

"Jenny? Why, she left for her date about an hour ago."

Everything in me freezes at the sound of that. "Her date?" I ask, my voice coming out sharper than normal. Jenny is out on a fucking date? On the very night that was supposed to be mine? What the hell is going on here?

The night that was supposed to be yours? Fuck, man, you haven't had the balls to tell her how you feel.

"Yeah," Mavis says, sounding very unhappy. "She went out with that Anderson boy. Jake I think his name is. I tried to talk her out of it, tried to get her to relax at home after her travels, but she wouldn't listen." Mavis purses her lips. "I don't like that boy. Something about his eyes. They look beady. Don't they look beady to you?" she rambles.

I'm not really paying attention to her. My brain seems to have stopped working the minute she said that Jenny was out on a date.

A fucking date.

I do know what boy she's talking about. Jake Anderson is a lazy, good for nothing kid who would rather get his dick wet than do a minute's worth of hard work. What in the hell is Jenny doing out with him?

Jenny might deserve better than me, but she sure as hell deserves better than Jake Anderson. An image of that asshole touching *my* girl flashes in my mind and rage fills me. If he lays a finger on her, I'll kill him. My hands curl into fists on their own accord and I squeeze them tight, trying to control myself. I need to be logical here. The problem is, when Jenny is involved, I'm rarely logical.

"Where did they go?" I bark out the question to Mavis. I see the way her pupils go round. I've shocked her. Am I betraying myself? Does she know how I feel about Jenny? I've done my best to keep it hidden, but I'm done with that. And acting like a fucking caveman right now is ensuring that she knows exactly my intentions for Jenny. Before tonight is over, everyone will know that Jenny is mine—especially Jake-fucking-Anderson.

"Carson, maybe—"

"Where did he take her, Mavis?" I growl. Every minute that Mavis delays is another minute that little lazy asshole could be trying to force himself on Jenny. There's no way she'd let him touch her willingly. I might be confused about the way Jenny is reacting now that she's back home, but I'm not wrong about this.

I can't be.

"She said they were going to Murphy's Grill for dinner and then maybe a movie..."

"How long ago did she leave?"

"Boss—"

"How long, Mavis?" I bark, very close to the end of my rope.

"About thirty minutes ago or so..." she whispers worriedly, wringing her hands. "You need to calm down, Carson. I've never seen you like this."

Calming down was sure as shit not going to happen.

Thirty minutes ago... While I was in the shower she'd left with that little prick. She didn't tell me she was leaving. She didn't talk to me about canceling our night. She left with him while I was in the damn shower!

She should still be at Murphy's. I grab my keys and turn toward the door. I have one thing on my mind, one fucking intention. *Getting my woman back.*

"Lord have mercy," I hear Mavis whisper in the background.

If the Lord is listening, she better pray He has mercy on Jake Anderson. Because when I get Jenny back, I'm going to spank her until her ass glows bright red. *And Jake?*

I'm going to kill that son of a bitch...*with my bare hands.*

6

Virginia

I stare at Jake from across the table, feeling out of place, slightly uncomfortable. I sent him a text just this morning, even though I knew I shouldn't have, and to my surprise he wanted to see me tonight. I should've postponed it, should've at least told Carson what I was doing and where I was going. But I didn't want to face him. I didn't want to tell him that I was going on a date.

Because admitting that to him, actually saying those words out loud, makes me feel like there really is no hope for me and the man that I really want.

"You barely touched dinner. Are you sure you're okay?" Jake leans back in the booth and smiles.

"I'm fine. Maybe just still tired from traveling."

That is a lie. I smile in return but it's a little bit forced. It doesn't feel right being here with Jake, even though he's been nice this evening.

He is a good looking guy, more with a boy-next-door kind of appearance, but I know better than that. I knew him from high school and how he really is. He has a wild streak, and although this town is full of hard-working people, Jake never really seemed to care about any of that.

"I'm really glad you agreed to come out with me tonight. I know it was short notice, but I'll be honest." He leans in and rests his forearms on the table, his smile widening. My skin tightens at that look, and I can't explain why a creepy feeling washes over me. "I never stopped thinking about you, Virginia."

I hate the way he says my full name. I've grown so used to Carson calling me Jenny that hearing Jake say my name makes me feel...gross in a way.

And then Jake reaches out and places his hand on top of mine. My entire body freezes, just tenses up. I want to pull my hand away, want to tell him that this isn't going to work. It would be different if I knew he just wanted a friendly relationship. But the way he looks at me, the way I notice his gaze lingering over my breasts when he thinks I'm not paying attention, tells me he wants something more than just being my friend.

I'm about to pull my hand away and just be honest with Jake, tell him that I don't want anything more than a platonic relationship. Hell, I will even admit that I'm in love with someone else. Because saying those words out loud to somebody else is the first step in me being honest and finally coming clean with Carson as well, right?

But before I can take my hand away I hear a commotion at the front of the restaurant. I turn my head and look toward the front doors, feeling my eyes widen as I see the man I'm madly in love with looking around with wide, crazed eyes and an angry expression.

I'm about to stand up and go to Carson to see what's going on, thinking maybe Mavis has been hurt, or maybe there is some other bad news which would make him come to the restaurant and find me.

But just as I'm about to stand I feel Jake add pressure to the hand he has over mine. And then Carson looks right at me, our gazes locking, his expression intent, possessive. I feel a light brush on my lips and snap my attention to Jake. I can feel his thumb running a small circle around my cheek, right next to my mouth. I look over at Carson again just in time to see him storming over, his gaze narrowed and trained right on Jake.

Oh God. I may not understand what's going on, but

I know that look Carson is wearing. Shit is definitely about to hit the fan.

7

Carson

It's as if this violent beast breaks free inside of me. I see that little asshole reach out and touch Jenny. The very thought of him putting his hands on *my* woman has this territorial need inside me rising up. I want to beat his fucking ass. I want him to know, without a shadow of a doubt, that she is mine.

I see Jenny's eyes widen, see her body straighten. I have no doubt she notices a change in me, probably wondering what in the hell I'm doing barreling toward her and that little prick. He still has his hands on my girl, oblivious to the fact I'm coming right for him. I see Jenny's mouth open and close, but she is still staring at me. I doubt she said anything to him. I doubt she's warned him.

I doubt she knows what's going to happen... But she will.

And then I'm right beside the table. I'm seeing red, can't focus on anything but how I feel in this moment. Possessiveness swirls inside of me, makes me a fiend. I find myself reaching out and grabbing his arm, pulling it away from where his hand is touching Jenny. It's as if I'm in someone else's body, not able to control myself with rationalization.

He looks over at me, the confusion on his face clear. And then I'm hauling him out of the booth. I can hear Jenny's voice but can't make out what she's saying. I'm too pissed in this moment.

"Don't ever fucking touch what's mine." I hear the growl in my words, and my focus is trained right on the asshole. The guy is nothing to be threatened over, but that doesn't mean I want him touching Jenny.

"Carson?" I look over at her then, the shock in her voice clear. Jenny's eyes are as wide as saucers and I realize what I said out loud. But I want her to know anyway. It's just I didn't envision the revelation going this way.

I look back at the guy I'm holding by the collar and narrow my eyes at him. "Do you understand what I'm saying?"

The guy nods and I can see the fear in his eyes.

Good. I let go of him and he stumbles back, landing on his ass in the booth. I turn and look at Jenny for a suspended second, then reach out and take her hand in mine. I'm not oblivious to the fact that people are staring at us, or that the cops have probably already been called.

I haul her out of there and once we are outside I head straight for my truck. My heart is thundering and the blood is rushing through my veins. The feel of Jenny tugging her hand from mine has me stopping and turning to face her.

"What the hell, Carson?" She's breathing hard, and I can see she's confused and flustered. I hate that I'm the one who's made her feel this way.

I exhale roughly and run a hand through my hair. I was like a caveman in there, which isn't how I typically act. I am easy-going, and don't let shit bother me. But when it comes to Jenny I can't let it go. I can't let the fact she is with another guy roll off my shoulders.

"We have a lot of shit to talk about." I finally say the words and stare in her eyes. She doesn't say anything, doesn't even move.

"Yeah, we really do," she finally says and closes her eyes. I can see her take a deep breath in. She glances back at the restaurant and I wonder if she's thinking about going back in there and making sure the little asshole is okay.

I wouldn't blame her.

But I could have done a hell of a lot more damage to him. As it is, I'm pretty fucking proud of myself for restraining from beating the shit out of him.

"You can't attack people like that for no reason."

Oh, I had a good reason.

If she wants to go in there I can't stop her, but that doesn't mean I won't go back in there for her.

She finally looks at me again and exhales. "I have some stuff I need to talk to you about too."

All I want to do is pull her in and kiss her, tell her that she's mine, that she's been mine for a long time. But instead I curl my fingers into my palms until the pain lances up my arms. First I'll tell her how I feel, and then if she doesn't run from me, or slap me across the face, then I'll pull her into my lap and claim her as mine.

Because at the end of the day Virginia *is* mine, and no one will tell me any differently.

8

Virginia

"We'll talk at home," Carson proclaims. My heart is thundering in my chest, so much so that I can hear the beat reverberate in my ears. My palms are actually sweaty. I have no idea what's going on—not really. If I can believe my gut instinct, I would think that Carson was jealous. *Could he be?*

Is that just wishful thinking?

"Carson—"

"Get in the truck, Jenny," he orders me, his voice carrying a deep warning tone that sends shivers down my spine. Shivers that make me feel...alive.

"But, Carson—"

"In case you haven't noticed, I'm not exactly in control right now. So either get in the damn truck now, or I can pick you up, throw you over my shoulder, and put you in there myself." His gaze is unwavering. "But either way we will discuss how you left the house knowing that you and I had plans—"

"Carson!" I almost growl, because he's not letting me talk.

"You let him touch you, Jenny," he barks, his voice accusing. Guilt swamps me and I squirm where I'm standing.

"He just touched my face," I defend, and it sounds lame, even to me.

"He shouldn't have touched any part of you," Carson growls.

"Carson, you're not being reasonable," I respond, at a loss on how to deal with *this* Carson. The man in front of me is different from the person I've known for longer than I care to admit. This Carson is almost ferocious.

"I'm not feeling reasonable, Jenny. You let him touch you—"

"But, Carson," I start, though I'm not sure what I'm going to say.

"You let him touch what's *mine*," he growls again and my heart stutters in my chest.

"Yours?"

"Yes. Mine. It's high time you accept it. I'm done holding back where you are concerned, Jenny."

"What does that mean, Carson?" I ask, feeling breathless. I want to believe that he wants me, that he's not just being protective right now.

He said I was his, though.

"What does that mean?" I ask again, my voice soft. I can hear how nervous I sound. I'm almost afraid to push him, just in case I'm wrong. Yet, everything about Carson right now tells me that I'm not.

"It means you either get in this damn truck right now, or I'll strip you bare and spank your ass right here in front of God and country."

My face heats and my heart stalls. "Spank me?"

"Exactly. I'll spank that perfect ass of yours for letting another man get near what is mine."

"Yours?" God, I feel like we are going back and forth with this, like I'm a broken record. Truth is, I feel like I'm in some other world, like I'd been dropped into someone else's life. "Carson, we've never... I mean, we don't have that kind of relationship. You're my guardian," I whisper, hope making my heart beat a wild melody in my chest at the very thought I could have him as mine.

"You've got about one minute to make your move,

Jenny. But I promise you that if you run I will come after you," he says, his voice dead serious.

"I... I'll just get in the truck," I whisper, trying to digest everything Carson just told me. I need to know what's going on, and leaving with him, talking to him, is how I'm going to find out.

9

Carson

I've got to get control of myself.

Hell!

I'm probably scaring Jenny to death. I don't want that. The last thing I want is for her to be afraid of me. But seeing another man dare to touch her... Yeah, even now I want to go back there and fucking kill him. Now I find myself coming to terms with the fact that I've let Jenny get too far away from me. I've just told her how I felt—in so many ways—in the middle of a damn parking lot.

Fuck.

One thought keeps haunting me now. It's something I don't want to give voice to. If I do, it will be proof that

I've been a stupid, blind asshole. It will be proof that Jenny will never be completely mine.

She doesn't speak as we drive down the old graveled road. I chance a look at her and see her staring out her window, biting on her nails. I know she has a million questions, but for whatever reason she's not voicing them. I want to scream out my frustration as I turn my gaze back on the road. This is part of the problem. Jenny and I have been too quiet, for too damn long.

"Have you let another man touch you?" I growl, finally asking my question and doing my best to ignore the way the mere words cut me inside. "More than what happened tonight?" If she's given away her virginity I'll find a way to get past it, but I can't guarantee that I won't hunt the fucker down and kill him.

"What?" she gasps.

I glance at her. Her face is pale and her eyes are wide with surprise—*but she didn't answer the question.*

Fucking hell! Is she dodging the answer?

"That's none of your business."

There's this bite in her voice and I grin. That's my girl giving me shit even though I need her to tell me the truth.

"Who did you give your cherry to, Jenny?"

"I... What... Carson, you're acting insane!" she huffs.

I look around and see the turnoff for the cornfield that I planted. The truck bounces over the dirt road, pot holes and bumps—mostly because I don't slow down. I come to a stop in front of the old metal gate that blocks the road. This is the back entrance to my farm. I have a key, but this is far enough off the road that Jenny and I can have this out. That's all that matters right now.

I shut the truck off and we sit there in the quiet and dark. The only sounds you can hear are the crickets outside, a stray hoot owl call here and there, and Jenny's erratic breathing. The moon is full tonight and it offers a filtered, pale light to shine through the cab of my truck. I tighten my grip on the steering wheel and try to calm down the raw anger and frustration inside of me.

Why did I wait so long to claim Jenny? Why did I assume she would be waiting for me, like I have for her?

Because I'm an idiot.

"Who is he?" I ask, doing my best to keep the words from sounding like a bitter accusation, but not sure I fully succeed. Truthfully, it cuts me open inside that she gave herself to another man. It will take me time to get over it. I'm still not letting her get away and even if I can't be her first, I'm damn well going to be the last man to crawl between her legs. I'll fuck her so hard she'll never think of letting another man near her again.

"He?" she asks, confused.

"The man you've slept with. Who is he, Jenny?"

"I really don't think we should talk about this,

Carson. I'm a grown woman and my sex life is not your concern—"

"Your sex life? Jesus Christ! Has there been more than one, Jenny?" I growl, feeling nothing but pain inside.

"More than one what?" she asks, exasperated.

"Have you had more than one man between your legs?"

"Carson! I just said I'm not talking about this with you!"

"You will answer the damn question. I'm done playing here. You haven't realized it yet, but you need to."

"Realize what?"

"You're mine, and I'm done waiting—apparently, I've waited too long already."

"I'm yours?"

"Exactly."

"When did you decide I was yours, Carson?" she asks, and I think I hear a hint of anger in her voice. I'm handling this wrong, I know it, but I've gone too far to turn back now.

"Since that night on your eighteenth birthday, when I first tasted your lips."

"Since... Carson."

"What?" I growl, not about to back down.

"That was almost four years ago! It will be four years in a day or so!"

"Doesn't change the facts. I knew with that one taste that you were mine, Jenny."

"Don't you think you could have told me?"

"I was trying to give you time to grow up and spread your wings a little. I owed that to your father and to you —even if it did kill me."

"I was eighteen! Most people consider that the age of an adult!" she huffs, clearly angry.

"You were a sheltered eighteen. You needed time to come into your own," I growl, getting frustrated. She'll never understand how much self-control it took to let her go to college after that kiss. How much discipline it took not to claim her right then. Nor could she understand how much it's killing me to know that she gave her body to another man during this time. I hate that I waited now. I should have claimed her back then and planted my child in her. If I had, Jenny would have never looked anywhere else for comfort. She would have had me and our child, and that's all she would have ever wanted.

I fucked up. I have to fix it.

"So you let me go, letting me think that the kiss was nothing...that you weren't interested in me...*like that.*"

"I had to. It was for your own good."

"My own good. How *nice* of you to decide what was

good for me, Carson! You could have at least asked me how I felt about your plan!" she growls and unbuckles her seatbelt, turning to look at me. "Did that thought ever occur to you while you were making major decisions about my life?"

"I was doing my job, Jenny!" I growl back, not thinking the words out and I wince at the way they sound.

"You job?"

"I'm your guardian, Jenny. It's my job to make sure you are—"

"That I'm what? That I get to spread my wings? That the first kiss I give a man feels like a rejection when he doesn't bother to react to it and proceeds to act like it meant nothing?"

"Jenny—you have to understand..." I start, feeling defensive.

"What I understand is that you're insane. You apparently decided I was *yours* four years ago, but you didn't let me in on the secret!"

"Damn it, Jenny!"

"Now you're acting like a caveman because some faceless man got what you claimed years ago, but again...*didn't bother to tell me!* Do I have that right, Carson? You know I'm not adult enough to figure these things out on my own, I need your help. It is, after all, your damn *job!*"

"Jenny ..." I stop, not sure how to explain things to her without making it worse. I get she's upset, but hell... so am I! Before I get the chance, however, she turns and opens the truck door. "Where are you going?" I bark.

"I'm walking home! I suddenly feel the need to spread my wings!" she mutters, jumping out of the truck and slamming the door.

She takes off walking, but she's going the opposite way of the house. If she thinks she can go back to that pretty boy in town, she's got another think coming. I get out and stride over to her, my long legs swallowing up the distance before she can get too far away from me.

"You're not leaving!"

"Watch me!" she huffs, not bothering to turn around.

I react on instinct. I hook my arms around her waist and pull her back against me. I pull her in tight so she can feel the hard ridge of my cock against her ass. I lean my face down close to hers, unable to resist a small kiss along the side of her neck, which turns into more of a bite, because after the night I've had I feel the need to mark her damn body.

She trembles in my arms, losing some of the stiffness in her muscles. Her ass even pushes against my cock. I doubt she realizes the invitations she's giving me, but I do. It's an invitation I have every intention of accepting.

"You're not walking away, Jenny. I may have waited too long to claim you, but whoever the fucker is that you gave your body to was an idiot."

"Because he took what you pushed away?" she huffs, her body going tense once again.

"Because he had you and yet he let you get away. Now you're here. Now *I* have you and you aren't getting away from me. *You're never getting away from me again*," I tell her and the words are a promise.

I spin her around and lift her over my shoulder, letting her torso drape over my shoulders and back, while I hold her legs and ass tight. I start striding through the corn, going straight to the house. I'll get the truck tomorrow. I need Jenny safely inside my house and I'm not risking letting her out of my arms until she's locked inside my bedroom, unable to get away.

Once I have her there, I have only one thought on my mind. I'll finally claim her body and do my best to obliterate any memory of a man before me and I'll bury my cock so deep in her, filling her so full of my cum that some have to take root. Before the week is out, Jenny will be pregnant with my baby and she'll never get away from me then. She'll never doubt who she belongs to again.

10

Virginia

I can feel the tension radiating from Carson, but I keep my mouth shut and let him control the situation. Yes, I have a lot of questions, the biggest one being what exactly he meant when he said I was his, and how far he is going to take that. Maybe it is obvious to some, and a part of me knows what it really means, but I want to hear him say it. I want him to admit that he desires me in the same way I do him.

I want Carson to tell me that, even though he said he's wanted me since I was eighteen, what he wants with me is more than just a warm body in his bed. And truthfully, that's my biggest fear. I worry that when this is all said and done, what he really desires is us rolling around between his sheets, making me just another notch on his bedpost.

We've been back at his house for the last twenty minutes, and although I feel a little dumb for walking off, I feel even more ridiculous that he felt the need to haul me over his shoulder like I was a sack of potatoes.

I'm a damn liar. I got so wet when he picked me up, like he was this caveman and he was hauling me back to his lair.

I watch as he walks over to the cabinet, opens it up, and pulls out two glasses. Then he goes over to the freezer and opens it, pulling out a bottle of whiskey. When he comes back to the table and sits across from me, my throat tightens.

He pours both glasses with a shot of whiskey and pushes one of them over to me. I stare at it for long seconds before finally picking it up and downing the whole thing. When I set the glass down, my throat on fire, my breath wheezing out of me, I see that Carson is staring at me with a smirk on his face. I wonder what he's thinking about right now.

But he doesn't say anything. He tosses back his own drink and refills both of the glasses.

"I figure we will both need a little kick in the ass after all the shit that went down tonight."

I nod and drink the second shot of whiskey,

coughing slightly once I have it swallowed. God, it's like liquid fire down my throat and settling like a rock in my belly. The warmth and buzz start immediately. I'm not a big drinker so I know these two shots will really loosen me up.

Good.

"Did I freak you out by what I said? I'm surprised you haven't packed your stuff and tried to leave." He looks away and I hate that.

"No, you didn't freak me out." He might have admitted that he wants me, but I haven't exactly told him how deep my feelings for him actually go.

And I want to tell him. I want to admit it all to him. I'm just too afraid, so scared that when I tell him I love him things will change.

I stand, not able to sit still anymore, not able to think clearly. I walk over to the sink and stare out the window, but it's too dark to see outside. Instead, I can see Carson's reflection. He's staring at me, watching me. He stands, but I don't turn around. It's then I notice I took the liquor bottle with me.

Despite the turbulent emotions running through me I am aroused, my pussy wet, and my nipples hard. Our gazes lock and I can't breathe. I turn around slowly, still staring at him, wondering what he's thinking about. I see him swallow, his Adams apple working as if he is trying to hold off from saying something. I clench my hands around the whiskey bottle, thinking about downing the whole thing, trying to stem off my arousal.

The death grip I have on the bottle seems to ground me, stabilize me. But I force myself to set the bottle aside.

"So, where do we go from here? Where do we stand?" My voice is thick, hoarse. I'm afraid, nervous... excited about his response. Carson doesn't say anything, and instead he moves closer, just a step, but I feel his body heat slam into me.

He takes another step closer. "I will always protect you, Jenny, always be here for you, no matter what. You know that, right?"

He hasn't answered my question, but I nod anyway.

Carson watches me intently, his breathing harder, faster. It matches mine. His chest rises and falls the closer he moves toward me. When we are mere inches from one another, I stare into his eyes, wanting to have the guts to just rise up on my toes and kiss him, to be the one to really start this.

Take me now, Carson. Make me yours.

"You're shaking," he says in a low, deep voice. He moves an inch closer, and I press my back fully against the counter.

"Tell me something you've never told anyone before," he probes, questioning.

I know I shouldn't say anything, but I can't help

myself. I need to have everything out in the open. I need to tell him how I feel. "I love you," I whisper, knowing I shouldn't have said that, but needing him to know the truth. And then after a few seconds he closes his eyes, braces his hands on the counter on either side of me, and breathes out roughly.

"I'm so much older than you."

My heartbeat is loud in my ears. "I'm not a girl anymore. I know what I want, and what I want is you."

He doesn't move, doesn't speak, and I wonder what the next step is. I've waited long enough to be with the man I love, to finally be able to express how I feel. This is my life, and I want this more than anything. I want Carson more than anything.

"No, you're not a girl anymore," he says almost to himself. "Believe me, baby, I've noticed." This lightness covers his face. "I love you, too, Jenny. God, I love you so fucking much it hurts."

Pleasure and heat fill me. And then he makes this low sound in his throat, grabs me around the back of my head, and pulls me close. He presses his mouth against mine, and this gasp leaves me. I'm frozen in place, unsure if this is really happening. But in the end it doesn't matter because the feel of his lips on mine, moving rough, hard, and demanding, has every rational thought leaving my brain.

The way he holds me, kisses me, makes me feel wholly feminine. He's had me since before he said anything, since before I knew this was what I needed. I can feel the hunger and need in his touch.

I am helpless to stop it, but I don't want to, ever.

11

Carson

When you wait years for something and you finally have it in your grasp, the feelings you get are indescribable. When I finally pull away from Jenny's lips, my fucking hands are shaking. So much has happened tonight that I'm busy trying to wrap my mind around it. But the only thing I really need to know is Jenny loves me. I thought I had lost her, but she's given me the words I've been dying to hear for years. There's no way she's getting away from me now.

I look over at her. Her eyes are wide in surprise and her hand is gently touching her swollen lips.

Lips swollen from my kiss.

"What are you thinking?" I ask her, my voice gruff.

"That this may be the best birthday I've ever had in my life," she whispers and for some reason that makes me smile.

"It's not your birthday yet, honey."

"It's not?" she asks, confused, her eyes still dilated. She's staring straight at my mouth. My smile broadens. I like knowing my kiss has affected her so much.

"Your birthday is tomorrow," I tell her.

"Oh," she whispers. "Will you kiss me for my birthday?"

I'm pretty sure she doesn't know what she's asking.

"You like my kisses?"

"So much," she whispers. "I've been dreaming of them forever."

"Do you dream of me doing more than kissing you?"

"Carson," she mumbles, her eyes moving to the floor, her face flushing to a deep pink. I take the small step forward, closing the distance between us, and put my finger under her chin to bring her gaze back to my face.

"Answer me, honey," I order her gently.

"That's not really fair, Carson."

"What's not fair?"

"You asking me questions and just demanding I answer them. What about you? Do you dream of me?"

"Every fucking night," I answer without hesitation.

"See... What?... Oh... You do?"

Seeing the different emotions flicker over her face is a treat I could watch for days. Yet, when my words finally register, it is the flare of desire I see that captures my attention.

"I live for the night, Jenny. Do you know why?" I ask, letting my finger move from under her chin and trail along the side of her face. I hear her drag a shuddered breath through her lungs and smile because it literally rocks through her body. She wants me, and she's not adept enough to keep it hidden—*thank God.*

"Why?" she asks, biting on her lip.

"Because all day long I work like a dog so I'll come home too tired to miss you."

"I... You miss me?"

"So fucking much," I murmur. "But working my ass off never works, Jenny. So I get in the shower and wash off the dirt and grime, wishing you were with me."

"You do?"

"Fuck yes. Why do you think I had the master bath redone a few years back?"

"I—"

"It was so that when the time came, and I finally claimed you, our bath was ready."

"Claimed... Our..." she repeats and I know she's weighing each word and understanding the gravity of them. *I want her to.* "What would it be ready for, Carson?"

"For the day I come in from working and you're in that shower with me."

"You want me to shower with you?" she asks. Shock is evident on her face, but it can't overshadow the desire that is there too.

"I more than want it honey, I crave it. I want your hands on me after a long day in the field. I want you touching me, holding me..."

"Carson—"

"Most of all I want to push you against the shower wall and fuck you raw," I tell her and the need in my voice vibrates with hunger.

"Oh, God," she says, trembling.

I place my hand on her stomach and press it flat.

"I won't rest until you're carrying my baby, Jenny. I want your stomach stretched with our child, knowing that a part of each of us is growing inside of you. Am I scaring you, Jenny?"

"No," she whispers, surprising me. "I love everything you're saying."

"Tell me, Jenny," I urge, needing her to admit to everything.

"I want all of that, Carson."

"All—" Before I can finish and tell her exactly what I

need from her, Jenny surprises me by doing exactly that.

"I want your baby, Carson," she whispers and finally it feels like everything I've ever wanted is within my reach. "I want you as mine."

12

Virginia

Before I know what is happening I find myself in Carson's arms. He smells so good, feels so good pressed against me. I run my fingers through his hair, pulling at the shorter strands until he hisses, but then lets out a deep, guttural groan of pleasure. I have no idea what is coming over me, but I don't want to stop.

I want to go as far as we can. I want to bring myself to the brink of going over the edge and not even caring if I finally fall and never reach the bottom.

"Are you sure about this, Jenny?" His mouth is by my ear, his warm breath teasing the shell. "Because once I'm deep inside your hot, wet pussy, there's no going back. I can't walk away from you. I won't." He's staring me in the eyes; the feeling that I am so lost consumes me. "You've always been mine, but once I claim you all bets are off." He goes back to kissing my neck now.

I can't find my voice so I nod, letting him know my answer. I press my breasts hard against his chest, not even caring that I'm being so bold in my needs.

"God, I'm burning alive for you, sweetheart."

"Take me to the shower, Carson."

He pulls back and looks down at me before cupping my face and stroking my cheek with his finger. Chills race up my entire body from that simple touch. Then he has his mouth on mine, his tongue between my lips as he mouth fucks me. There is no other description for what he is doing. My inner muscles clench and a fresh gush of wetness leaves me. I want him, need him so badly right now. "Please, Carson. Be with me."

And then he picks me up in his arms and strides to the bathroom he renovated just for us. I still can't get over it, still can't wrap my mind around the fact he's done all of this for me. He's wanted me for as long as I've wanted him.

When we are in the bathroom, he sets me on my feet. I wobble slightly, my arousal so intense it makes me dizzy. The bathroom is incredible. It's the first time

I'm seeing it since he renovated it, but I can see how much time and work he's put into it.

Glass, marble, chrome. All of it looks so damn fancy given the fact we are in his farmhouse. The shower is massive, with black tile that covers the floor and walls. It's got two shower-heads, one on each side, and there's even a Jacuzzi style tub beside the shower, one little entity.

"Carson, this is incredible," I find myself whispering, knowing my eyes are wide, my shock evident. I would have never known about the work and detail he's done in here if he hadn't told me. I don't come into his room, despite the fantasies of doing just that bombarding me. I turn around, not sure what to say or do next, but before I can utter a single word, my mouth snaps closed. His shirt is unbuttoned, his hard muscles on display, the six-pack I've seen countless times as he's working out in the field shirtless, filling my vision.

"You can't look at me like that, Jenny." His voice is low, and so damn deep. I feel a chill race up my spine.

"Look at you what way?" Did he even hear me? My voice is whisper soft, but the way he growls, the look he gives me, tells me he heard me just fine.

"Like you want me to fuck you, Jenny. Like you want me to take you up against the shower wall, my cock deep in your body, our mouths fused together."

Heat the likes of which I have never felt before fills

me. And I find myself nodding. Yes, I want all of that and more. And then he's in front of me, his shirt already fully off his body and lying on the floor in a pile. I go for my own clothes, not caring how fast all of this seems to be moving. I need to have him up against me, both of us bare, no more trying to hide how we feel.

But he breaks away from me far too soon. He moves over to the shower and cranks it on. Within minutes, steam is filling the bathroom. A nice, warm heat surrounds us, and I am totally undressed. I stand there nude, not feeling the least bit embarrassed that he sees every intimate part of me. I want this more than I've ever wanted anything before.

Finally, he removes the rest of his clothing. I take in the sight of him, the fact he's so much bigger than me, his muscles on clear display from the hard labor he does day in and day out. I can still remember the feel of his slightly calloused hands on my body. And the way he looks at me makes me feel as if he's touching me, running his fingers along my nipples, between my thighs. My gaze stops on his cock. It's so huge...so massive and hard it makes my knees weak.

"Come here, baby girl."

I go to him instantly. He leads me into the shower and I let out an involuntary moan as the warm water covers my back. Carson pulls me in close, his touches soft, gentle even. I don't want that though. I don't care if this will be my first time, that me being a virgin means I'm inexperienced. I want rough and hard. I want whatever Carson wants to give me.

I take the reins then, placing my hands on his chest and moving us so his back is to the tile wall. I rise on my toes and place my mouth on his, kissing him softly, trying to be all sweet. Of course I don't want that, but I'm hoping that the strung-tight tether I know Carson has on his desire right now will snap and he'll lose control.

"God, baby girl, you're killing me," he groans against my mouth. "I can't keep myself in check much longer, Jenny."

"Then don't" is all I say.

Before I know what is going on, he growls like an animal, turns me around so I'm the one pressed to the tile, and has his hands on my ass. He squeezes the globes before dropping to his knees and lifting my leg up so it's over his shoulder. I'm panting now, knowing he can see my exposed pussy, wondering how he feels, what he's about to do.

He stares between my legs for long seconds before looking up at me. "I'm going to fucking devour you."

And then he does just that.

13

Carson

My first taste of Jenny is one I will never forget. *Sweet, hot, innocence.* If I have to describe it, those are the only words that come to mind. She's every dream I've ever had—every fantasy come to life.

And she's mine.

I have her leg over my shoulder to give me more access. I run my tongue flat against the outside lips of her pussy. She's bare, clearly waxed. A flash of jealousy runs through me. I don't want anyone seeing this sweet little snatch but me. *It's mine.*

I use my fingers to pull her lips apart. Her clit is

throbbing, the juices of her pussy coating it. She's so excited I can almost hear her ragged breathing over the running water. I give her one last look. She's like a goddess of water, with her head tilted back against the wall, droplets running over her body like a gentle caress, dripping from her rounded breasts. I take my other hand and place it flat against her stomach, holding her there.

Right there.

Right where my baby will be inside of her.

I use that hold to pin her against the shower wall. I don't want her to move until I have her coming in my mouth and begging me to stop.

I lick her clit, gently and with no pressure—more of a light stroke. Her body tries to thrust toward me, but my hold keeps her still.

"Carson," she moans.

I let my fingers slide from the lips of her pussy between the wet valley, teasing her tender walls. I can feel her quiver beneath my touch and my dick stretches, so hard it's physically painful.

"You're so fucking beautiful, Jenny. I wish I could tell you how long I've dreamed of touching you like this, of loving you." I groan right before I slide my fingers inside her pussy. She's so damn tight that her muscles cling to my fingers both welcoming me inside and resisting me at the same time. *Christ.* Getting my dick inside this tight little hole will be an exercise in torture, the sweetest torture I've ever known.

I push my fingers so deep inside of her, knowing she's a virgin by the tightness of her. God, she's pure, all mine, and I am going to claim her. My dick fucking jerks and I know there's cum leaking from the head. I have to fight down the urge to slam inside of her now. I can't do that. She's a virgin, this is new to her and Jenny is too special to rush. I have to make this good for her.

When I rake my tongue against her clit, curling it around the throbbing little button, I begin gently moving my fingers in and out of her. I let my fingers do the fucking, slowly at first, getting her used to the invasion.

I look up between her legs and watch as she lets her head go back, a cry leaving her, and her hands slapping against the wall of the shower. She's completely lost to her passion. I don't think from this point. I grab her by the hips and move her so she's basically sitting on my face. I tunnel my tongue inside her sweet pussy, all while working in tandem with my fingers and managing to tease her clit. She grinds down on my face, seeking her own pleasure, her hips undulating a broken rhythm, demanding more, while taking everything I give her.

I dig my fingers into her lush ass, knowing I'm bruising the soft skin as I take control of her body, eating my fill, fucking her with my tongue, and nibbling on her clit. I'm doing everything I can until finally she explodes for me. Her sweet arousal coats my taste buds. I drink her up, petting her pussy with my tongue in reward for being such a good girl.

When I've brought her down from her high, I slowly stand, holding her body close to mine. The water in the shower is starting to cool and I reach over and turn it off, then I gather Jenny up in my arms, intent on nothing more than getting her to my bed.

"Carson?" she asks, her voice soft, exhausted and full of pleasure.

"I need you, Jenny," I growl, unable to say anything more, or give her the soft words she deserves. All I can think about is getting inside her tight little pussy and burying my cock so deep against her cervix that I can put my baby inside of her. I want to give her everything.

Including my child.

14

Virginia

Carson has me on the bed, the damp towel tossed to the side, and both of us naked and ready. He's so hard for me, his cock thick and long, and all because of me. I am done waiting, done pretending that I can hide how I feel. I want Carson and from this point forward I'll make that known.

"Please, I need you," I moan.

I might be a virgin, but the only man I've ever wanted was Carson. He's the only man I'll ever want. He takes a step toward me.

"I've wanted you ever since you turned eighteen and I realized you were a woman. I have held back, though, baby. I have wanted to let you live your life, meet a nice boy your age..."

I see the way his jaw clenches after he says that.

"But no more. I won't pretend that I can stand back any longer. You're mine, and always will be."

"I'm yours."

I want him to devour me, to make it known, body and soul, that I was his, just like he said...forever.

"I'm not letting you go. Not ever, Jenny."

I'm so worked up, so wet for him...so primed.

"There is no way I am going to last tonight, not once I am deep in your hot, wet, virgin pussy."

My heart races at his words.

"I want you," I say again, wanting him to know I really do need him like I need to breathe. He groans and I see how he clenches his jaw again.

"I'm trying to show restraint."

I shake my head. "I don't want you to."

He growls like an animal and I get wetter.

"I'm starving for you, so fucking hungry I don't know if I can go slow." He moves closer.

"I don't want slow." And I don't.

"Tell me what you want." He moves closer. "I want to hear you say you want my big, thick cock in you. I want to see your lips form the words as you tell me you want me to pop your cherry, to claim it as mine."

I am breathing so hard and fast I feel lightheaded. "I

want to be yours in every way. I want you to claim my virginity, to make it so no one else ever touches me, but you, Carson. *Just you.*" I lick my lips, my throat so tight and dry.

"You're so fucking pretty, Jenny." He's nearly on me now, and leans forward to run his tongue along the seam of my lips.

I could have climaxed from that alone.

He grinds his hard dick right up against my belly. I can't stop myself from gasping.

He growls in approval. "You feel that?"

I can only nod.

"You see what you do to me? You see how hard you make me?"

I nod again, my breath coming out of me in hard pants.

"God. I need you, Jenny." He leans down and runs his tongue along the side of my throat. Can he feel the way my pulse jumps? "You feel good, baby?"

"Yes," I whisper.

"Good, but I'm going to make you feel even better." He licks at my throat again. "Hold on to me." I lift my hands and place them on his biceps, digging my nails into his flesh. I feel his cock jerk against me.

"I want you as mine forever." He goes back to dragging his tongue up the column of my throat.

I want that too.

He thrusts his cock against my belly. He's like a madman in this moment, causing me to get lost in the moment as he finds his pleasure while giving me mine.

He looks his fill of me despite the fact I know he's seen every inch of me already. He starts at my toes, working his way up my body, over my legs, lingering his gaze on my pussy, over my belly, and finally stares at my breasts. I feel like I'm on fire just from his gaze alone. I need more from him—so much more.

"You're fucking perfect." He looks at my face then, and I can see how dilated his pupils are.

"You want this in you?" he says between clenched teeth and grabs his cock, stroking the monster from root to tip.

I can't answer, can't find my voice.

"I'm going to fill you up, make you take it all. I'm going to put my baby inside of you, have you tied to me forever, so we are one."

Maybe his words should scare me, have me running in the other direction. But I want everything he is describing and more.

"Do you fucking want this in you, stretching you, making you cry out in pleasure?" he says and I look down at his cock. "Do you want me to shoot my load deep in your body?" My mouth dries. "Do you want me to pop that cherry of yours?"

"Oh. God," I moan. I am so ready for him, and I

know as soon as he claims me there is no going back. "I want all of that and more."

I will be his irrevocably.

15

Carson

I'm driving myself crazy making her admit over and over that she wants this. Maybe somewhere in the back of my mind I'm feeling guilty for taking her, maybe even hoping that she'll call this off so I don't feel like I'm corrupting her. She deserves better than a broken down farmer who is years too old for her. I can't stop myself, though, and I can't let her go—not anymore.

"I'm going to do my best to make sure I don't hurt you, Jenny."

I move beside her, keeping her on her back. For a minute I just take in the fact that Jenny is finally on my bed. That she's finally here and she's finally mine. I commit it to memory. A picture in my mind that will always be there. Her pupils are dilated with desire, her hair is fanned against the pillows, and her naked body is bathed in the pale light of the room. I take it all in and I know that as long as I live, nothing will ever be as great as this moment. *Nothing will ever touch it.*

"You couldn't hurt me, Carson. You'd never hurt me," she whispers, her trust in me so complete that I can feel it in her words. It settles inside of me, soothing me as nothing else can.

I move my fingers over her body. My hand is darkened from years of working in the field under the hot sun. It looks even darker against her pale white skin.

I let my callused fingers slide down her neck, across her breasts to her stomach. Taking my time and committing it all to my memory. I've wanted it for so long, I need this time. I can't rush this.

Slowly I make my way between her legs, to the very center of her. I let my fingers drift against the outside of her pussy. The lips are wet, coated with her desire for me. Her breathing is ragged, echoing in the room even louder than my own. With each breath her stomach moves, and her fingers, which are digging into my hips, flex. Her gaze is glued to me—watching everything I do and waiting for more.

I let my fingers slide between the lips of her pussy, her desire gathering on them. Her soft gasp of need is music to my ears.

"You're wet for me, Jenny."

"Carson, please. Stop torturing me. I need you," she cries softly, her head pushing back against her pillow, her hips thrusting out to try and take my fingers deeper. I don't let her. I can't let her hurt herself. I need to make this good for her.

"I just need to make sure you're ready for me, Jenny. I'd rather cut off my hand than hurt you, sweetheart," I explain, even though the feel of her pussy clinging to my fingers and the gentle sway of her hips trying to ride me is enough to drive me insane.

"I'm ready, Carson. I've wanted you forever. I need you," she whispers, her hand coming up to gently hold the side of my face. I press my lips to hers. A gentle kiss, because the love I feel inside for this woman right now outweighs even my need. Our tongues dance slowly, intricately, and caress each other. It's unlike any kiss I've ever given a woman—but then I've never loved anyone but Jenny.

When we break apart, I move so that I am over her. Her hands grip my biceps and I look down into her soft gaze, hoping she can see how much she means to me.

"I'm claiming you, Jenny. You're never getting away

from me now. From this moment on...*you're mine.*" I tell her, for the simple reason that I can.

I position my cock at her entrance. Our gazes lock with one another.

"I've always been yours," she whispers.

"Keep your gaze on me, Jenny. Don't look away. I want to watch your expression as I take your virginity," I order her. My voice is gruff. The tight leash I've kept on my desire is nearing a breaking point. It's killing me to be sweet with her now, but this is her first time. She deserves this and more. It's my job to make sure she's always protected now, that she is always happy and cared for—that she knows how special she is.

I push my cock inside of her, so achingly slow my balls hurt, knowing I'm tearing through her innocence. She's gasping, holding onto me tightly, but her focus is trained on me just like I want. Each inch I push into her is an exercise in torture.

"Fuck, honey. You're so damned tight," I groan.

This is it. The moment I make her mine, the moment I've been dreaming of for so damn long.

"Carson... God, you're so big. I don't know if I can..."

I can't allow her time to second guess what we're doing, to worry. Her body is already starting to tense and that will only make things more painful for her.

"I promise I'll make you feel good, honey. I'll make this so fucking good for you you'll think you're flying in the stars," I say to her and I don't care if it fucking kills me. I will make that true for her.

Then, before she can panic further, I thrust the rest of my dick inside of her, claiming her virginity and finally—*fucking finally*—making her mine.

16

Virginia

His big body rests against mine, pressing me into the mattress, sending a lovely, heavy sensation coursing through me. Carson is so muscular, so big and heavy that I feel the breath leaving me. Warm, hard male flesh molds into me, making the sweet anticipation of release just a reach away.

"You feel so fucking incredible, sweetheart." He curls his fingers around my upper arms.

"So good. You're doing so good." He kisses the top of my head and continues to push in and out of me.

The stretching and burning sensation is intense, but when he is fully inside of me I sigh in contented pleasure. The feeling of being completely filled by the man I love is breathtaking, and then when he cups both sides of my face and kisses me possessively, I feel my pussy clench around him.

"Jenny..." he says softly, but harshly, and starts moving back and forth in me, slow and easy at first. Each time he gets to the entrance of my body, the broad head of his dick stretches my unused muscles as he pushes into me again. He does this over and over again until I am sweating and breathing hard. With every inch he sinks into me, I feel claimed.

"So good, baby." He leans back slightly and watches himself push into me and pull back out. "You're mine. This sweet fucking virgin pussy will only ever be mine. I claimed you, took your cherry, and I'm shaping your tight little pussy to fit my cock. *Only mine.* I'll never let you go now." He thrusts back into me.

Over and over he does this, slow and easy thrusts that have me lifting my hips in hopes he'll go faster.

"*Christ,*" Carson says harshly. He pushes himself up, leaning back on his haunches, and grips my inner thighs. He pushes my legs wider and stares down at where his cock is lodged into my body. "So fucking perfect," he murmurs to himself. He places his thumb on my clit and rubs the bundle of nerves back and forth, over and over.

Lights flash before my eyes as my orgasm claims me.

Carson doesn't let up. He thrusts in and out of me, drawing my climax to the peak then keeping it there until I can't breathe. I stare at him, seeing the wild, untamed expression on his face.

Before I can even think straight, Carson moves onto his back, his cock still buried deep in my body, and has me over him, straddling him. His hands are on my waist and he lifts me, causing his cock to almost slip out. All I can do is brace myself with my hands on his chest as he fucks me in this new position.

He groans out his pleasure and the sounds he makes only grow louder as the seconds move by. I know he's close. I press all the way down on him and grind my pussy against his pelvis. I am so sensitive, sore even, but I am not going to stop this. I can't. I want him too much, want this too badly.

"Yeah. Fuck, baby girl." He tightens his hold on my waist as I take over and ride him. Up and down I move, sinking harder and faster on his cock until my head grows dizzy from it all.

I am going to come again.

On the next down stroke I grind my clit against him. The explosion inside of me rivals the one before. I throw my head back and cry out as my pussy clamps down on his cock. Carson digs his fingertips into me, and his low, animalistic grunt signals that he's found his own release.

The sensation of him growing harder, thicker inside of me has me gasping out. I bounce on him faster. Then he comes in me, filling me up with his seed. I love feeling him come deep inside of me. I can't help hoping I get pregnant with his baby. I can see that same need in his eyes, as well. We both want this, even if it's kind of crazy.

I collapse against his chest, our skin sweaty and our breathing loud in the otherwise silent room. He wraps his arms around me and together we roll to our sides, facing each other. The heavy length of his cock is still buried inside of me, and spasms of pleasure continue to move through me. I close my eyes and rest my forehead on his damp chest, loving the sound of his rapidly racing heart.

I can't believe we just did that. I can't believe that Carson is really mine.

He kisses me on the forehead again, and I love this gentleness in him. "I've never loved anyone the way I love you."

I smile. "I love you too."

17

Carson

A year later

I look out over my farm with a sense of pride. I've always been part of this land, but since having Jenny by my side there's a peace inside of me I never knew existed. This is where I'm supposed to be. This is the life I'm supposed to live. This land and Jenny —most of all Jenny—are the reason I was put on this earth. The reason I draw air.

We've been together a year now and every day that passes I fall more in love with her. The only dark spot in our life is the fact that Jenny hasn't got pregnant yet. It's not from lack of trying either. I fuck her every damn chance I get. I don't let her rest at night.

We're both hopeful now, though. She's over a month late right now. We did a home pregnancy test a couple of days ago and it came out positive. The look on her face when she saw the results made my heart swell with love and pride. She wants my child as much I want to give her one.

I'm taking her into town tomorrow to the doctor. We found a female OB with a good reputation. I want her to have the best, but I'm also a fucking bastard who doesn't want another man looking at what's mine. Jenny belongs to me. Her body is mine and no one else is looking at her sweet little pussy but me. Hell, I'm a jealous bastard. I don't even want a female doctor touching her, but I can deal with that more than if it was a man.

I park my tractor in the barn and lock it up for the night. I'm quitting a little early, but then, since Jenny has moved in I do that every night. There's not a second I don't want to spend with her. I look at the wedding band on my finger, and the gold shines under the evening sun. I married her the day after I took her virginity. I didn't want our child born out of wedlock. It might be an old fashioned idea, but then that's who I am.

"Jenny, I'm home," I call as I walk through the front door. Right away I know something is wrong. Usually when I come home she's in the kitchen cooking supper and humming. She's taken to being a farmer's wife like I wouldn't have believed. She loves everything about being a wife and helping me work the land. I was worried I should let her go to have a better life, and every day she proves me wrong. She was made for me. If there are such things as soulmates, then that is definitely me and Jenny. I think even her father would agree...*after he beat the hell out of me for touching his daughter.*

My heart rate speeds up when Jenny doesn't answer me. Her new SUV I bought her is still in the driveway, so I know she didn't leave the house.

"Jenny!" I call out again, as fear begins to take hold. The farm is remote. I made her promise to keep the doors locked and to never let a stranger in, but she goes outside to sit on the porch and work in the yard through the day. What if someone grabbed her?

What if someone hurt her?

Different scenarios keep flashing through my mind, feeding my fear and panic. If something were to happen to Jenny, I wouldn't want to live. I couldn't—not without her. I need to...

All thought stops when I make it to our master bedroom. I don't see Jenny, but I hear her.

And she's crying.

I follow the sounds into the master bath. Jenny is curled in the corner of the shower, the water beating down on her and she's crying so hard her body is shaking with the sobs. I throw open the glass shower door and the cool spray hits me immediately. I look at the dial and despite it being turned all the way to the hot setting the water is frigid—which means my Jenny has been like this for a while.

I turn the water off, and I don't think, until that moment, Jenny even registered that I was here. But with the water off, she looks up at me and the heartbreak and tears on her face cause physical pain to flash through me.

"What's wrong honey? Talk to me," I tell her gently. I grab a towel and gently wrap it around her. She just sits there looking at me, blinking past the tears pouring from her eyes. Her body is shuddering from the force of her tears and the frigid water. "Jenny?" I question again, my voice hoarse because I'm choking on my fear.

"Carson!" she cries, but says nothing more. A shiver runs through her body and I pull her into my arms, feeling how chilled her body is.

I gather her against me, holding her like the precious gift she is, and take her back into the bedroom. She's too upset and weak to stand, so I sit her on the bed and begin drying her off. I do this quickly, intent on nothing more than getting the excess water off and warming her up. Once I've done that I turn the covers down on the bed, strip out of my clothes quickly and then wrap her up, bringing us both under the covers and giving her my body heat.

Jenny is a rag doll through all of this. She lets me do what I want, and though the sounds of her tears and the force of sobs have quieted, she's still crying. Each tear feels as if it is cutting my heart out. I hold her close, letting her absorb my body heat, and kiss the top of her head, whispering soft, nonsense words to her. Words that have no rhyme or reason. They are just meant to comfort her—to calm her.

I don't know how long we're like that, to be honest. It could have been half an hour or even an hour or longer. Eventually, she's out of tears, and I kiss the side of her face. Her hand wraps around my larger one, which is resting at the base of her neck. I have my fingers on her pulse point, the beat reassuring me that she's okay even if she is upset. Whatever is wrong, I'll fix it, but I just need to know she's here... Her pulse is strong... She's okay—*at least physically.*

"Talk to me, Jenny. Let me fix whatever is wrong," I whisper into her ear, placing a gentle kiss against the shell.

"I need to get up," she says, her body going stiff against me like it never has before. She tries to push away from me, but I hold on tight—stubbornly refusing to let her go.

"No you don't, honey. Not until you tell me what's going on so I can fix this."

"Some things even you can't fix, Carson."

"Bullshit," I growl. By God, Jenny should know that I will move heaven and earth to make sure she is happy.

"Let me up!" she cries, pushing against my body harder.

"Jenny—"

"I started my period, Carson!" she cries when she manages to break away. We lie there looking at each other, our gazes locked on one another. Mine is shock and hers is a mixture of regret and pain.

"Jenny, we can try—"

"Please don't," she whispers. "I love you, Carson, but please don't tell me we can try again. Just don't tell me that, not right now. I just can't hear that," she says brokenly. She slides off the bed, her arms wrapped around her upper body like armor as she walks back to the bathroom...leaving me feeling helpless.

"There are other options, sweetheart." I don't move from my place, giving her space. She needs that, it's clear, even though it eats me up to stay away. "Adoption, fertility treatments—"

"I know," she says and looks over at me. "Just give

me some space, okay?" She smiles but it looks forced, weak. "I just need to be alone right now."

And as hard as it is for me to get up and leave her there, I'd do anything for Jenny, even if it's like a knife to my heart.

18

Virginia

"Jenny, we need to talk," Carson says.

I look up in the bathroom mirror and see him in the reflection. He gave me the space I needed, albeit it was only for a short time. Carson isn't one to stand on the sidelines. It's one of the things I love about him. He's a stubborn man, but he knows what he wants and always wants to fix a problem.

But some things just can't be fixed.

He's standing by the bathroom door. He's slipped on his jeans, the top undone, and his feet bare. He doesn't have a shirt on and his hair is all rumpled. He's beautiful—*absolutely beautiful*. He could have any woman he wanted, and he chose me. But that was before, when he thought I could give him babies. With each month that goes by, the hope inside of me fades. Carson has never said anything; he never makes me feel bad about the fact that I haven't gotten pregnant yet—but I know.

If I didn't before, I definitely know now. When I went a month without a period and I took that home pregnancy test... His eyes lit up. He was so happy. He hollered, picked me up and... *God.* It hurts to even think about that day now. I feel like a complete failure. I feel like I'm failing Carson. Worse. I feel like I'm standing in the way of the one thing he wants more than anything in the world. *A family.*

A false positive. I could curse out that little pregnancy stick for giving me hope. For giving us hope.

"I don't think there's anything to say," I whisper, washing my face, not wanting to talk about it. Talking about it only upset me. Before I would be sad, but now I'm just...fucking pissed.

"The fuck there isn't. You're hurting."

"Nothing you can say will make that better, Carson. You can't always fix everything."

"Honey. It's only been—"

"It's been over a year, Carson. It's time to face the facts. I can't get pregnant."

"You don't know that. Besides, if there's a problem..."

"I think it's pretty clear that there's a problem, Carson," I answer, suddenly feeling very tired.

"It could be with me. Did you ever think about that, Jenny?"

"There's no way it's you, Carson. You're too virile and—"

I stop talking, because I don't have the answers. The truth is it could be him. Just because he's the manliest man I've ever encountered, it doesn't mean he can spawn a whole town of babies. But in the end, it doesn't matter. Whether it's him or me, the fact remains that we can't get pregnant on our own.

"I know you went off to college, but I sure didn't realize you were a doctor."

"Quit being a smartass," I mumble, finally turning to face him, because it's clear he's not going to let this drop. I tighten the robe I had put on earlier, and let my hands play with the sash.

"Then quit trying to shut me out. I know you're disappointed, sweetheart—"

"Don't try and pretend you're not, Carson. I was there the day I took that test. You were on cloud nine."

"Damn it, of course I'm disappointed," he growls and the pain that slices through me at his words is nearly unbearable.

I lean on the sink because it's a blow that could bring me to my knees.

"Carson, I think it's time we talk about separating." I'm running on emotions right now, saying things I'm not sure I really mean. Maybe I want him to feel the pain I feel, even though I'm sure he does. He just hides it so much better. I love him with all my heart, but I don't want to be the reason he's held back.

"What the fuck are you talking about?" he growls and I jump at the anger suddenly in his voice.

"I can't be what you need, Carson. I can't give you want you need. And you deserve a family, a big one. I don't want to be the reason you're in a childless marriage. I can't handle that." I exhale, the words hurting me so damn badly. I don't want to say them, but I want them out there. I want him to know he isn't stuck with me. "I think it's best if we just... separate," I whisper, choking on the words, my heart breaking. I hold my head down, trying to get control of my emotions, because I feel like I'm dying.

"What the fuck, Jenny?" Carson growls suddenly right in front of me. His hands grab my hips, the pressure bruising.

"Carson," I gasp, the anger on his face is the likes of something I've never seen from him before. My heart kicks against my chest.

"Is it that easy for you? Can you throw me away like yesterday's garbage like that?" he yells.

"I... *No!* Carson, nothing about this is easy! I *love* you!"

"Then what the fuck are you thinking?"

"I'm thinking of you! I'm trying to give you what you want." The last part comes out of me on a whisper.

"I wish to hell you'd explain how you leaving me does that. You're my fucking world."

"You want a baby. You want a family. Heirs to leave this land to. You've said that for as long as I've known you!" I yell back, anger pulling me out of my misery as nothing else could.

"Do you not fucking listen when I talk, Jenny? Have you not heard me for the past year when I told you that you have given me the world? As long as I have you, I don't need another goddamn thing. You're it for me, Jenny. You always have been. I love you." He says the last part with so much emotion I feel like crying.

"I love you too," I cry. "I just want you to be happy."

I would have thought I had no tears left, but I'm wrong, because now I'm sobbing my eyes out.

"Jenny—"

"I need you to be happy, Carson. That's all I want," I tell him in between tears and shuddering breaths.

This morning I was so happy... And now it feels like my world is ending.

"If I'm not with you I'm not happy," he says and strokes my cheek. "If I don't have you by my side there's no reason to keep breathing."

And I know he means that, because I feel the same way.

19

Carson

"Baby girl, look at me," I tell Jenny, my body shaking with fear.

I'm not afraid to admit it. The thought of Jenny leaving me scares the fuck out of me. She's my world.

I put my hand under her chin, and apply pressure to get her to raise her head to look at me.

"Carson," she whispers, her gorgeous eyes shining with tears.

"If I don't have you, Jenny, nothing else means a goddamn thing," I tell her softly.

"You want a baby..." she whispers.

"I want *you*, Jenny. If it ever came down to it and I

had to choose you or this damn land, I'd choose you, every fucking time."

"But..."

"I wanted a baby to tie you to me. A part of both of us that would always connect us, Jenny. I'm a selfish bastard and I wanted that so you would never think of leaving. And don't get me wrong. Seeing a baby we created looking up at me, knowing we made that together, has pride filling me, has longing choking me. But, honey, you have to know that the only thing I need in this world to make me happy...is you. I love you," I tell her, my voice thick.

"Carson, you're crying," she whispers, surprised. Her fingers come up and brush my face. She's right. I am crying. Even thinking of a world without Jenny beside me...unmans me.

"Don't leave me, Jenny. Don't ever leave me."

"Is that really what you thought? That a baby would tie me to you?" she asks with a deep breath, her thumb brushing my face.

"It would. You'd want your child to have both parents. You'd always—"

Jenny brings her lips against mine so I stop talking. It's more than effective and I kiss her back, my hands coming up on each side of her face, my lips plundering hers slowly but intensely, trying to show her without words how deeply I love her.

"Carson, you own my heart. You're a part of me. I'd never leave," she says when we break apart.

"Jenny, you just told me you wanted to separate," I tell her, getting control of my emotions now that it's becoming clear that Jenny still loves me.

"Only for you, Carson. So you could find someone who could give you a child," she answers, looking downward and stumbling on the words.

"We'll go to the doctor tomorrow and have her check us out," I decide.

"But—"

"And I need you to ask yourself something, Jenny."

"What's that?" she answers, looking back to me in question.

"If I'm the reason we can't have a child, would you leave me? Would you find another man who would give you what I can't?"

"What? Of course not. I don't want anyone but you. I..."

"And that's exactly how I feel about you, Jenny. You're everything to me."

"I was stupid," she whispers, her face coloring, trying to avoid my gaze.

"You weren't. You were hurting. But what you don't understand is that when you hurt, I hurt. Whatever life throws at us, Jenny, we have to face it together."

"I love you, Carson," she whispers and finally the fear I've been dealing with leaves.

"You can prove that to me," I grumble, picking her up and carrying her back to our bed.

"But, Carson. I'm on my period..."

"I don't care. We both need this. I need to know you're still mine," I tell her, lying her down on the bed. I unzip my pants and my cock slides out, already hard and leaning towards Jenny and her beautiful full lips.

"I'll always be yours," she whispers, just before she takes me into her mouth. I close my eyes and let those words settle inside my heart...inside my very fucking soul.

20

Virginia

I'm wringing my hands together and looking around the exam room, trying to calm my breathing. I don't know why I'm so nervous. Carson's right. We have each other and that's all we need. We could always adopt a child. Whatever happens, as long as we're together it's fine.

I keep repeating that to myself and I truly believe it. But at the same time I'm scared of what the doctor will tell us. She did an initial exam and drew some blood. That was over thirty minutes ago and she hasn't come back in. I was just worried about not having a child, but what if something is wrong with my health? What if—

"Jenny, stop," Carson says, his voice tender and soft

as his hand stretches out over both of mine. "Everything is going to be fine."

"I know. I'm just...worried."

"There's no reason to be, sweetheart. We've been through this."

"I know, Carson. I do. I don't even know why..."

"I'm sorry, Mrs. Haynes. I had an emergency with a patient," the doctor says, coming back into the room. Carson squeezes my hand reassuringly and I curl into his side as the doctor walks around her desk to sit down and face us.

"That's okay, doctor. I hope everything is okay."

"Oh, everything is fine. I just needed to reassure a patient who's about to become a mother for the first time. Now, I've prescribed you some vitamins and for the next few months I want you to take it easy. Make sure you—"

"I'm sorry, doctor. I feel like we're missing something here. Is there something wrong with my wife?" Carson asks.

"What? Oh! You don't know? I asked Dr. Moore to come by and tell you the results."

"What results?" I ask, before Carson can. "Am I sick? Are we able to have children?"

"You're perfectly healthy, both of you. Although you may start to experience some nausea in the coming weeks..."

I feel everything in me freeze. Did I just hear her correctly?

"Can you tell us what the hell that means?" Carson growls, his patience at an end.

"Oh, I'm sorry. I've made a mess of this. There's not a thing wrong with your wife, except she's pregnant."

The silence stretches on between us, and I glance at Carson, not sure if I heard the doctor correctly.

"I'm...*pregnant?*"

"By our estimation, Mrs. Haynes, you're about two months pregnant."

"But I can't be," I say, confusion clear in my voice. Then I start crying. Big, wet, sloppy tears.

"But you are."

"Maybe you should make sure you have the right file? My wife started her period yesterday and we're here because..."

"I assure you both, I have the right file. I understand how stressful this all must have been on you, but you are very pregnant."

"But the bleeding..." I whisper, afraid to let the hope inside of me completely free.

"Sometimes it happens, but you said yourself that today it's almost stopped. It's something we'll watch closely, and one of the reasons I want you to take the next few months easy, but this does happen. I once had a patient who came in five months pregnant and had no idea because she had a period every month just like normal." She smiles at us and I can see she's trying to be reassuring. "But because you have the bleeding I am going to schedule you for an ultrasound, just to make sure everything is okay."

"I can't believe this," I whisper and Carson pulls me up from my chair and into his lap. I should chastise him, because we're in a doctor's office, but the truth is, I don't care. I want to be in his lap. I want to be close to him right now. *I need his arms around me.*

"Jenny..." he whispers, his face brushing mine gently. I look into his eyes and they are bright with unshed tears. He's smiling.

"I'm pregnant."

"You're pregnant," he repeats.

"I'm having your baby," I whisper, reality finally settling inside of me.

"You're having *our* baby," he corrects me.

"I love you, Carson," I tell him through my tears.

"And I love you, Jenny," he reassures me and when he kisses me, I get lost in our kiss. I guess we both do, because neither of us notice the doctor leaving the room.

We break apart a few minutes later and Carson puts his hand on my stomach. I cup mine over his and close my eyes.

"For as long as I can remember, Carson, I wanted to be your wife and have your babies."

"Jenny—"

"Thank you for making my dreams come true, Carson. Thank you for loving me."

"I'm the one who should be thanking you, sweetheart. You've given me the world," he whispers, kissing me again.

I don't argue with him, but he's wrong. He's the one who has given me the world. He's given me a family.

EPILOGUE ONE

Carson

The room is silent, dark, and the only thing I can focus on is the clicking of the ultrasound tech working on the machine. She starts putting gel on Jenny's belly, and I stare at the monitor in front of us, my heart in my throat, my palms sweating. I squeeze Jenny's hand and she does it in return.

And then the tech starts the actual ultrasound and I'm in awe at what I see. It doesn't look much like a baby yet, but I see limbs, the head, and a tiny body. It looks more like an alien, but hell, that's Jenny's and my alien growing inside of her.

I squeeze Jenny's hand and look at her. She is

staring at the monitor, this wide-eyed expression on her face, tears sparkling in her eyes.

God, I love this woman so much.

And then we hear the rhythmic sound of a little heartbeat. It's fast for something so tiny.

"That's our baby, Jenny."

She laughs, this watery sound, and I can feel the happiness in her come through to me.

I can't stop myself from cupping Jenny's face and kissing her. I don't give a shit if the tech is seeing this. I want the world to know how deliriously happy I am.

Once the tech prints off some pictures for us, and has Jenny cleaned up, she leaves us in the room. I place both hands on either side of her face and lean in to kiss her.

I pull back and stare at my wife, my soul mate...my Jenny. "I love you, sweetheart."

She smiles in return. "I love you, too."

God, what I feel for Jenny grows every single day, and I know it won't stop. I know I'll love this woman until the sun stops setting and rising.

And fuck, it's the best feeling in the world.

EPILOGUE TWO

Carson

I am living my dream. Without love, family, and happiness there was no point to life. I am the luckiest fucking man in the world.

The sound of the fire crackling in the hearth, and the glow from the flames makes the room seem relaxed, comforting. I pull Jenny closer to me, and bury my face in the fall of her long, sweet smelling hair. I slip my arm around her and span my open palm on her belly. She is big and round with our second child. After we had our first baby, a little girl, we thought it would be another journey to get pregnant again. But we were both surprised when she got pregnant fairly easily. We hadn't been trying, and because she was nursing and hadn't gotten her period, we didn't know she was pregnant. But to our utter surprise and elation we found out she was carrying a little boy.

A son and daughter. A wife and soul mate. I am living the fucking dream.

I look down at Jenny. She will always be mine, no matter what. I start rubbing her belly and feel the baby kick. God, I love this. I rub her belly once more, and my little boy kicks again.

"You think you can handle a baby boy, Jenny?"

"If he's wild like you, maybe not," she says and chuckles. "But if I can handle you, I can handle anything."

I shift on the couch and pull her onto my lap so I can kiss her. I stare at her face. "If I could marry you all over again, I would."

This woman and my children are the reason I live, are the reason I work so hard. I want them to want for nothing.

She leans forward and kisses me softly.

"Do I still make you happy?" She smiles at me.

"Always."

I pull her in and hug her, just keeping her close. This is the life...what living is all about.

The End

Jingle My
BALLS

JORDAN MARIE
JENIKA SNOW

JINGLE MY BALLS (Hot-Bites Novella)

By Jenika Snow and Jordan Marie

www.JordanMarieRomance.com

support@jordanmarieromance.com

www.JenikaSnow.com

Jenika_Snow@yahoo.com

Copyright © December 2017 by Jordan Marie and Jenika Snow

First E-book Publication: December 2017

Photographer: Wander Aguiar Photography

Cover model: Jonny James

Photo provided by: Wander Book Club

Editor: Kasi Alexander

Cover Created by: RBA Designs

Nick

My firm has been hired to make sure Holly gets her biggest Christmas wish.

The rules are simple:

Seduction and fantasy, and absolutely no sex.

But, the moment I get a look at the delicious redhead, all rules go out the window faster than Santa's sleigh on Christmas night.

I shouldn't touch her, but it is the season of giving, after all.

And I really want to give Holly a night neither of us will ever forget.

The problem is, once she wraps that sweet little tongue on my candy cane,

I want much more than just one night.

Warning: Welcome to Jenika and Jordan's Hot-Bite Christmas where the packages are big, the stockings are definitely hung, and snow isn't the only thing that gets plowed. We've decided you've been too good this year. So pull up a chair and enjoy a quick, dirty little cup of Christmas Cheer.

1

Holly

If I hear one more Christmas carol, I'm going to hurl. That's it. I hate this time of year. It's cold, it's miserable, and people are just plain rude. I tried Christmas shopping today—*I really did*. Fifteen minutes in the store with holiday music playing in the background, people pushing and shoving, getting mowed down by shopping carts, and I was done.

Which is why I'm limping on the sidewalk, with not one shopping bag to show for my trouble. Some woman inside the department store ran into me with her cart. She didn't apologize; she just huffed, like I was the one who caused the accident.

I find a bench close to the park and sit down to

inspect the damage. I bend down to look at the back of my leg and wince at what I see. My stocking is torn and there are these gigantic runs in the nylon going up my leg. The heel of my foot is bloody and has been ripped open at the exact spot the back of my Jimmy Choos slide against. My favorite pair of heels didn't exactly escape hell either. They're scuffed and have serious damage. If I had it to do over I wouldn't have walked away. I would have given that lady a dirty look and thrown my shoe at her before giving her the finger.

"Looks like you've been trampled by Santa's reindeers," a deep voice says to my right. I turn and look at him and everything in me stills. Chills run down my back and the voice seems to vibrate in the very center of me, sending instant awareness through me and making my body hum with need. Which is unusual for two reasons. One, I've been on a break from relationships and men in general for the last five years. My last breakup was not good—so not good that the thought of trusting another male scares the hell out of me. The last and most obvious reason is the one that takes precedence, however. I don't know this man. I don't know him at all and worse... He's wearing a Santa outfit.

Great, I've reeled in a nut job.

"Do I know you?" I sound like a cranky old bitch right now, but I'm not in the mood for some guy dressed up to try and get me in the holiday spirit, not matter how good looking he is.

"I'm Santa, can't you tell?" he says, drolly.

I rest my back against the bench and look at the stranger, feeling my eyebrows lift up in sarcastic disbelief. Yeah, he's wearing a Santa suit, a cheesy red one that looks like it's made out of crushed velvet and that's trimmed in white fake fur. I suppose that's not strange; 'tis the season and all that. What doesn't fit the part, however, is when he yanks off the beard and hat and pulls off the white gloves, I can see that his large, masculine hands are covered in ink.

I draw my attention back to his face. Now that the fake beard is gone I see he's sporting a black beard with a bit of gray sprinkled in. Dark, almost obsidian eyes stare down at me. They look intense, mocking and yet at the same time somehow bored with life. He pulls out a cigarette and then lights it, cupping his hand against the cool New York wind.

"I don't think Santa is supposed to smoke," I tell him.

"Sweetheart, Santa does a lot he's not supposed to do," he smirks and something about that look on his face makes my body heat.

"Whatever. You should make sure your boss doesn't see you do that," I mutter, annoyed because he's making my traitorous body react when it shouldn't.

"Santa has no boss."

"God, can you drop the act? I've about had it with Christmas and the last thing I want to do is hear you tell me how you spend your days on the North Pole playing with your reindeer," I huff.

"I make the elves stroke my reindeer horns actually," he smirks. "What's got your panties in a twist?"

"You mean besides being mowed over by a woman with a cart and ruining a pair of pantyhose and my favorite pair of heels?"

"Who was she? I'll put her on the naughty list," he asks and at this point I just shake my head.

Who is this guy?

"Will you give it a... *What are you doing?*" I feel my eyes grow big as I watch him get down on his haunches in front of me.

"I thought that was rather obvious. I'm checking your injury out," he murmurs, ignoring my protest and pulling my leg up into his lap—despite me trying to pull it away.

I brace myself on the bench, because if I don't, I'm going to end up falling to the ground. I try to kick at him, but he holds my leg firmly, not allowing the movement.

"Will you stop? I don't know you! And besides that, this dress is too short. You'll have me flashing half of New York." My voice has risen by this point.

"Stop being dramatic. My body is completely blocking you." He dismisses my objection and then he looks at me—*really* looks at me. His eyes bore into mine, and his hand on my leg becomes tighter, almost punishing in his hold. "Are you wearing panties?" he asks.

My body jerks in reaction. I should be repulsed. In fact, I should be panicking that a man I don't know, a man dressed in a Santa suit, with a cigarette trapped between his lips and his big—*huge really*—ink-covered hand wrapped around my leg, is asking me if I'm wearing panties. What I should not be is turned on. And, if my damp panties are any indication... *I am definitely turned on.*

"You did not just ask that!" I cry out, desperately trying to pull away from him. *I can't be turned on by a stranger—a very weird, sexy as sin stranger. I cannot be talking about my panties with said stranger and most of all, I can't spread my legs a little wider for him.*

"Black... nice," he says almost to himself, obviously having looked at my panties. I'm not sure how much he can see because of my pantyhose, but despite it all I feel my face heat, even though the air has a wintery chill to it. "Damn, honey, I'd say the shopping cart won your war," he mumbles around his cigarette, yet somehow managing to make each word clear.

"Will you let go of my leg please?" I growl out,

unable to pull away from his firm grip. I'm thinking that what I thought might be padding to fill out the Santa suit is actually just plain muscle. If his hands are anything to go by, he's huge.

What is it they say about large hands again?

I squirm uncomfortably. I really shouldn't be thinking about that at all.

2

Nick

I've been fucking bored out of my mind all day...until now, that is. I run Dreamers, a premiere shop on the Upper Eastside that specializes in making dreams and fantasies a reality. Christmas is our busiest season. A lot of that is because there are a ton of lonely, bored women during Christmas. Case in point, one Ms. Keni Preston. A bored ex-housewife whose biggest wish for Christmas this year? To be seduced and romanced by Santa.

Now, don't get it twisted. I don't sell sex. I sell the fantasy. Ms. Preston paid to be picked up by Santa in Central Park, taken home and fed a romantic dinner in a penthouse suite and cuddled all night. No sex involved. Now I know what you're thinking, but cuddling is *not* sex. There are even these people who proclaim themselves professional cuddlers.

People I hire for this shit are extensively vetted, thoroughly interviewed, and paid handsomely for their help. I only hire the best of the best, except for Brian Flannigan. He called in sick this morning, leaving me short one fucking Santa. I have a small staff, all of which are booked solid. It was either cancel Ms. Preston's fantasy at the last minute, or fill in myself. Fuck, I hate doing this shit, and I never do it, to be honest. I should have canceled. It would have been the professional thing to do, but one look at this hot piece of ass has me thanking myself for not pulling out at the last minute.

I snort at that though. There won't be any pulling out at the last minute where it concerns her.

In the spirit of Christmas—and the hope of never getting a bad fucking review on Yelp or some other asinine site, I stepped in, and I'm damn glad I did —*now*. I hadn't met Keni previously because my receptionist does all the booking. I have to say, however, if I had known what she looked like beforehand, I would have totally taken this job out from under Brian. She's a stone cold fox. Legs that fucking go on for miles, tits the size of cantaloupes and so fucking perfect they reach out and beg you to hold them. The black dress she's wearing is professional and severe, but it's sexy and shows just enough cleavage that you want to grab each side of the V-neck collar and rip it away from her body. *And fuck.* That damn red hair she has on her head is like a fucking crown of beauty. Makes me wonder if the curtains match the carpet.

She's got all those locks bound up in a damn bun, but you can tell it's long and wavy. Shit is bronze, and auburn and other colors I can't begin to name. It's like she's got the fucking sun trapped inside of it.

Perfection.

I expected her to give in to me right away, but she must like the game we're playing. I can dig it. I always did like a woman with an imagination. So when she starts squirming I decide to go with my instinct. Usually women wound as tight as this one have a bit of a freaky side to them. I swat the side of her thigh hard, and keep pressure on her leg.

"Keep still," I order her, making my voice deep, commanding. If she wants to play this game then she needs to know I'm in charge. And because she paid for the Santa fantasy, I add, "Or Santa will put you on the naughty list."

"Are you deranged?" she asks, pretending to be outraged. She can't hide the tremble in her body, however. She can't hide the way she shivers from the contact, or the way her calves tighten under my hand, or even the way her ass and hips curl into the air toward me. And she really can't hide those fucking nipples, which push against her dress.

"Santa has to punish naughty girls." I grin and stand, taking the cigarette out of my mouth and crushing it under my boot. "What's your name, honey?" I ask, ignoring the fact I already know—after all, I'm playing a role here.

"Holl—Holly," she whispers, clearly flustered. It surprises me that she doesn't give me her real name. But I like that she's sticking to the fantasy and apparently the Christmas theme, using the name Holly. She fits the description on the ticket, red hair, green eyes, wearing black fuck-me heels, and carrying a briefcase. I dismiss the thought that maybe, just fucking maybe I got the wrong girl. She likes to play and I'm definitely in the mood to play—*with her.*

"Holly, I think it's time I show you exactly what Santa does with bad little girls."

"I... You do?" she asks, her eyes opening wide and getting round, showing off the green beauties that a man could get lost in.

"I do indeed," I tell her, letting my hand move farther up her leg. Her body tenses, her hand going half-heartedly to stop me, but when I push under her dress, going high on her thigh, she doesn't protest.

"What does... What does Santa do?" she asks in a

whisper-soft tone and I send up a thanks to the powers that be that Brian called in sick.

"Santa makes them wet." I grin, letting my finger graze against the silky fabric of her pantyhose. I really want to tear the fuckers away so I can touch her panties —ones I know are nice and soaked. I bet she's all primed for me. But even though her hose are keeping me away from what I really want, I can feel how damp they are. Her face turns pink and I know exactly how my touch is affecting her. I know her dirty little secret now. She's definitely into her fantasy and she's ready for more. I'm going to take her back to the penthouse I reserved and I'm definitely thinking I'll give Holly more than she paid for. It goes against every rule my company has, but Holly is making me forget about all of that. She's even making me feel generous.

She's got my cock harder than fucking steel.

If little Holly here plays her cards right, this Santa might just decorate her pretty little body for Christmas...

With my cum.

3

Holly

I cannot believe what I am doing. I followed Santa out of Central Park and to this swanky building, his big muscular body draped in that hideous red crushed velvet outfit, yet still making me so wet I am not about to say no to what is going to happen. I should though. I don't know him, which makes this crazy. Yet he ignites this fire inside of me the likes of which I've never experienced before.

The rational side of my brain says he could be a serial killer, tempting me with his holiday sexiness and making me forget the whole stranger danger rule.

But then another side of me, the one that controls the fact I want him to fuck me so hard he makes me sing *fa-la-la-la* in a high pitched scream, overrides everything else.

And that is how I find myself in this penthouse suite, staring at a man I know I want between my legs more than my next breath, and praying his candy cane is as big as I am picturing.

Neither of us says anything for long seconds, but he has this cocky smirk on his face that tells me he knows exactly how I feel, maybe even what I am thinking.

A shiver races up my spine at the way he looks at me, the way he checks me out. He rakes his gaze over the entire length of my body and I curl my hands into tight fists at my sides. I can feel how hard my nipples are, and there's no doubt in my mind that they're pressing against the material of my shirt, like tight little buds begging for his mouth.

"How bad do you want your stocking stuffed, Holly?"

His use of holiday jargon should turn me off, but it actually has the opposite effect.

I clench my thighs together, trying to stem off the flow of wetness. My panties are well into the soaked territory, and I know my pantyhose are damp as well. But I can't answer him, can't find my voice. None of that matters, though, because the grin he gives me tells me that I don't need to say anything.

He knows exactly what I want, exactly what I need to turn this shitty day right around.

He give me a shit-eating grin, his straight white teeth flashing, and then he goes for his red coat with the white fur trim around the collar. When the jacket is removed all I can see is hard golden skin covered in dark tattoos. His washboard abs have the feminine side of me rising up, and my belly clenches painfully.

I'm so aroused right now that all I want to do is tell him to rip off my clothes and fuck me raw. I want to be sore in the morning. I want to have trouble walking because he pounded into me like a madman.

Oh God. I'm such a dirty fucking woman. I cannot believe I'm thinking this raunchy shit about him.

I guess this is what happens when you're celibate for too damn long.

He doesn't say anything as he walks over to a leather chair and sits down. He spreads his legs, the motion causing his belly to clench and show off his perfect six-pack. His biceps are huge, and all I can imagine is that tattooed flesh above me.

He pats his leg and I feel my eyes widen.

God, please do not even go there.

"Come sit on Santa's lap and tell me what you want for Christmas."

I should find this whole situation funny, but it's having the opposite effect on me. Am I that much of a lunatic that Santa roleplaying is turning me on this much? But when I look at his crotch, see the massive bulge good ol' Saint Nick is sporting, I know that what I want for Christmas is what he's sporting under those red velvet pants.

"Don't make Santa ask again. You want to stay on the nice list, right?" He lifts a dark eyebrow and my mouth dries. That shouldn't turn me on as much as it does. He pats his thigh again, and like a good girl, I find myself walking over to him. "Wait," he says and I freeze. "Take off the heels and panty hose."

I swallow the lump that suddenly lodges in my throat. I do as he asks and feel my flesh tighten as the chilled air moves over it.

"Now come here and sit on my lap." His voice has gotten deeper, more demanding.

When I'm right in front of him he could have pulled me onto his lap, but instead he waits for me to sit down. When I'm in the position he wants me in, both of my legs draped over one of his, I have to force myself to breathe normally. I can feel the outline of his monstrous cock under my ass, and I try not to squirm.

I try and fail.

"You feel what I have for you, that big fucking gift I'm sporting between my thighs?" He smirks at me again and lifts his hips slightly, digging his dick against my ass. I gasp softly. "You must have been a very good girl this year to get this present from Santa. Weren't you, Holly?"

I find myself nodding, getting swept away in this role-playing fantasy that I never knew I could actually enjoy. And before I know what is happening he has his hands on my waist and turns me around so I'm facing him. The new position has my legs now spread, hanging over his muscular thighs, and his big shaft pressed right between my thighs. My skirt has risen up, and I know if he looks down he'll be able to see my panties.

He leans in so our mouths are only inches apart. "I can smell how ready you are for me, how much you want this." His words have this growl laced with them. "Ask me to fuck you, Holly."

And as much as I should have said "fuck you," I actually find myself licking my lips and saying, "Fuck me."

4

Nick

I need my head examined. These are the nightmare stories you hear that can topple businesses. It's sad to admit, but at this point I'm not thinking with my head. I'm thinking more with my dick and my balls, which are so fucking tight and heavy right now it's a wonder I'm holding back. I have the urge to throw her on the floor and sink deep inside of her. I'm resisting that—*barely*. At least I made her ask me to go further. I mean, it's not much, but for some reason my conscience feels better with that small admission.

She's looking at me, her green eyes cloudy with desire and need. It's an expression that a man could get drunk on. Hell, I'm already there. I reach up and begin taking the clips out of her hair, not wanting to go one step further until I've released the auburn locks from their prison. It should be against the law to keep hair like this up. I let my fingers drift through the strands once they are free, loving the feel of it against my skin.

"Hurry," she whispers, urging me on, and I can't help but grin. She thinks she has some control here. Time for me to show her the truth... *She has none.*

"Get on your knees, Holly."

"But..." she says, her face showing confusion. She's beginning to second-guess herself, which is probably wise. I find myself doing the same, but I'm hoping she doesn't stop.

"On your knees. Now, Holly," I repeat, my voice leaving no room for argument.

She slides to the floor, hesitantly. She's biting at the inside of her lip nervously and there's a question in her eyes.

Is she about to call this whole thing off?

"I didn't plan on doing this," she whispers. Is she about to blow the fantasy? For some reason that disappoints me. I'm enjoying this role-play more than I thought I would. "I don't even know your name," she adds. She does, however, stay on her knees, those big, beautiful green eyes looking up at me as her gaze locks on mine.

"Undo my pants," I growl, my dick throbbing for her touch.

Her hand quivers slightly as she reaches to untie the drawstring on these damn pants.

Once she has the ties undone I see her eyes widen. I grin. "You're not wearing underwear," she says in surprise.

"Santa likes to have his balls free so they can jingle all the way home...*inside* of you."

"Jesus," she murmurs. "I can't believe I'm about to do this with a man who is probably convinced he's Santa."

"Do what? Suck my candy cane?" I smirk—definitely pushing my luck.

She wraps her hand around my cock, pulling it out. The bulbous head is painted with my pre-cum. Large, rigid veins throb in my shaft. If she doesn't wrap her lips around me soon, I might just come all over her face. She holds me tightly, her sweet little hand stroking upward. I groan in pleasure.

"You like that?" she asks, and suddenly she doesn't seem timid at all. It's like she's almost challenging me.

"Very much," I tell her, reaching out and stroking my finger along her jaw. She's beautiful. Her lips and the delicate features of her face call to me like nothing and no one ever has before. She's gorgeous, but she'll look even better when those lips are stretched open around my cock and her face is pressed right up against the root.

"Tell me your name... Give me at least that," she says, squeezing my cock tight with her hand, causing me to growl out in ecstasy.

Suddenly roleplaying doesn't seem as important as hearing her scream out my real name as I'm ramming home inside of her.

"Nick. Call me Nick," I tell her, pulling on her hair to try and angle her head down, tired of talking.

"As in St. Nick?" she asks, but she flattens her tongue out and licks along the underside of my cock.

"I'm no saint, Holly, and I'm about to prove that to you," I growl, wrapping her hair around my fist and deciding it's time for me to take over.

I need that mouth on my cock...*now.*

5

Holly

His cock is hard and long, thick and a little intimidating. I'm sure as hell not a virgin, but just the thought of having Nick's big shaft deep inside of me makes me feel like this is my first time.

I still have my hand wrapped around his cock, my fingertips not even able to touch because of his girth. I tip my head slightly back and stare at his face. He's leaning completely back on the chair, his forearms resting beside him, his eyes at half-mast. He looks a little bit drunk, and I know it's because of the pleasure coursing through him.

I feel intoxicated myself.

"Go on, Holly. Suck on Santa's big candy cane."

The roleplaying is really turning me on, and I don't know if that means I'm twisted in the head, or if I'm so in need of some deep dicking that I'm willing to play along.

Either way, I don't plan on stopping this.

"Go on. Do it." Nick's voice gets harder, more demanding. Shivers race along my body at the tone.

I look back down at his dick, the slit at the tip already dotted with pre-cum. I find my mouth watering for a taste of him. And then without waiting anymore, I lower my head, part my lips, and suck the crown into my mouth.

Male saltiness explodes on my tongue, and I moan in pleasure. He tastes so good, woodsy and clean, potent and all male. I close my eyes and moan around him as I start bobbing my head up and down. I take as much as I can into my mouth, and when the head hits the back of my throat and I gag slightly, I hear him groan.

"That's it," he says in a raspy voice.

He has his hand on the back of my head, keeping me right where he wants me. I keep sucking on him, running my tongue along the underside of his shaft, working my mouth over his throbbing dick. My eyes are watering, and my mouth is salivating. He feels like he's gotten harder while I've been sucking on him, and the continuous taste of his pre-cum on my tongue has me wanting to reach between my legs and rub myself until I get off.

I start to do just that when he says, "Don't you fucking touch yourself, Holly. You haven't shown Santa that you've been a good girl and deserve a gift."

I want to tell him that I do deserve a gift, a big one...like the monster he's sporting between his legs. But I continue to give him head, humming around his cock and wanting him to shoot his load deep down my throat and really give me the holiday spirit.

And just when I feel his body tighten, knowing he's about to come, he pushes me away. His dick slips from my mouth with a resounding pop, and I look up at him, my chest rising and falling as I breathe heavily. My lips feel swollen, slightly numb. I wonder how red they are.

"How much do you want me to fuck you? How much do you want me to shove my big dick right up your tight little snatch?"

His words are so vulgar...so damn arousing. I can't speak, I can't even move. I'm on my hands and knees, my skirt pushed obscenely up my thighs, my panty-covered pussy on display. I can see Nick is staring right between my legs.

"Go on, tell me." He's looking at my face now. "I want you to tell me how much you want my big fucking shaft deep in your tight little cunt."

I can hear my heart racing in my ears, and my palms

are starting to sweat. The arousal I feel is like nothing I've ever experienced before.

"I want that." He doesn't respond, but I can see he expects me to say more. I lick my lips and glance down at his erection. "I want your big, hard cock shoved deep in my pussy." I look up at his face again. "I want you to stretch me until it hurts, until the pain and pleasure mix into one. I want to forget the fact that I don't even know you, but that I'm so aroused right now that I don't even care." My throat tightens and I know I won't be able to say anything else that will make sense. Hell, I'm surprised I got that out.

He doesn't say anything for long seconds, and as the silence stretches on I wonder what he's thinking about.

"Stand up and get undressed." His words, tone, broker no argument. "Show Santa what a good little girl you can be."

And just like that I do exactly what he says. I'm that desperate for a good old-fashioned fuck.

6

Nick

I watch Holly get undressed, my hand wrapped around my cock as I slowly jack myself off to the image. If I'm not careful I'm going to come before I get inside of that pretty little pussy. When she's completely naked, she stands there looking at me, her face flushed with a mixture of need and embarrassment. Considering what we're doing here, and what brought us to that point, her shyness seems out of place, but that's clearly what it is and I like it. It appeals to me as nothing else could right now. Still, I'm a big enough bastard that I'm going to exploit that shyness until it disappears. I want her so mindless to passion she's a slave to whatever I desire.

"Touch your tits for me, Holly."

"I—"

"Do it and make Santa happy."

She lets out a long, shuddery breath and then she moves her hands under her breasts, cupping them. I watch as she squeezes the globes, her teeth biting into her lower lip as she tries to control her excitement.

"Tease your nipples," I instruct.

Her tongue comes out, wetting her lips, and I watch her throat work as she swallows down her nerves—but she does it. She's got perfect tits and her nipples are the size of a dime...nice and round and so hard at the moment they're begging for my attention.

"Slide your hand down your body, Holly," I command softly and then I watch as she does just that, slowly dragging her fingers across her chest and then lower to her stomach. She pauses there, as if she isn't sure what I want.

We both know what I need.

"Don't stop, Holly. You know what I want," I urge her, and in this minute there's no role-play. There's nothing but me and her and what I need her to give me. I think she may actually stop our play, that maybe I've pushed her too far, but then she slides her fingers between the lips of her pussy and begins playing with her clit.

Her gaze stays focused on me, and I let my focus

move from watching her fuck herself to looking in her eyes. My balls tighten with the need to come. I want to bend her over and take her from behind. I promise myself I will do that before the night is over. Right now, there's no way I can hold off that long. Plus I want to see her face when I fuck her for the first time.

I shift around so I can access the pocket hidden in these ridiculous Santa pants. I have no idea where tonight is going, but I always stay prepared. I find my billfold and it only takes me a minute to fish out one of the condoms I keep stashed. I take it out and show her.

"Put it on me," I growl, hoping I can handle her wrapping my cock up. I'm not a fucking horny teen that can't control himself. I've had my fair share of women, but I can't remember any of them right now, and I sure as hell can't remember ever being this worked up over one.

"Thank God," she mutters and I find myself smiling. I have no idea what it is about this woman that I connect with so much, but I like it.

She takes the condom out of my hand and goes to her knees in front of me, looking at me as she wraps her hand around the shaft of my cock.

"What are you doing?" I ask, which might be the stupidest question I've ever asked in my life. The answer is crystal clear when she flattens her tongue out against the root of my cock and proceeds to lick up the length until she gets to the tip.

"Making sure you're nice and slick for the condom," she whispers against my dick and I can feel the vibration of her words all the way to my fucking balls.

I wrap my hand in her hair, twisting the strands around my fingers and hauling her up so her lips are right against mine.

"If you don't hurry there won't be a need for lube or the fucking condom because my cum will be all over your face and tits," I growl.

"I like that," she whispers and the look on her face confirms her words. It's tempting, but not as much as the idea of getting inside of her.

"Later," I promise, thinking if I do everything I want to do to her tonight, my balls will be sore as hell tomorrow. "Slide the condom on, Holly. Santa wants to take you for a ride."

She moves her hand over my cock, her motions telling me she's nervous. But then she's ripping open the condom. You can tell by the way she unrolls the latex that she's not real skilled at doing it—it's almost as if it is new to her. Which, considering what we are doing, is endearing.

She rolls the rubber down my cock with gentle care, and again her sweet side surprises me. I reach out, grabbing her around the waist and pulling her close. I capture her lips with mine and slide my tongue deep into her mouth, claiming it with a groan. Her tongue wars with mine, our kiss hungry, savage, and full of need.

"You really know how to kiss," she gasps when we break apart.

"Climb up on my lap, Holly."

"So you can take me to the North Pole?" she laughs, giggling at our game.

"Fuck the North Pole, baby. Santa has a different kind of pole for you," I respond. "One that's real hard."

I hold my shaft still for her to slide down onto it. She lets her hand go over mine, as if to help. There's something so fucking satisfying about the feel of her fingers wrapped over mine. It's like it's a sign that whatever this is, whatever we're doing, we are doing it together.

"My, Santa, what a big candy cane you have," she whispers, her voice breaking as the tip of my cock pushes inside of her.

"Go slow, Holly. I want to see my dick disappear inside of you inch by fucking inch," I order, unable to follow her game. The feel of her pussy squeezing the head of my cock is just too fucking good. I shift her so she's leaning back, my hand on her ass holding her in place. Then I train my gaze on where my dick is lodged deep inside of her.

"Oh God..." she whimpers. "You're so big. You're *stretching me.*"

Fuck. I'm right there with her. Nothing has ever felt so fucking good. Finally, my cock is all the way inside of her and her ass has settled against my lap. I lift one of my hands and cup her tit, squeezing the mound tightly. I try to stop myself from doing what I really want to do —which is fuck her hard until we both explode. I want to make this last. I need to. I hold one of her breasts out, letting my tongue tease the large nipple, making it glisten, while I knead the other with my hand.

"Fuck yourself, Holly. Use my cock to bring us both to the edge," I tell her, wanting to watch her ride me, needing it more than I need air right now.

"I'm so full I can't breathe," she cries, but she rises off my cock.

I bite down a moan as I feel the flutter of her muscles caress my shaft. She lifts until I'm almost outside of her, and then she slides back down. I let her do that a couple of times mostly because it's pure torture, but the kind I fucking like. Eventually, though, I can't take it anymore. I grab her hips and as she begins her downward slide, I slam her down on me so hard my balls bounce against her ass. She screams out as my cock touches her fucking cervix. She curls her hips forward, my dick scraping the sides of the walls of her pussy. I can feel the cum pushing through my cock. I'm close to the end. I need to make sure she's with me. I slide my fingers down, finding her clit as she grinds down on me.

She shatters into a million pieces, her pussy clenching my cock as she screams out her pleasure, pulling me into the orgasm with her. I can feel my cum jet out into the condom, and for a minute I curse the latex blocking me from filling her up. I close my eyes and imagine my seed painting the walls of her cunt and pooling against her cervix as I empty every last drop I can.

God, what the hell is going on with me? This woman is already turning my fucking world upside down.

7

Holly

"Ride me. Milk the cum from me with that tight cunt of yours." Nick's words are harsh, guttural. He wraps his hands around my waist, digging his fingertips into my hips. "Use me to get off," he groans out. "Let me feel you come. Let me feel your pussy walls clench around my dick."

I lean forward, my breasts pressed to his hairy chest, the feeling incredible. I moan, my pussy contracting along his cock on its own.

"God, do that again, Holly."

I brace my knees on the chair and rise up, the pleasure making me feel drunk. Placing my hands on his pectoral muscles, I do what he wants, clenching my pussy on him over and over again. The sound of his teeth clashing together is strong. With his hands still on my waist, I feel him dig his blunt nails into me. The sting is there and it mixes with my pleasure.

Nick is breathing hard, his wide chest moving up and down, his restraint clearly slipping.

"I'll never get enough," he says, and although this is the first time we've been together—most likely the only time we will ever be together—I can't help but believe him. "I want you to ride me until you're bouncing on my cock, until we're both sore tomorrow."

"Oh. God," I whisper and start rocking back and forth on him. I push fully up and rest my hands on his pecs, bracing myself. Then I start bouncing on him, up and down, harder and faster.

"*Christ.* That's it."

His voice is rough, full of need.

"Now, you watch as we fuck." His voice is so commanding that I can't deny him. I won't because I want to see as well.

"Look down, Holly. Watch as you fuck yourself on Santa, as you bring that sweet, primed cunt of yours down on my cock."

There has never been a time in my life when I felt this kind of arousal. I know when this is all said and done Nick will have ruined other men for me.

I rise up but keep my focus on where we are

connected. When his cock becomes visible, I see how glossy it is from my pussy cream. Everything in me tightens at the sight. He's stretched me so good, and the burn of the pleasure is still there. I don't want this to end.

"So hot, Holly."

My breath leaves me and my arms are shaking from holding myself up, but still I ride him.

My pussy sucks at his cock, and his big dick stretches me wide, making me feel like I am going over the edge.

I move up and down, the breath leaving me in uneven gasps, and my tits bouncing. My orgasm rushes forward once more and I feel him get harder inside of me.

I don't want to stop it.

And then I see the change in him. His body becomes tighter, harder. Sweat covers his chest and forehead, and his jaw clenches tightly. I know he's going to come. The question is how long will he restrain himself?

"You see what you do to me?" he says, but it sounds like he's speaking to himself. He's fucking me still, or really, I'm the one doing the fucking. But I can see that he's right at the edge. I don't know how much longer I can last, so I know I have to get him off so we can both find oblivion together.

I clench my pussy muscles around his dick and he groans, tossing his head back and closing his eyes. His fingers are digging deep into my skin, and I know there will be bruises tomorrow. Good, I want that mark, that reminder that I actually did this.

And then he starts lifting me up and slamming me back down on his cock. The wet, sloppy sounds of our sex fill my head, making me drunk from it all. I don't think about anything else but this moment. I don't care that this man is essentially a stranger, that after this one-night stand I'll have to do the walk of shame. But I don't care. This moment is everything I've needed. I've been sex free for far too long, and Nick is definitely putting the holiday spirit back in me...literally.

He slams me down hard on him once more, stilling, his fingers biting so deep into my flesh that I hiss from the pain. He groans, his necks muscles standing in stark relief, his body seeming bigger than life in this moment. I swear I can feel him coming, and I mourn the fact that the condom is keeping it from me. I want his cum. I want all of him—no matter how crazy that is.

The feeling of him coming, and the sight of him lost in passion has me climaxing again.

I collapse on his chest, both of us panting, our skin sweaty. I can hear the thunderous beat of his heart. It matches mine. I want to ask where we go from here, but I'm too embarrassed...too afraid of what he'll say.

Instead I detangle myself from him, both of us making a sound as his cock slips free from my pussy. I can't help but glance down at his dick, the tip of the condom filled with so much cum. The sight has me aroused all over again.

I can't look him in the face, not after what we just did, not when I'm afraid of the disinterest he'll cast my way. Instead of making a fool of myself, I gather my clothes, hastily put them on, and get the hell out of there.

But I swear I hear him call out my name just as the door shuts behind me.

8

Nick

I'm a fucking fool. There's no other word for it. I just let Holly walk away. I didn't even try to stop her. I warred with myself. I mean, this was just a fast afternoon quickie. It's not like we really know each other.

It's just sex.

That's it.

Except I can still feel her riding my dick. I still hear her breathy sighs in my ears and I can still smell her in the room... I miss her.

Isn't that a fucking bitch. I don't think I've ever missed a woman in my damned life.

I get up and jump in the shower. Yet, even as I'm

doing it, I hate the fact that I am washing Holly off of me. Then again, her name isn't Holly. Nothing about what we did here was real. I need to remember that.

But everything felt real.

It sure as hell felt real when her tight little cunt was squeezing my cock and milking it dry. I move my hand to my dick, letting the lather of the soap slide around my shaft and jack it a couple of times, but it feels nothing like the real thing. It feels nothing like Holly.

Holly was unique... *She was special.*

She *is* special.

Nothing has ever felt like she did...

Fuck. I sound like some kind of lovesick fool about a girl who didn't even give me her real name and rode my cock after hiring me for a fantasy. I need to snap out of it. I finish up my shower and throw the clothes on I was smart enough to bring with me, instead of that fucking damn Santa suit. I glance over at the red velvet glob on the floor.

An image of Holly undoing my pants flashes in my mind and my cock stretches against my jeans. I want more of her. I don't care if her name is Keni or Holly. I don't care if it was just meant for one stolen afternoon. I want more of her and I have her information. She had to give it to sign up for a fantasy. If she thought she could hide from Santa, she's sadly mistaken.

Ho, ho, son-of-a-bitching-ho... Santa is fucking everywhere and she'll learn that soon enough.

It's time little Holly—or whatever the hell name she wants to use—finds out that Santa is coming to town. And, when I get there, I'm definitely coming...*in her.*

9

Holly

The next day

I shift on my chair, a soft hiss leaving me. I'm sore, my pussy clenching on its own, the memory of exactly what was shoved inside of me vivid. Although I'm sore and full of partial regret, I can't deny I wish I was with Nick right now. I didn't want to leave yesterday, didn't want to pretend I could just walk away. But I will be damned if I am going to make a fool of myself and want something more with him when he probably just wanted some easy sex, and he sure as hell got that tenfold.

I exhale and lean back, not sure exactly what to do

next. I don't even know his last name to try and contact him, if I was going to go that route. And even if I did know where to find him what would I say?

"Hey, remember me? We had some kinky Santa role-playing sex." Yeah, not going to happen.

"Hey."

I glance over and see Michael standing in my office doorway, his smile wide, and the "fuck me" look he's giving me pretty intense. I know Michael wants me, and he makes no secret about it, but with his greasy slicked-back hair and reputation of trying to bang every female in the office, I've never been more put off by a man.

Well, and given the fact I've just experienced a real man in Nick, roleplaying or not, Michael is more of a turnoff than anything else.

"Hi, Michael," I say with absolutely zero interest in my voice. I know him well enough to understand even a slight smile in his direction makes him think you want him in your bed.

"A bunch of us are hitting up O'Hare's after work. Wanna join in?"

I should say no right away, but he's making it sound like it's an office affair, which I wouldn't mind, especially since it will help keep my mind off Nick. "Who is all going?"

"Kelly and Mitch, Randall, Shellie, and I think Donald. I'm sure we'll get a few others to go, but after the Anderson account has been wrapped up we all need to let loose a little." He wags his eyebrows at me and I don't even try to hide my distaste.

"Maybe. I have to see if I have anything going on." That's a lie. I have nothing going on, but it's sounding a little more appealing to just go home and finish off a bottle of wine while I soak in a bubble bath...and of course think about Nick and all the things I want him to do to me still.

Michael doesn't leave right away, and I close my eyes, knowing I am totally screwed either way. I want to see Nick again, but I have no clue where to even start, where to even look.

Then it looks like I'm shit out of luck. Looks like I just need to move on, and hopefully if I ever find another man he won't be so disappointing that all I keep thinking about is a damn one-night stand.

"Yeah, okay. Getting out with everyone will be nice." I don't bother looking at Michael, but I can practically feel his excitement fill the room.

When he finally leaves I look back out the window. I can't see much but skyscrapers and a murky sky from the winter weather swiftly approaching, but I need something else to focus on besides a certain Kris Kringle-playing hottie who happened to be covered in tattoos and made me sore the next day.

Yeah, Nick definitely ruined me for all other men.

I SIT around with a handful of co-workers, the martini in front of me only half drank. The pub is packed, with bodies almost shoulder-to-shoulder, and the scent of sweat and alcohol filling the air. I swear I can even scent sex lingering, as if all these people are waiting for the liquor to kick in before they take a random stranger home and fuck them.

Kind of like the scenario I keep daydreaming about.

I lift my drink and down half of it, feeling the burn travel down my throat and settle in my belly. "I'll be right back." I grab my coat and excuse myself, heading out the front, pushing my way through the thick throng of people crowded in the pub. Once outside, I wrap my jacket around myself a little tighter and lean against the side of the building.

The air is crisp, the winter already here and biting me in the ass. I stare at the crowds of people, shopping bags in their hands, the late night not stopping them from getting their shit done. This is New York, the city that never sleeps, my home, and a place that has over eight million people residing here. There's no way in hell I'll ever see Nick again.

The odds are definitely not in my favor.

10

Nick

How the mighty have fallen.

I'm fucking standing outside a brownstone at nine in the morning, on a Saturday, banging on the door because no one answered the damn doorbell. This is not just any brownstone, however. I look down at the file I'm holding, pausing my knocking—just in case the neighbors in the adjacent townhouses are tempted to call the law.

This brownstone belongs to Keni Preston. That's why I'm a fucking freak. I'm chasing a client down—a client I had an ill-advised one-night stand with. A one-night stand that could get me sued and destroy my business because I'm being a stalker. And a memory that I've jacked off to for the last three days.

A one-night stand I'm starting to think I'll never be able to forget.

I'm about to turn around and say forget it when the door opens. I'm practically holding my breath—I'm that anxious to see Holly again. Disappointment fills me when a woman with red hair opens the door. She's definitely not Holly. Her red hair isn't a vibrant crown on her head. It's pretty, but it doesn't have the depth of color Holly's does. She's pretty, but she's not my Holly.

Fuck.

My Holly.

My dick is sewn up over a woman I don't even know. A woman who probably doesn't believe my name is actually Nick. A woman who fucked me because of a Santa roleplaying scenario. *Shit.* I've had women fuck me for a lot of reasons. Admittedly, most of them have either fucked me for the size of my dick or the size of my wallet—but absolutely none have fucked me because I was wearing a red velvet coat.

And I can blame my lack of control where Holly is concerned over the fact I haven't been with a woman in far too damn long. With my business being successful, and the workload keeping me busy, I have no time—or interest—in taking anyone to my bed. But then I saw

Holly and everything changed. She made me break a cardinal rule about not getting involved with a client.

"Can I help you?" the woman asks and I notice her eyes are a pale blue. Maybe they would have been pretty before the heated look in Holly's branded me.

Fuck.

"I'm looking for Holly...uh...Keni Preston?"

"I'm Keni," she answers, and the look on my face must have frightened her because she steps back behind the safety of the door.

"No. I'm talking about the Keni who hired Dreamers for a Christmas..." I see the way her eyes widen in surprise. She's silent for a second and I wonder exactly what the fuck is going on.

"Stop!" she cries, looking around. "That was me," she hisses. "But I'd rather not have my neighbors know. How did you find out? *Who are you?*"

What the fuck is going on here? I'm starting to get a sick feeling in my stomach and for once it has nothing to do with the fact that Holly isn't underneath me—at least not entirely.

"I'm... I'm sorry, you're the one who hired—"

"Who are you?" she repeats again and I definitely see panic in her face, but she's not lying. I'd bet everything I own on it.

"I'm Nick Jones. I own the company."

Her throat works as she swallows. "You own Dreamers?" she asks, looking confused. Hell, she's not the only one.

"Yes, and we were following up on the Christmas order placed by Keni...uh, you. Was the fantasy for you or for a friend?" I ask, praying she tells me it was for a friend and gives me the name. That's the only explanation for the fucked-up situation I am now in.

I start to relax, thinking I have it all figured out. Holly—and just maybe that's her real name—might think she can run away from me, but I've got her now. Maybe when I finally get her in my grasp again, Santa will have to spank her for being a naughty little girl. Fuck. Maybe I can make her naughtier? A quick image of Holly tied to my bed, my cum painted across her face, her tongue licking it off her lips while I'm still getting off across her tits, slams to my mind. I swear my cock swells rock hard. If I don't find Holly soon, my fucking balls are going to explode. I've heard the term *bust a nut* my whole life, but not until this woman have I realized what the fuck it means—and the agony that comes with it.

"No... I mean, it was for me, but I just changed my mind. I chickened out, okay? I shouldn't have ever booked it. It's just this was my first Christmas as a single woman. My son is spending Christmas with his father and new stepmother and I just...panicked. I couldn't go through with it, though. I didn't think anything else about it. I mean, you had my deposit and... Shit. I should have canceled." She's rambling now, clearly nervous. "Am I responsible for the whole fee? That hardly seems fair, considering I didn't show. I mean, maybe I should have called when I decided not to show up, but I didn't actually decide not to—at least not until it was time to go there. I figured by then it was just too late. You know?" She's breathing hard and fast.

I want to assure her things are fine, at least where she's concerned, but she won't let me get a word in.

"Is that why you're here? To collect the outstanding amount? Is that standard practice? I mean, this is my home. If you had billed me—or even called, I would have come in," she huffs, blathering on so much that I lose track.

Really, I stopped listening when I discovered she didn't have a friend show up at the park in her place. I stopped listening when I realized that I have absolutely no idea who Holly is or how to find her.

She's lost to me forever...

11

Holly

Two weeks later

I should just leave, but because this is a work function, and basically mandatory or I get the "Where the fuck do you think you're going?" looks from my superiors, I am trapped. It's like a damn prison, a fancy, champagne flowing, rare caviar serving, expensive dress and tuxedo wearing prison. Hell, I don't even know ninety-nine percent of the people in this damn ballroom, but I smile and act like I'm best friends with all of them. Because this is work, and even though I loathe being here, I have to play nice.

I finish off the champagne in my flute but don't wait until a server walks by with a tray filled with more. I head over to the bar and lean against the smooth, glossy wood counter. My mind drifts to Nick, and to the fact that even though it's been two weeks, I still want him. I still think about him, about the possibility of just running into him and things falling right into place. I have a better chance of resurrecting the Lost City of Atlantis than running into Nick in New York City.

Instead of letting my mind be consumed with all things Nick, I focus on the fact that my feet are killing me in these stilettos, and that this dress is a size too small.

"Champagne, please," I say to the bartender and turn to survey the ballroom. This place drips of money, and every year around the holidays they throw this ridiculous party, trying to schmooze with all the big-shot businesses around the city. It is really everyone getting drunk and bragging how they have more money than the next.

It is always a suffocating night, with the stench of overpriced cologne filling my head, and drunken old men trying to get me to go back to a hotel room with them.

There is only one man I want to go to a hotel room with. Nick.

What I need to do is get the thought of Nick out of my head. Because at this point I'm starting to not only feel ridiculous, but also pathetic.

I take the champagne glass and push my way through the people, heading toward the balcony. The doors are closed because it's cold as hell outside, but I'm sweating, and need the fresh air.

When I get on the balcony I look out at the skyscrapers and the lights that fill the city. It's bright, and I can't see the sky clearly, or make out any stars. But I love this city, even with the thick population, and everything else that comes with being crammed into an asphalt and steel world.

I lean against the railing and look out at the scene, hearing the blare of car horns honking, seeing the spots of red and yellow from the lights below. I take a sip from my champagne, not able to help letting my mind wander to Nick again. Where is he right now? Has he been thinking about me, too?

Thinking about me? Am I that desperate?

I close my eyes and shake my head. I need to just find another guy. That will help me forget about Santa and the massive candy cane he's sporting.

I PULL AT THE BOWTIE, this fucking suit strangling my entire body. I toss back the whiskey, needing another one. As if my prayers are answered, a waiter comes by with a tray filled with the little fuckers. I grab one and start walking away from the group I've been speaking with. This corporate parry is not my scene, not in the least, but it is good to mingle with big shots and let them know I am not someone to fuck with. It is good to let other assholes know that I am a bigger one if need be.

I finish off the whiskey in a matter of minutes and start making my way toward the bar. I am already feeling pretty buzzed, and although I should stop, I can't. Over the last two weeks I've tried finding out where Holly is. I haven't found shit though. She's disappeared, or hell, maybe Holly isn't even her real name. I know I should put all of this behind me, chalk it up to a one-night stand, but I just can't.

All I can think about is Holly, and I know until I find her I can't walk away. I won't.

Just as I reach the bar I glance toward the balcony. The outside lights make it easy to see the few people mingling around, but it's the flash of red hair that makes my heart freeze right in my fucking chest. I know that it's most likely not Holly, but God, that shade is not something I'll ever forget. The color of Holly's hair is engrained in my brain, and the woman who is leaning against the balcony railing has the exact same shade as the woman I am desperate for.

As if on instinct I find myself moving toward her. I'm not sure what I plan on saying when I get there, but I'm also not about to fucking stop myself.

12

Holly

"Holly?"

I gasp. My body goes solid, my heart lodges in my chest. I know that voice.

I've been dreaming of that voice.

Still, it can't be Nick. There's just no way. To prolong my own agony, I take my time turning around. If I don't look, I can pretend it's him.

"Fuck. It *is* you," he growls and my knees go weak. I literally have to lean on the railing of the balcony. If I don't, I'm afraid I might fall.

"*Nick?*" I ask, and I have to blink several times to make sure it is him and not just some figment of my desire-laden, wishful thinking brain. He looks so different wearing a very expensive tuxedo rather than his Santa outfit. But he looks good, so damn good. Even though he's covered from neck to toe, I can still see the tattoos that cover his hands, and even the ones he has on his throat. They turn me on like nothing else can.

He turns me on like no one else ever has or ever will.

"Motherfucker!" he growls and then takes three large strides to me, eating up the space between us.

He grabs me by my upper arms, his fingers biting painfully into me—but nothing has ever felt so good.

"Is it really you?" I ask, still not quite believing.

"I've been looking for you everywhere, Holly. You have a lot of explaining to do."

"You have? Wait. What do you mean *I* have explaining to do?"

"You walked out on me," he growls.

"But, well, it was over. I mean... Well, we were done and..."

"I wasn't done with you, Holly, not at all."

"You weren't?"

"Santa had some more packages for you."

"Nick... Is that even your name?"

"It is, and is your name really Holly?"

"Yes... How... *Why* are you here?"

"You should know, Holly, Santa is everywhere," he says with a smirk.

Any other time I would have found that sexy, but not right now. Right now I feel like the earth under my feet is literally trying to disappear. Heck, I'm even dizzy.

"No. Not this time. This time no more games," I argue, and maybe he can hear the panic in my voice. I know I can. I'm scared I'm going insane. That's the only explanation for the fact that the man I've been dreaming about for weeks suddenly appears at a business holiday party.

Before I can question him further, Michael is standing beside us. I should have known he would have followed me outside and, as always, his timing is impeccable.

"Holly? Is this man bothering you?" he asks, eyeing Nick up and down like he can really take him if it comes down to it. I snort at that thought.

Michael does his best to make his voice sound threatening. I hold my head down, because Michael is the last person I want here. I *need* to be alone with Nick —I need answers. Besides, it's kind of ridiculous. Michael is a good foot shorter than Nick and looks downright skinny next to Nick's muscular form. I clench my fingers involuntarily against the firm, hard muscles of Nick's biceps.

God, I've missed him.

"Who are you?" Nick asks, bringing my attention

back to the moment at hand. His voice is hard, slightly pissed off.

"I'm Holly's boyfriend," Michael answers, and my body goes stiff as shock flows through me. I snap my head in Michael's direction, knowing my eyes have got to be as big as the fucking moon. Oh my God! I always knew Michael was insane, and now I have proof. Before I can speak up, I look up at Nick's face and discover I may have bigger problems. He looks like a volcano about to blow.

Oh shit.

13

Nick

I still can't believe it. I fucking found her. Elation fills me, because honestly, I had given up hope. Now that I have Holly in my grasp, I'm not about to let her slip through again. Maybe it was stupid to remind her of our little holiday *"game,"* but I couldn't help myself—probably because I can't wait to resume playing with her.

Fuck, there's so much more I plan on doing to Holly.

I'm about to tell her exactly that when some asshole comes up and puts his hand protectively on Holly's shoulder. I've never been territorial in my life, but right now I am about half a step away from ripping that fucker's arm out of its socket for daring to touch what's mine. This might have started off as a game, but Holly is definitely mine.

"I'm Holly's boyfriend," he announces. The urge to break his neck so he stops breathing is there. It's raw and dark, but Holly reduces my thoughts to caveman-like processes. She's mine. What's mine stays mine. I manage to beat it down, but it's not fucking easy.

"You're her what?" I growl, and I can feel Holly's body tremble beside me. Her hand cups the side of my neck, trying to draw my attention. Any other time I would look at her, but right now, all I want to do is—

"Holly and I are dating," he announces.

"No fucking way," I growl.

There's no way in the world this pipsqueak has touched my girl.

"You are not," Holly answers, her voice hard. "We're not dating, Michael."

"You're here at the party with me," he answers, his tone filled with annoyance and his face flushed.

"Is that true?" I ask Holly. I don't really give a fuck. I'll deal with this jerk and she will be coming home with me.

"Not the way he's making it sound," she mutters. "I met up with some coworkers and we arrived together. Michael and I work at the same place. That's it."

"That sounds a lot different than the story you're painting, man."

"Do you know this guy, Holly?" Michael asks, ignoring me.

"Nick? Yeah. I know him," she whispers, and this time I look down at her, because I have to. Her voice is sweet and she's blushing. Her gaze centers on mine and I can tell her head is as full of memories of our time together as mine is.

"Damn straight you do." I grin. "Trust me, buddy. She knows me and I know her in ways you'll only ever dream about," I add, goading the little asshole.

"I don't believe that," he responds.

"I don't really give a fuck what you believe. But you will be going home alone with your hand, and I'll be going home with Holly's legs wrapped around me all night and her tight little pussy wrapped around my cock," I answer with a shrug, like I don't have a care in the world.

Holly gasps and I know that will probably piss her off, but I don't like that this idiot is trying to lay claim on her. The easiest way I know to shut a man down who is talking out of his ass is to go for blood early.

"You're disgusting!"

"Maybe so, but Holly likes everything I do to her. Now, move your hand away from my woman." I look at her. "Let's go, Holly. You and I have some things to talk about." I turn my attention back to my woman, wanting nothing more than to take her back home and have her again... *and again.*

Hell, I may never get my fill of this woman. After weeks of being without her, I'm pretty sure I won't.

"Holly, you can't really have anything to do with this guy!"

"Let's go," she whispers, ignoring this Michael asshole, but the jerk isn't going to let it go.

"Holly, do you know who he is?"

I ignore him. She's agreed to go home with me and that's all I need. I take her hand in mine and pull her close.

"Holly! His firm is one of our clients. He gets paid to have sex, for God's sake."

Holly freezes, her body going rigid. She looks up at me and, understandably, her expression is full of questions. They are questions I don't like, even if I do understand them. I have, however, had enough of this fuckwad. I pull away from Holly and slam my fist into his face, instantly breaking his nose. He goes back holding said body part, blood spouting down his face. That gives me some small satisfaction.

"Nick?" Holly asks. People are starting to gather around us. There's even a couple seeing to the idiot, but I ignore them.

"What's going on here?" Cedric Moak comes out of

the doors. "Andrews, what are you doing on the ground?" he asks, helping the guy get up.

"He hit me!"

"Michael was—" Holly starts, but she doesn't get to finish. I won't let her. I want this shit handled and I want out of here.

"He work for you, Cedric?"

"He and Ms. Kline here are attorneys on our corporate floor."

Holly Kline. She'll never get away from me now.

"Ms. Kline is not an issue. I'm talking about him." I have a hard stare on my face, letting them all know I'm fucking serious.

"Michael Andrews, yes, he's been with our company for the last year," Cedric answers, frowning.

"He just slandered my name, accusing me of sleeping with clients. If Moak and Sons wishes to continue having my company and my personal business on retainer, I want him gone." I make sure to hit them where it hurts.

"You can't do that," Michael yells.

But I can and I definitely will.

"He's gone," Cedric answers without a second thought. I didn't imagine there would be. I'm one of his biggest clients and his son's biggest contributor when he ran a successful campaign for U.S. Senator. Losing my business and my personal interest would be one of the stupidest moves they ever made.

"Good. Then we have no issues. I believe I'm done here for the night. I think Mr. Andrews has pretty much ruined mine and Holly's evening."

"I'll have him escorted from the building. I wasn't aware that you knew Ms. Kline, or were in a relationship with her," Cedric replies. He's fishing now, but I let it go. Instead I look at Holly. Her face is a mixture of shock and confusion. It looks damn good on her.

"I don't divulge information about my private life, Cedric. But, if you must know, Holly lives with me," I announce. Holly's mouth falls open in shock. Before she can start arguing with me, I take her hand. "Let's go, Holly. Cedric, I'll be in touch." I give him a slight nod of goodbye. Holly follows me, even though I'm sure she would rather ask me a million questions. I'm thankful. I'd rather handle her questions in private.

"You can't do this to me. I'll sue all of you. This is wrongful termination and I'll sue for assault! I'll own your business before I'm done," Andrews screams. I look at him with a cold smile. Before morning I'll know everything there is to know about Michael Andrews and there won't be a rock big enough for him to crawl back under. He fucked with the wrong guy tonight.

"If you're brave enough, try me, asshole," I warn him, and that's the only one he will get.

With that, I take Holly and head out of there. I can't wait to have her alone and under me.

14

Holly

"Will you slow down?" I gasp.

Nick is so much taller than me and he's taking these long strides across the room that are impossible for me to keep up with. He has a tight hold on my hand, which essentially means if he doesn't slow down, he will be dragging me soon.

He stops abruptly with a growl and then he leans his body in and down. His hand moves against the bottom of my ass and before I realize what he's doing, he's pulled me up his body so that my torso is hanging over his back.

I panic, trying to make sure my dress doesn't rise up

and flash the world. Luckily, it's pretty tight and that's not a huge issue.

"Nick. What are you doing? Put me down!" I mumble, feeling a little lightheaded—probably from being carted around and hanging upside down like I was a sack of potatoes.

"Holly, I just watched another man say he had a claim on you. I saw his hand on your shoulder. If I put you down, then I will be fucking you against the wall and everyone in this damn party will get to see the show."

"I... Maybe we should talk before there's any... *fucking*."

"You better talk fast then," he growls and even in my confusion, a shiver runs through me and centers between my legs.

"What did Michael mean when he said you get paid to have sex?" I ask, almost tripping over the words. I don't exactly trust Michael, but considering how Nick and I met, I need Michael's accusation explained.

Nick doesn't answer, however. Instead he slides me down his body so that I'm standing in front of him. I figure we're finally going to talk and as much as I enjoyed the thought of him carrying me out of here and fucking me—we do need to talk. Yet Nick surprises me. He all but spins me around. I have to brace my hands on the sides of the brick wall by the entrance of the ballroom to keep from falling when he moves me so fast. Then, before I can question him, his hand comes down hard on my ass.

I gasp at the shock of it and the sting of the sharp pain. I can barely form a thought before his hand comes down again. I'd like to say I'm horrified that Nick is spanking me in front of my co-workers and my boss. Not all of them are here, I'm sure, but quite a few are. I don't turn and look though. I concentrate on remaining standing. My knees are literally weak. A visible shudder runs through me and I lick my lips as I feel my panties getting wet as he spanks me again. Heat spreads through my body. I push my ass out against his hand, unable to stop myself. The simple truth is, I want more.

"What are you doing to me?" I ask, my voice shaking, husky and full of need. I'd like to say I was asking about the spanking, but I'm not. Instead I'm wondering how Nick has this way of turning me into this sexual being who lives for his next touch—however it's delivered.

"Punishing you for thinking I'd fuck you—or anyone—for money. You just earned a one-way ticket to the naughty list, Holly."

"What was he talking about? And then Mr. Moak... None of this makes sense, Nick," I whisper softly, because by this time his hand is moving up under my dress. He wraps his fingers tight around my thigh, and it feels so hot—almost as if he is branding me. I can feel the tips of his fingers push under the lace of my panties. I try to look over my shoulder to see who is watching us, but Nick doesn't allow me that freedom.

"I own NJ Industries. Are you familiar with my company, sweet Holly?"

"I... I've worked some with that account. You own...a lot of businesses." I gasp as his finger strokes softly against the lips of my pussy. "Nick, you can't, people are watching," I protest as a full body shudder moves through me. I may be asking him to stop—but I don't want him to.

"I can do anything I want to, Holly. You're mine. I'll stop, though," he says, his voice deep and his hot breath fanning against my skin as he whispers into my ear.

"You will?"

"All you have to do is tell me you haven't missed me since we've been apart."

"I have missed you, Nick," I answer, unwilling to lie to him. "I've missed you so much I ache with it."

"Then I'm taking you home and I'm going to fuck you and once I've come enough so that I'm in a better mood, I'll let you choke on my cock and apologize for leaving me alone in the hotel that day."

"Nick, maybe we should—"

"Or I could fuck you here, Holly. You're so damn

wet, my cock would slide into you smooth and easy right now. I could sink into you up to my balls."

"Oh God," I whimper, closing my eyes and literally seeing everything he's describing. I feel so empty without him and my pussy is hungrily trying to hold on to his fingertips to ride them.

"Choose quick, Holly."

I close my eyes and hold my head down against the wall. My body is warring with what I need to do and what I want. I want him to fuck me right here, *right now,* and as much as I want to tell him to do that, I find the willpower not to. When I give myself to Nick again, I want it just to be the two of us.

"Take me home, Nick. I want to go home with you," I tell him and this time when he picks me up in his arms and holds me to his body I don't protest at all. I curl into him, resting my head against his chest, and listen to the steady beat of his heart.

God, I have missed him.

15

Nick

O nce I have Holly back at my place I don't waste any time. There is no point; both of us are too worked up. Hell, we barely made it through the door before I had her dress up around her hips and my face buried between her legs.

"Come for me," I murmur against her soaked, hot flesh, her pussy so damn sweet. I'm addicted to her already.

"*God, Nick*," she whispers, her pleasure my own. She lifts her ass up a little more, and a tremor works over her entire body as she comes for me. Yeah, this is exactly what I want from her. I want her to always be at the precipice of pleasure when she's with me.

When her orgasm fades, I take hold of the root of my cock and stroke the fucker for long seconds. I don't have to keep up with the Santa roleplaying, but I get a kick out of it, and truth is it turns me on playing with her like this.

"You want Santa's big candy cane?"

"Have I been naughty or nice?" She smirks, playing along. *That's my girl.*

"You've been really fucking naughty, but that's what Santa likes." I groan as the ecstasy slams into me. I don't hesitate now that I'm finally between her splayed thighs. I position my cock at her pussy and stare into her eyes. Without thinking or talking, I push into her, just shove my thick, big dick deep in her body.

"Yes," she hisses out and closes her eyes.

I am buried in her wet heat, unable to go slow. I need her like I need to fucking breathe.

"*Christ.*" I pound into her, pulling my cock out before slamming it back in. Her tits shake from the fierce motion, and I am riveted to the sight. "Look at me," I demand, realizing she has closed her eyes.

She obeys instantly. When she's looking at me, I groan.

"I don't think I can hold out, Nick," she moans.

I grunt. "Good, because I can't hold off either, baby." She arches her back, her tits thrust out. I lean down and run my tongue along the underside of her throat. She's so fucking sweet. I feel her pussy clench around my dick, and can't stop from going over the edge. Thank fuck she's already getting off.

And then I feel my orgasm approach. It's a tightening in my back, a tingling in my balls. It moves quickly through me, and I fucking let it. I fucking love it. I'm wearing a condom, but fucking hell, one of these days I'm going to go bare in her, just really fill her up with my seed, make her take it all.

"Fuck, yes." I rest my face in the crook of her neck and let myself go over the edge. I feel her pussy milking me, drawing the cum from my balls.

Holly is mine.

When my orgasm has waned and I can't hold myself up anymore, I roll off of her, not wanting to crush her. Before she can move away, I put my hand right between her thighs, rise up on my elbow, and look down at her.

"This is mine," I say and add a little bit of pressure between her legs.

She makes the sweetest noise for me. "I'm all yours."

I growl like a fucking animal.

She closes her eyes and hums, the content pleasure clear in the way she's acting.

She rolls onto her side and curls against me. I know there is a lot of shit we have to talk about, but we have time. We have so much of it and I'm not going to waste a second.

"Will you hold me, Nick?"

"I thought you wanted to talk, about all that shit..." I respond, kissing the top of her head and holding her close.

"Not now. Later. I just want you close."

As much as I love the dirty fucking we've done, I want to be gentle and sweet with her too.

I squeeze her gently, giving her exactly what we both need. I sure as fuck don't deserve her, but I have her, and I am not going to fuck this up. I want Holly in my life too damn badly.

EPILOGUE

Nick

One year later

It's been one year since I unceremoniously made Holly mine. There wasn't ever a chance in hell of her ever getting away from me, not when I finally found her. I knew she was the one and I haven't doubted it since—*not once.*

Today I finally make her mine, forever.

I feel her fingers flex against mine and I bring my gaze slowly back to her. She's beautiful every day, but today in her white wedding gown, with her bronze hair around her face in waves, she nearly takes my breath away.

"It was a beautiful wedding," she whispers as she sways to the music.

I look around the reception and I feel peace fill me completely. I married Holly today. Finally, she has my ring on her finger and she has my name.

"This damn reception is lasting too long," I grumble.

"You don't like dancing with your wife?" she whispers.

The room is transformed into a winter wonderland, complete with fake snow, sparkling Christmas lights, and red, festive ribbons. It's truly beautiful, but it pales when compared to my woman.

"I love dancing with my wife, but..."

"But?"

"I'd rather be fucking her," I groan, leaning down to kiss her lips. I had her this morning, but I want inside her again. Even a year later, I can't help but feel this possessiveness with Holly—this need to be a part of her.

I am the luckiest bastard in the world, that's for damn sure. I might have thought it was a bad idea filling in for one of my employees a year ago, but it's been the best fucking thing to ever happen to me.

"We could leave. I doubt anyone would miss us," she replies. "I do have a surprise waiting for you in the penthouse suite of this hotel..." She grins wickedly.

"What kind of surprise?"

"Let's just say I think it will get you in the Christmas spirit," she laughs. Her laugh reminds me of the sound of bells ringing softly in the night. It fills me with joy.

Without further thought, I pick her up and carry her out of the ballroom, toward the elevators. She laughs harder, wrapping her arms around my neck and kissing my neck.

Yeah I'm the luckiest bastard in the world. I have everything right here in my arms and I'm never letting her go.

Holly

I MARRIED NICK. I can still hardly believe it. He's unlike any man I've ever known before. He screams bad boy, with his big, muscular frame and ink that covers almost every inch of him. I never thought I'd ever be with a man like Nick, but the ring on my finger says otherwise.

My heart says otherwise.

Nick holds me tenderly to his body as he carries me from the elevator to the penthouse suite we reserved for the night. We'll be honeymooning in Greece, but our first night as man and wife will be here...in the same room where it all began. I feel so small in his hold, and can't help but lean against him and close my eyes. He goes all caveman on me more times than not, but I love that about him.

I pull back, not sure what I am about to say, but before any words can leave me he leans down and kisses me.

"I love you, Holly."

His words bring even more joy. I feel tears stinging my eyes.

"I love you too," I whisper.

I feel Nick move his hand down the length of my spine, over the small of my back, and finally along the curve of my ass.

"What's that doing here?" he asks and gives my ass a squeeze. My body goes liquid for him instantly.

I follow his line of sight and smile when I look at the red velvet Santa suit neatly folded and pressed on the sofa. *My surprise for him.* I grin.

"I was hoping I'd get to sit on Santa's lap," I answer, biting on my lip and wondering if my man is going to play along.

He gives my ass a smack, shaking his head—but he's smiling and it might be my imagination, but I think I see a Christmas twinkle in those eyes of his.

"Has little Holly been nice or naughty this year?" he asks, and joy fills me as he slips into the role that brought us together in the first place.

I probably would hate this game with anyone else, but Nick isn't just anyone. He's everything and I love anything we do together. I think that's just another sign he's the one. Even if others think we are jumping into this, I know this is the right move.

We belong together.

Nick pulls me impossibly closer and makes this low growling sound. "I fucking love you, baby. You're perfection, Holly baby."

I feel my cheeks heat, because even after being with Nick for a year, the butterflies never leave, and I know they never will. There will never be a Christmas that goes by where I don't try to make my way onto Santa's very, very naughty list.

The nice list is overrated anyway.

The End.

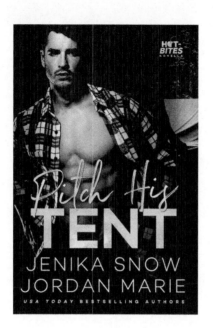

Pitch His
TENT

JENIKA SNOW
JORDAN MARIE

USA TODAY BESTSELLING AUTHORS

PITCH HIS TENT (Hot-Bites Novella)

By Jenika Snow and Jordan Marie

www.JordanMarieRomance.com

support@jordanmarieromance.com

www.JenikaSnow.com

Jenika_Snow@yahoo.com

Pitch His TENT

JENIKA SNOW
JORDAN MARIE
USA TODAY BESTSELLING AUTHORS

She's my best friend's little sister and completely off limits.
But I'm not going to stop until she's mine.

Beau

I pushed Lexi away years ago.

I've regretted it every moment since, but a man can't live in the past forever.

I decided to go camping to clear my head and plan my future—a future without Lexi.

Imagine my surprise when she's already there.

Lexi knows nothing about camping, that much is clear.

That's okay, I'll use it to my advantage.

I have a second chance and I'm not going to waste it.

First, I'll share my sleeping bag with her and eventually I'll teach her exactly how to...

Pitch My Tent.

Warning: They're back! Jenika Snow and Jordan Marie have teamed up to bring you another hot little number. This time they're taking you out into the wilds. But don't worry, the only thing attacking here is a hero alpha with his eyes set on his woman. A guaranteed safe read that is hot enough to melt your Kindle. It may not teach you how to survive in the wilderness, but if you read closely you might learn the correct way to anchor those tent poles.

1

Lexi

"Camping? Like real camping where you're sleeping in a tent in the middle of nowhere, peeing behind trees, and eating beans out of a can? That kind of camping?" Sherry, my best friend since grade school, says in the most disgusted voice she can muster, I'm sure.

Even at twenty-two years old she still gets on my nerves, but makes me laugh at the same time. I stop packing and sit on the edge of the bed. I stare at my hands, knowing that this idea is slightly insane, but something I really need to do for myself. "Believe me, I know how crazy that sounds."

"No, I don't think you do." Sherry gives me a

sympathetic look. "Have you even ever been camping before? You do realize you have to have supplies? It's not like you can go to the campsite and they have everything already set up for you." She was smiling, teasing me.

"I'm not a complete moron." I smile back at her. Even though inside I am telling myself there are other things I can do to relieve stress.

"You know if you need to talk I'm here. I'm always here."

I smile back. "I know. I just need to get away for a little while and clear my head."

She nods in understanding. "Yeah, I get that. How long are you going to be gone?"

"Just the week. I borrowed a bunch of camping gear that my brother had stored away, so I'm all set. I just need to get away from the city, from the bullshit of Eddie flaunting his new relationship in my face like I give a shit." I think about my ex. We've been broken up for a month already, yet working with him, and seeing how he nearly fucks the new co-worker right in front of me, as if trying to somehow get back at me for "breaking his heart" grates on my nerves more than I want to admit. Hell, it shouldn't bother me because I'm the one who broke up with him. But I think the stress of work, and the bullshit of Eddie being an asshole has been my tipping point.

"You should just report his ass. Surely him groping his new fling is sexual harassment."

I shrug. "I don't know if it counts as sexual harassment if she's doing the groping too." Sherry makes a disgusted face and I laugh. I get back to packing, and haul the last bag downstairs. I may be only going to be gone for the week, and probably over packed, but I want to make sure I have the comforts of home as I relax.

I toss the last bag in the back of my car. I turn and stare at Sherry. "I'm going to hit the road and get an early start. That way I can set up everything before it gets too dark." I give her a hug and thank her for listening to me bitch. She's the one person I trust implicitly. She's always been there for me, especially in the times I'm feeling like my life is spiraling out of control.

"Oh, I forgot to mention I saw Beau the other day."

Just the mention of my brother's best friend has emotions rising up in me. He's back? Is he on leave? Was he discharged? It's been years since I saw him, years since he and my brother left for a tour with the army. My brother Brooks came home on leave, but I never saw Beau.

I've tried to keep hidden, keep submerged. Beau Sterling is my brother's best friend, his army buddy, and the man I love. He's a guy I grew up around, one who, just looking at him, makes me want to set something on fire. He is arrogant, sure of himself because he knows he's so damn good looking. All through the years I've wanted to slap the smirk off his face, and then pull him in close and kiss him.

It's been a long time since I've spoken to him, yet I'm still consumed with my feelings for him. I can still remember that night all those years ago, right before he left, at the party my parents threw for him and Brooks. I can still remember my lips on his... I shake my head. Nope, not going there.

He's only ever seen me as Brooks' little sister, even when I wanted to be so much more than that. I think that's why I get so pissed thinking about him. Because he never saw me as the woman I am, the woman I grew up to be. He still sees me as that little girl who probably got on his nerves.

But then there's the fact—the secret fact—that even though he pisses me off, I want him. God, I really want him.

I love him.

I've been in love with him since I knew what that word even meant, since I felt my emotions for him rise up and threaten to strangle me.

"I swear," Sherry says, this lustful look in her eyes. "If Beau wasn't such a cocky bastard I might've gone after him." I snort at that. "No, probably not. He's not my type, not in the least." She wrinkles her nose. "But he was wearing a tight black shirt that showed off every muscle." She starts fanning herself. "I love guys in the military, but it's a shame he got injured."

At the mention of that my heart cracks in two slightly.

"And the worst part about it all is he knows how damn good-looking he is."

I laugh, hiding the fact that just thinking about Beau like that gets me all hot and bothered. I feel my face start to heat as I think about him, about how much I hate him ... how much I want him. I say goodbye again quickly and get in my car, not wanting Sherry to see how I am reacting.

Because the last thing I need is for Sherry, or anyone for that matter, to know exactly how much I want Beau Sterling. All that will accomplish is to leave me with a broken heart and nothing to show for it.

2

Beau

I throw the last of my crap in the back of the truck with a grin. The old truck looks like a rolling wreck, but eventually I'll fix it back. It's a symbol for me. Proof that even battered, with miles on you, you can always start over. When I get this truck restored it will have exactly what I'm giving myself: a new beginning.

Next week I start fresh. After being discharged from the army, I've been at a loss on where to go with my life. Nothing feels right. I miss the military life, but a bum knee that I got as a result of taking shrapnel ended that dream.

My best friend Brooks is still serving and in a lot of

ways that makes it worse. Brooks and I have done every-thing together from grade school up. Where one of us was, the other would be close behind. Brooks' grandfa-ther used to say we were brothers, but I think we were closer than brothers. Hell, I have a brother now I never speak to and, even with Brooks being stationed in Afghanistan, we still talk once a week.

I've been in a rut. It's time I start getting my life back together. That begins with getting my head straight and starting to live again. Since being discharged, that's something I haven't been doing. I had a purpose in the army. Outside there was nothing for me—nothing I could have anyway. There was plenty I wanted... what I've always wanted and denied myself.

Alexandria "Lexi" Clark.

Brooks' younger sister has haunted me since she was five. At first she was annoying. A cute annoyance that Brooks and I put up with, but an annoyance just the same. As she grew up, that slowly changed. She had a quick sense of humor, she was smart, and she made me laugh. There hasn't been much in my life to laugh about, but Lexi always managed it. Still, I never saw her as more than a kid, my best friend's sister. That's it. Then Beau's parents held a going away party for us the night before we were to be shipped overseas. At twenty-four, I wasn't prepared for what was waiting for me across the sea. I sure wasn't prepared for Lexi following me outside that night when I broke away from the party to get a breath of air.

I can still remember it as if it was yesterday. From the yellow and white sundress she wore, to scent of lemons and sugar that clung to her skin.

"Are you scared about going into war, Beau?"

"We're not in war anymore, buttercup. We're just helping that country get on its feet again."

"People die over there all the time."

"People die everywhere."

"You're not scared?" she asked again and I studied her face—really studied it. Her features were etched with concern, her hazel eyes sparkled with emotions I was afraid to name. I knew Lexi had a crush on me. Brooks knew it too. He made me swear to stay away from her. I laughed it off, telling him she was too young for me and wasn't my type.

I was lying out of my ass.

"Not a bit. I aced all my training. Those soldiers overseas won't know what hit them," I bragged, but inside I was scared. I had never admitted that to anyone. I barely admitted it to myself. Being cocky was how I got through my own issues, how I hid my own fear. I also knew it grated on her nerves, but I didn't want to show her that a part of me was afraid. I was scared to leave the only place I'd ever called home. I was afraid to leave her.

"I'm scared. I don't know what I'd do if something happened to you, Beau."

"You'd barely notice, buttercup." I dismiss her words, even as they make me feel raw inside. No one in my life really cared if I lived or died except for three people. Brooks, his grandfather and Lexi. Of those three, none of them made me ache like Lexi. She made me yearn for more. So much more.

"I'd notice, Beau. I'd be destroyed. I love you," she whispered and then she kissed me.

I pull my mind away from the past. I can't live there and when it comes to Lexi, I want to. Other women may have kissed me in my life. Hers was tame and innocent really. She was only seventeen at the time. I pulled away immediately. I was seven years her senior and she made me want to forget that. That one kiss has been a memory that has lodged deep inside of me over the years. Fitting, since Lexi Clark is the one woman I've never been able to forget.

She's only one more thing to put behind me.

Next week I start my career as an officer of the Montana division of the fish and wildlife agency. It's a new career and a new world before me and it's way past time that I forget the life I used to have and the memory of a kiss from a girl I should have never kissed.

I jump in my truck and turn the key. The engine roars to life and I smile. Things will be different now. I just have to stop living in the past. I'll use this week to clear my head and burn the bridge to my past. I won't look back.

What better place to do that then up on Boulder Ridge, camping and getting back to nature? It's the perfect way to kick off this new chapter and leave the past right where it belongs.

Behind me.

3

Lexi

"Son of a bitch," I hiss and toss the hammer across the ground, cradling my busted thumb to my chest. It's throbbing because I was a dumbass and hit the digit instead of the spike that would hold my tent down.

I sit on my ass and stare at my half-erected home for the next week. I still have no idea why in the hell I decided to do this. It sounded like a good idea at the time, but now I'm seriously having my doubts.

Exhaling and scooting back so I'm leaning against a thick evergreen, I tilt my head back and stare up at the sky. There's a break between the tree line, which shows a beautiful swatch of blue and white. I hear nothing but the rustling of wind through the leaves, the scurry of some animal off in the distance. I close my eyes and let the wind brush over my skin. The scent of pine and dirt fill my head. This is a very beautiful place, scenic and relaxing. Peaceful.

Now I remember why I needed to do this.

I don't know how long I sit here, but it's the sound of an approaching vehicle that draws my attention. I lean forward and stare at the vehicle I can see in the distance. And as it comes closer I realize it's an older truck, one that looks very familiar. My heart starts beating hard and fast, and just when I think it'll drive past, it actually pulls into the camping spot beside mine.

God.

It can't be who I think it is.

My position makes it hard to see exactly who the driver is, especially with the glare from the sun covering the windshield, causing a reflection of the trees all around.

I wanted peace and isolation, but with my new neighbor I doubt I'll get that now. It's not like I can just up and leave, not unless I want to lose all the money and time I spent in planning this damn retreat.

The driver's side door opens and from my position I can only see a boot emerge. It is big and worn, scuffed, and clearly masculine. And then the guy comes fully out, slams the door shut, and proceeds to stretch. My heart jumps into my throat when I see who it is.

Beau Sterling.

Has hell frozen over right now? I look up at the sky to see if pigs are flying. How in the hell is Beau Sterling parked in the campsite beside me? Is this some kind of cruel, sick joke? He has yet to notice me, or if he does he is clearly ignoring me. Maybe that is for the best.

I can't hide the fact I do have feelings for him. He is strong and smart, and does have a caring side that I've seen a handful of times. He served in the army, got wounded because of it.

I made a fool of myself over him years ago. I was young and naïve and I just want to forget that kiss, forget the way he acted uninterested in me. I don't know how long he's been home, but I hate that he didn't come see me.

It looks like my luck has just run out in keeping my emotions locked down, in pretending I can not be in love with him.

He turns his head and looks right at me. My heart jumps to my throat, my belly clenches tight, and every erogenous zone in my body tightens up. He's big and strong, tall and muscular. The jeans he wears are slightly loose, but they fit him perfectly, showing off his masculinity. The T-shirt he wears is snug, showing the ripples and dips of his muscles, the ridges of his six pack.

His dark hair is short, slightly disheveled. And his eyes, like two pieces of onyx, seem to look right into my very soul, knowing all my secrets. I feel my face heat and wonder if he can see me blushing. My nipples tighten, beading up under my shirt. And I'm wet, God I'm so wet between my thighs my panties are becoming soaked.

How in the hell am I supposed to camp with Beau Sterling right next to me?

4

Beau

"Fuck!" I growl before I can stop myself. It's a kneejerk reaction and the word springs forth the minute I see Lexi. I watch her flinch at what I said and I instantly regret it. The thing is, when I'm around her I can't seem to stop myself from being an asshole. It's my way to push her away, to pretend she's nothing more to me than Brooks' little sister. I've spent my life pushing her away, it seems. "What are you doing here, Lexi?"

"Charming as ever," she mutters. She gets up off the ground, turning away from me. I bite down a moan when she bends over and her ass stretches against her jeans. Sweet mother of God, there's not a woman alive that can fill out a pair of pants like Lexi.

She turns around, holding a hammer in one hand. I should probably worry she's going to use it on me. Lord knows I've given her more than enough reason to.

"What are you doing here?" I ask again.

"Gee, I don't know, Einstein. Camping?" There's a bite in her voice.

"Camping?"

"That's what I said," she mumbles, walking toward the heap of material lying on the ground that I think is *supposed* to be her tent.

"Lexi."

"What?" she asks, looking over at me.

"You don't camp. Hell, you cringe at the thought of using a public bathroom, let alone going out in the woods." I look around. She's alone. She came out here alone? I don't fucking like that.

"You don't know me anymore, Beau. You never did, really," she says, avoiding my eyes.

She's wrong, of course. If she had any idea just how much I know about her, she would freak out. There was a time in my life where I lived for daily updates about her. Shit, maybe I still do, but I need to stop. Lexi is not mine and she never will be. This week is all about starting fresh and putting the past behind me. Just because the biggest problem with my past has shown up here, nothing has changed. It's just a sign from the cosmic universe that moving on is long past due.

"You still with that Eddie boy?" I ask her. I remember she was with some loser named Edward Winslow the Third. Brooks would bitch about the little asshole daily, and I'd grit my teeth thinking of Lexi with someone other than me. He never fails to remind you of *the third* part either—which is rather stupid, since the dude used to work as a night manager at the local 7/11. Why she ever saddled herself with that waste of space I will never know.

She snorts. "No," she says firmly, trying to ignore me and look at the mess that is her tent. She's staring at the metal pole that loops in the ends of the tent like it's a creature from outer space. I'd laugh if my heart wasn't beating in my chest so hard that it's painful.

"You finally kicked the guy to the curb?" I ask her, alternating between hoping I'm right and praying I'm wrong. It was hard enough to stay away from Lexi before. If she's single... *Fuck.*

"We broke up, if you must know."

"Brooks never mentioned it," I mumble, more to myself than to her.

"Why in the world would he mention it to you? Besides, I'm not sure he knows."

"Why wouldn't your brother know?" I rub the back

of my neck, hating that the fact of Lexi being single is getting to me so deeply.

"It may surprise you, Beau, but my brother doesn't really want to hear about my personal life."

"You can tell me all about it," I tell her with a grin, doing my best to not let her know that the news of her being single has shaken me.

"Why? Do you need to take notes?" she asks, sweetly.

"Trust me, honey, notes on your personal life is the last thing I need," I tell her, getting annoyed at the thought of her with anyone. Shit, all I can think about is showing her exactly how much I want her ... as long as Brooks never found out about it. Christ, I can't camp beside Lexi; there's no way I'm going to survive.

She stretches the tent pole she's holding. Too bad it's the wrong part of the tent and she doesn't have the pole set.

I bite back a laugh when once she has it stretched she takes a step back to admire her handiwork and the tent collapses in a sorrowful, sad mess. I look up at the clouds in the sky and sigh. If I don't get a move on with my own tent, we're both going to be sitting out in the rain. If I do get my tent up, Lexi will probably wind up in it with me... which will be a different kind of hell.

5

Lexi

Istand back and watch as Beau puts together my tent. It's safer this way. I'll end up just screwing something up. He finally came over after me cursing like a sailor for the last hour, trying to put the damn thing together. I had been about to say screw it, that I would sleep in my car, or even head into town and stay at that rinky-dink little motel I passed coming up here, but Beau stepped in and saved the day, something he is good at.

I don't know why I thought camping would be a good idea. And to make matters worse, Beau will be in the site right beside me, like fate is trying to say something. Or maybe it is wishful thinking on my part, like I want things to just fall into place.

"Okay, you're ready to go." He stands and wipes his hands on his jeans, dusting off the dirt. The sun is already starting to set and I feel really bad that he's been working on my stuff instead of getting his own set up. Although he got his tent set up for the evening already, thankfully.

But still, I want to do something to say thank you. "Can I make you some dinner, as a thank you for helping me out?"

He grins, flashing a set of straight white teeth. "I'm not gonna turn down some food, especially if you're making for me."

I feel my cheeks heat and turn away before he sees. For the next ten minutes I set everything up, get the little propane stove ready, grab the can of beans and a can of fruit. I even brought some burgers that I'll grill. It didn't even occur to me to light a fire, but I look over my shoulder and see Beau is already on it. Although dinner won't be a feast, it will be a warm meal and hopefully things can get a little less awkward between us with some conversation.

Another twenty minutes passes and dinner is ready, the fire is roaring, and Beau has two foldout chairs placed around the pit. I walk over to him, a plate in each hand, and give him one. I see he's brought over a cooler, and he pops the lid and wraps his fingers around the necks of two beer bottles. He hands me one and I take it with a grateful smile.

We eat in silence, me just staring at the flames licking over the logs, very aware that Beau is sitting right next to me. Although I'm hot, it has nothing to do with the fire in front of me.

His presence makes me feel very self-aware. I sneak a glance over at him and see that he's already watching me. I feel my face heat even further and look away quickly.

"Tell me what's been going on, Lexi."

Hearing him say my name does all kinds of things to me. He was the first person to ever start calling me Lexi. After that it just kind of caught on with my friends, even Brooks. I shrug, still not looking at him, still not able to make eye contact.

"Nothing really." That's the truth. After he and Brooks left for the military I basically puttered around. I finished school and got my associates degree in business, but I'm not exactly using it.

I look Beau in the eyes and this strong feeling overcomes me. I want to tell him how much I love him, want to tell him that him being away all these years was hard. I want to ask him how long he's been back. I want to ask him why he didn't come see me.

But even though all these questions are running

through my mind, I know I'll never ask them. I'm too afraid, too frightened of his reaction, of his response. I've dreamed so many times about telling him, and he reciprocated my feelings, pulled me in close and told me he loved me. Those were the dreams of a silly girl, though, and I told myself that every time.

But what if? What if I was finally honest and the attraction wasn't just one-way?

6

Beau

I finish up my food, feeling disappointed. I hate that things between us are stilted. I realize it's partly my fault. Lexi is still upset because I rejected her after the kiss all those years ago. It's probably for the best she thinks that way.

"I guess I'll go finish setting up my camp, Lexi. Thanks for dinner."

"You're leaving?" she asks and she sounds surprised. It can't have escaped her notice that we're barely talking to each other.

"Yeah I need to get my camp ready or I'll be sleeping on the ground." I grin. "The weather report predicted some heavy rain coming in late tonight."

"It did?" she asks, and it's clear she had no idea. What kind of person plans a camping trip without checking the weather? I could have laughed. She's too damn cute.

I pinch the bridge of my nose and hold my head down. Does Brooks even know what his sister is up to? How could he allow her to be out here camping all alone, without any protection? He didn't want me to touch her, then the least the asshole could have done was to make sure she didn't do stupid stuff like this. She needs a man to take care of her.

"Yeah. It did. When most people decide to camp, Lexi, they check the weather so they are sure to be prepared." I exhale a breath of frustration and let it go. Lexi is not the kind of girl to like the outdoors. She'll be gone tomorrow and this won't matter.

"Anyway, it's not like you're really talking to me, so I'm going to go," I growl, turning into an instant asshole because she needs a man to take care of her, and I know it can't be me.

"I was talking! Maybe you're just pouting because I'm not falling at your feet like most girls do."

"I didn't realize you'd been watching what other girls do," I respond, looking at her. I'm watching her closely so I can see the minute that the flush enters her face, even when she moves, putting away her trash, trying to avoid my stare.

"I wasn't. Not really. I just know what Brooks tells me."

That answer annoys me instantly. Hell, Brooks hasn't seen me since I was discharged. He's still living the life I thought I would. Deployed overseas and well on his way to being a general. There's a part of me that resents him for that, but he's my best friend. He's not responsible for the shambles my life is in. Brooks may have made it clear his sister was off limits, even if he didn't know I wanted her, and I might be honoring that, but shit, I knew Lexi cared about me. I could see it in her eyes and the way she looked at me. I never wanted to hurt her—even inadvertently. Lexi has always been in my heart.

Which can only mean that Brooks has been spreading lies to drive Lexi further away from me.

"Do you believe everything you're told?"

"Brooks wouldn't lie to me. Besides, it's not like it is any of my business. You made it clear how you felt about me years ago, Beau."

"Just because I told you that I...that we shouldn't..."

"You told me not to kiss you anymore, that I was a kid, even though I wasn't. You told me I wasn't your type. Trust me, Beau, I remember. I got the message back then loud and clear, and I get the message now. Thanks for helping me with my tent. I think I'll turn in."

"Why does everything with you end in a fight?" I growl. "It's good you'll be leaving tomorrow. I came up here to get peace, not more stress."

"I'm not leaving tomorrow. I have this campground rented for the whole week and that's exactly how long I'm staying."

"You? You're planning on staying out in the wild all week? No fucking way."

"What's so hard to believe about that?"

"You forget I know you, buttercup."

"Don't call me that."

"You used to love it when I called you buttercup."

"I don't anymore. I've changed. *You* don't know me anymore, Beau."

"I know you don't like living without modern conveniences. I know your idea of roughing it is spending the night without internet, *not* indoor plumbing."

"Like I said, Beau Sterling, you don't know me anymore," she says, dismissing me without looking back and making her way to her tent.

I don't know what pisses me off more. It could be the fact that she's walking away from me, it could be the fact she asked me to stop calling her my nickname, or it could even be the coolness she's treating me with. I think, however, it has more to do with the fact that she's right. I don't really know Lexi anymore. I've been spending my life pushing her away and avoiding her. I didn't want to. I did it out of respect for Brooks and his wishes, but I still did it.

I've regretted it every day, but more so right now than ever.

"I'll tell you what I do know."

"What's that?" she asks, not bothering to turn around and sounding very bored.

"I know that cheap little pink tent you bought isn't going to stand up to the thunderstorms we're supposed to get. If you don't leave tomorrow you're going to end up really wet and cold."

I watch her body tighten and jerk with my words. Still, she doesn't turn around.

"Goodnight, Mr. Sterling," she says and disappears behind the closing flap of her tent. A minute later I hear the zipper move on the door.

I frown. When she called me Mr. Sterling, all I wanted to do was bend her over my knees and spank her ass.

I warned her. That's all I can do. I wasn't kidding about the tent, nor the rain headed our way. She's going to end up wet, cold and miserable...

Or worse, she doesn't leave and I forget all the reasons I need to stay away from her, and then make sure she's wet, hot and completely filled.... *with me.*

7

Lexi

I t is the crack of thunder that wakes me up. My tent is shaking, the wind howling outside fierce, violent. A droplet of water falls onto my head. I gasp and sit up, seeing rain coming through my cheap tent. This is the one thing I purchased on my own. Everything else I got from Brooks' storage unit. I bought a cheap, yet pretty tent, and now I am paying for it.

I grab my purse and start looking for my car keys. Looks like I am sleeping in my car tonight. And of course, because my luck totally sucks, I can't find the keys.

Of course.

Another flash of lightning causes the interior of my tent to illuminate. Seconds later the thunder booms.

I cry out on instinct then immediately slap a hand over my mouth. What the hell was I thinking coming out here? No way I can last a week.

More lightning and thunder ensues, but because I can't find my keys I'm stuck. I wrap the blanket around me and put the material over my head, the water now coming through the tent. God, I cannot believe I bought such a shit item.

"Lexi?" I hear Beau's voice right outside my tent, and part of me wants to ignore him, wants to be proud and act like I didn't totally screw this up. "Lexi, buttercup, I know you're getting soaked in there. Come out and get in my tent until the storm goes away."

I'm tempted to say no, but another splash of water seeps through the blanket and onto my head. I start shivering. I grit my teeth, grab my purse, and head out of the tent. Beau is standing on the other side with an umbrella, a grin on his face. Damn, I hate when he's right.

"Come on, sweetheart." He holds his hand out, and even though he pissed me off earlier, I find myself slipping my hand in his much bigger one. He closes his fingers around mine and together we go to his tent.

The rain is really coming down hard, the sound of it beating against the tent almost deafening. His tent is spacious, and as I sit in one corner and watch as he digs around for another lantern he's got in his bag, I can't help but appraise him.

Beau is so attractive, big and strong in that hard-working kind of way. His biceps flex and I feel my body heat. I grow wet between my legs, and my nipples become so hard I'm surprised they don't rip through my T-shirt.

I grab the material and pull it away from my body. The fabric is slightly damp from the rain, and the fact that I'm not wearing a bra just now hits me. I feel my face heat, know I'm probably red as a tomato. I reach for one of his blankets and pull it up to cover my chest just as he faces me. He looks at me for a second, cocks an eyebrow, and a smirk covers his face.

Damn, he either can read me well, or he already saw the outline of my nipples when we first got into the tent. I glance away, not wanting to look at him because some pretty filthy things are running through my head right now.

He doesn't say anything, thankfully, and a second later the tent gets brighter as he turns on the lantern. For long seconds we sit there in silence, and when he starts rifling through his bag again, he produces a dry shirt and a pair of sweats.

"Here." He hands the items over to me. "You're

soaked and you'll get sick if you stay in those damp things."

I look at him like he's grown two heads.

He exhales. "Lexi, we're adults. I'll look away if you want, but change out of the damn clothes and don't be stubborn about it."

What I'm really thinking about is getting naked in front of him. So many things have gone through my head over the years, things I imaged—fantasized— about doing with Beau. I want to be his, want his hands on me, his mouth on mine. I want the world to know that he loves me, the same way I love him. But those are just that ... fantasies. It's not reality, and I really need to get that through my head.

I don't bother to wait until he turns around. I drop the blanket and lift the shirt above my head. We are adults, as he says, and it's not like he's never seen a pair of breasts before. I could almost chuckle at the shocked way he looks when he sees me getting dressed, before he turns around. When I have the shirt on I go for the pants next. He does turn his head away then and I grin.

"Shit, Lexi," he says under his breath.

Good, it's about time I'm the one making *him* uncomfortable.

8

Beau

"Something wrong?" she asks. I can hear the laughter in her voice and though she's trying to play innocent, we both know she's trying to tease me. She has no idea what she's doing. If she knew what was inside my head right now, it would scare the fuck out of her. I want her pretty damn badly, especially since the image of her nipples poking through her damp shirt is engrained in my head. Did no one ever teach her she shouldn't poke a damn bear? And I feel pretty feral right now. I have to clench my damn hands to keep them from shaking.

"You should be careful who you flash your tits to, buttercup," I growl, turning around just as she's pulling my jogging pants over her ass. I glance at her once more, seeing her bent over, my gaze now glued to the way the material slides over her tanned, firm hips. Hips that I've dreamed of holding onto, bruising with my fingers as I sink inside her tight little body.

Jesus.

I may not survive tonight. My dick is so hard that my jeans are suffocating the damn thing.

"It's *you,* Beau. We're both adults like you said," she says with just enough sass that I want to smack her hard on the ass and leave my handprint. My dick is dripping; I can feel the pre-cum on the head—that's how fucking close I am to coming. Lexi has no idea what she's playing with.

I move up to her, and I can't stop smiling. My clothes dwarf her. There should be nothing sexy about the way my shirt hangs off of her or how she's holding the material at her waist to keep my sweats on her sweet ass. But I don't think I've seen a woman look better. I reach over and grab a towel I had lying on my cot, and hand it over to her. Then I move my hands down to hold over the one she has clenched, holding her pants on.

"Are you having fun teasing me, Lexi?" I ask, not bothering to hold in the growl that leaves me. I know it's not my imagination when I hear the way her breath rushes from her lips. I grab the waistband of the sweats, her skin warm against my fingers. I begin folding them down, and cinching them to make them tighter against her stomach.

"I think I am," she whispers, and her gaze is clouded with desire. I'd have to be a fool not to see it.

"I'm not a boy like you're used to dealing with, Lexi. I'm a man. You shouldn't tease a man—we might bite back," I warn her and I turn her around gently so her back is to me now.

"I doubt you could dish out anything I couldn't handle, Beau," she says and she's putting on a good front, but her voice is threaded with need and as I move my hand down her back, she shivers—and I'm pretty fucking sure it has nothing to do with the cold.

I move even closer to her, and I let my hands brush against the plush cheeks of her ass before they rest on each of her hips. I'm the one testing her now, seeing how far she'll let me go. My body is against hers now, and when she tries to move away from me, I assert pressure on her, not letting her.

"No," I say in a low rumble that seems to vibrate through me.

"What are you doing, Beau?" she asks, her voice tender.

"I'm just drying your hair, Lexi. That's okay, isn't it?" I whisper against her ear. I have no fucking doubt in my mind she knows I'm not really trying to dry her damn hair.

"I...yeah. That's okay," she answers.

I get the towel and carefully use it to get most of the moisture from the darkened tresses.

"You have beautiful hair, Lexi," I tell her. I shouldn't, but I can't seem to help myself. The same way I push against her ass, wondering if she can feel how full and heavy my cock is—even through my jeans.

"Beau," she moans, pushing her ass against my cock.

I could take her now. Take her and make her mine —the way I should have years ago—the way I was always meant to.

I wrap my hand around her hair and tilt her head back, desire filling my body. I'm on a razor's edge and I'm so tired of holding back.

And then an image of Brooks flashes in my mind.

Brooks. My best friend. The man who saved my ass more than a few times in Kandahar while on patrol. A man who gave me a family when I was younger, when I had none.

I owe him. If nothing else, I owe him loyalty. He doesn't want me with his baby sister. As quick as that, my desire turns to anger.

Anger at Brooks, anger at the situation, and anger at Lexi for teasing me. Most of all I am angry at myself.

"You feel what happens when you tease a real man,

Lexi?" I ask. I pull her body hard against my raging cock. There's no way she can help but feel it now. "You better be careful what you ask for, you just might get it."

I hurl the words at her, doing my best to keep the anger out of them, but instead making them sound like I'm mocking her. It's not easy. It nearly destroys me and my cock is so hard it aches. I gently push her body apart from mine.

She turns to look at me, shock evident on her face.

I do my best to hide the torture I'm in and smile at her, daring her to push me further.

"I hate you," she whispers and that one sentence is enough to wipe the fake smile from my face.

Fuck.

9

Lexi

I can't sleep, and it has nothing to do with the storm raging outside. Over the last couple of hours the weather has only gotten worse, with the water beating against the tent, the wind shaking it.

I shift so I'm now facing Beau. He's got his back to me, his chest rising and falling underneath a thin blanket over him. His upper back and shoulder are exposed, and I cannot believe he's not chilled not wearing a shirt.

Although I'm not complaining about the view.

The weather outside is pretty cold due to the rain and wind, but inside the tent is nice and warm. It's clear he didn't cheap out on shelter like I did.

He left the lantern turned on, but on a low setting so that there is a dim glow inside the interior. I look at the dips and curves on his bicep, the strength and power that come from him clear. He is so muscular, with the sinew and tendons bunching under his golden skin.

I didn't lie when I said I wasn't teasing him earlier tonight, that I didn't want to get under his skin the way he did with me. But I was angry when he denied me, when he acted like what was going on between us was wrong.

I heard the self-anger in his voice, even though it was clear he tried to hide it. I have a feeling that this all had to do with Brooks. Maybe there is some loyalty there, with Beau feeling he would be crossing lines with my brother if he were with me.

Or maybe all of this is in my head. Maybe he really doesn't want me in the way that I want him.

The latter frustrates me. I felt the evidence of his arousal for me, could see it in the way he looked at me. But he is fighting it, hiding it. Even now I am aroused, my pussy wet, my nipples hard and aching. I wonder if he's actually sleeping, or if he is just as worked up as I am. Because I must be a fool, crazy, or hell, both, I find myself reaching out and running my fingers along his arm. His skin is warm and smooth, and I shiver, wanting to be pressed against him, feel that warmth for myself.

This isn't just about sex. This is about me loving

Beau, wanting him in my life as more than what we've been, and praying he feels the same way I do. But I'm so afraid of screwing things up, that being bold, like I was earlier tonight, and teasing him, could ruin what little relationship we really have.

I know he is like a brother to Brooks, that he doesn't want to cross lines and fuck things up there, but I'm a grown woman and I know what I want. I want this man lying right beside me. I want to feel his naked body pressed to mine, keeping me warm, letting me know that I'm not the only one feeling these things. I want things to be more than me poking a sleeping bear with a stick and seeing if I can get a rise out of it.

Something in me opens up and I feel stronger, braver. I won't let this opportunity pass. If it ends up ruining everything, then at least I tried. At least I was able to say I went after what I wanted.

I sit up, the blanket falling from my body and pooling around my waist. I start to sweat despite the chilled air outside this tent, beads forming between my breasts and down the length of my spine. Can he hear how heavy I'm breathing? It sounds like a freight train to me. My pulse is beating in my throat, pounding hard, threating to burst free. Am I really going to do this? What if this all blows up? What if he rejects me?

I have to try.

I slip off the oversized shirt, the one that smells like

Beau. My nipples instantly harden further as the air hits them. I start to shiver, but it doesn't have anything to do with being shirtless. I'm nervous, afraid of what's to come, if I'm making the right choice. I shimmy out of the sweats, and soon I'm naked, Beau still facing away from me, my heart beating a mile a minute. I reach out and place my hand on his bicep, his muscles flexing beneath my touch.

"Beau," I say softly, gently. I curl my fingers into his skin a little harder, and he stirs, turning around and facing me. I can see that he wasn't asleep by the wide-eyed look he gives me. Or maybe he's surprised to see me sitting beside him naked. I could have laughed at the latter. Of course he's shocked to see me like this. But I exhale slowly. "I want to cross that line," I say softly. "I love you, have loved you for longer than I want to admit." I swallow the thick lump in my throat.

He doesn't say anything for long seconds, and I'm afraid that this is where he tells me nothing can happen between us. And then he sits up, his chest coming into full view as his blanket slides off of his body.

"Lexi." He says my name in a deep, gruff voice. He reaches out and pushes a stray piece of hair from my cheek, his finger brushing my skin. I shiver. And then he wraps his hand around my waist and hauls me onto his lap. My bare breasts press to his chest, a gasp leaving me. I can feel how hard he is, his dick like a steel pipe between my thighs. "Lexi," he growls, and then he slams his mouth on mine and fucks me with his tongue and lips.

All I can do is wrap my arms around his neck and hold on.

10

Beau

I shouldn't do this. Fuck, I know I shouldn't, but I'm face to face with every fucking fantasy I've ever had in my life. It would take a stronger man than I've ever met to turn Lexi away. When it comes to her I'm weak as fuck, and I'm tired of pushing her away. I know there will be hell to pay and Brooks will probably kill me, but I can't let her go this time.

I can't.

I devour her mouth and the sweet, smoldering taste of her makes me ache. Her warm, naked body rubs against me, teasing my dick. I've fantasized about her for years, but nothing ever came close to how this feels.

I move my hands down her body, memorizing the

feel of her under my touch. It feels as if she's branding me, but, hell, she branded me a long time ago. It's always been Lexi... *Always.*

Lexi is grinding her ass against my hard cock, torturing me, and I doubt she has a clue. If she doesn't stop, I'm going to come in my pants and that's not how I want tonight to go. I break away from her, standing us both up. Thank fuck the tent is massive and we have plenty of room for what I have planned. Her eyes glow right now; there's so much desire and emotion in them, they captivate me.

"Lay down for me, Lexi," I order, my voice vibrating with the hunger I feel as I squeeze her breasts in my hands.

This is it. The moment I expect Lexi to falter, to run away. I half expect her to. I've not given her the soft words that she deserves. I can't, not yet. I have to hold myself back. Maybe because I expect this all to blow up soon. Why would she pick me to spend forever with? She wouldn't. She may want me right now, but Lexi is too good for me, too special. She deserves the best. Not a broken down ex-soldier with nothing on the horizon. When Brooks finds out, it will fall apart. She will push me aside under Brooks' demands. She's always done what her big brother wanted. Brooks knows and I know that I don't deserve Lexi, but I can't stop myself from taking the gift she's giving me now.

Her big eyes look up at me, so raw and full of love my gut clenches. She's perfect in every way.

"Like this?" she whispers as she lowers herself on the bed. She lays down on the sleeping bag, her hands covering her breasts.

"Spread your legs for me, Lexi. Show me your pussy," I order, hypnotized by her.

She bends her legs and holds them apart, her feet flat on the ground. A fine blush runs over her entire body and I can see she's embarrassed, but she still gives me what I want. I ache at how innocent she looks. I wish I hadn't pushed her away all those years. I lost my chance to be her first, to be the man who claimed her virginity. Her first... It's for the best that didn't happen. If I had claimed her back then, I would have been her first and her last. There's no way I would have let her get away from me. Still, it hurts me that she was with a man who didn't deserve her. I'm glad she kicked him to the curb.

I mourn the loss of tasting her innocence, but if she was a virgin I couldn't have her. That would make her completely off limits. At least this way I can have her... until reality intrudes and she pushes me away.

"Touch yourself for me, Lexi," I order, pushing her further—testing her limits. I slide my pants down, my dick so hard it hurts. I step out of them and wrap my hand around my cock, stroking it as I look down at her.

"Oh... God," she gasps, her focus on my dick. She moves her hand down her stomach to her pussy. I watch its path, every perfect fucking inch, and my cock weeps for her. A large drop of cum drips off the head and slides down the shaft. I stroke myself as Lexi clumsily touches her pussy. She's nervous. I smile, liking that I'm pushing her to her limits. "Maybe we shouldn't... I'm not sure you'll..."

"I'll what?" Just knowing what she was about to say turns me on even more. "Trust me Lexi, I'll definitely make you feel good," I tell her, not about to let her back out now. I'm too far gone. If she wasn't sure she should have never offered me a glimpse of heaven.

I get down on my knees between her legs and move my cock against her entrance, her juices sliding against my dick, the heat of her pussy beckoning me. She's so fucking wet and I've not touched her yet. How good will she feel when I finally get inside? I lean over and suck one of her tight nipples between my teeth, biting gently and using my tongue to tease it. Lexi's body jerks in response, her nails biting into my neck as she tries to hold on to me. She jerks under me, her hips thrusting and causing the lips of her pussy to wrap around my cock. It feels so fucking good. I suck hard on her nipple while pinching the other one. I'm rewarded with her cry of pleasure as her back bows up off the sleeping bag.

She's so fucking responsive.

"See, Lexi? There's no going back. I'm going to make you feel good," I vow, still teasing her tits with my hands, while she desperately grinds her clit against the shaft of my cock, trying to make herself come.

"I didn't mean that," she gasps, pushing against me, trying to her body closer to mine. "It's just you're so big," she adds, as another shiver rolls through her body.

Damn, if I wait much longer she's going to come like this. I have to get inside of her.

"Play with your tits, Lexi. I want to watch as I fuck you," I order, taking her hands from my neck and putting them on her breasts. She does what I ask, her chest heaving up and down as she pulls on her nipples. I can tell she's so fucking close to exploding. Jesus.

I wrap my hand around my dick, using the tip to tease her swollen clit, pressing it against her.

"Oh God, that feels so good, Beau," she whimpers. Her hands are almost violent on her tits now. She's lost to passion in a way I never expected.

"You don't have to worry, baby. My cock will fit inside of you and it's going to make you feel so good," I tell her, dragging my dick through her sweet juices and positioning myself at her opening.

"You will?" she breathes.

"Look at me, Lexi," I order. She brings her pleasure-filled gaze to me. "I will, honey. You keep your eyes on me. I want to see you when I get inside your pussy. I want to see your face as I claim you."

"O-okay, Beau," she whispers, her voice thick from her lust.

"You're so fucking perfect, Lexi. You're everything. I'm going to give you so much pleasure, you'll forget you ever had a man before me," I growl right before I thrust deep inside of her.

"But, there's never been anyone else," she cries as I thrust my cock in. "I've never wanted anyone but you," she adds as I seat myself deep inside of her. Her body is rigid, her eyes wide, her mouth parted. Shit. She didn't need to tell me. I felt it as soon as I thrust in her body. I am Lexi's first. I'm the first man to claim her.

She's a virgin.

And I just took her cherry like a wild man. Fuck, I know I hurt her. I do my best to hold perfectly still, mentally beating myself up, but all I can think is I'm Lexi's first and I'll be her fucking last.

She's mine.

11

Lexi

I can't breathe, can't even speak. The pain, burning, and stretching is unlike anything I've ever felt before. But that discomfort doesn't take away from the immense pleasure I feel. I am wet, achingly so. My nipples are hard, erect, and tingling. And the fact Beau is above me, his dick thrust deep inside of me, claiming my virginity, pushes everything else to the back.

I can see by his expression he's startled to realize I am a virgin. I hadn't wanted to tell him because I hadn't wanted to ruin things. Would he have said no if he knew he would be my first? *I want him to be my only.*

"Fuck, Lexi, baby." His voice is deep, harsh, guttural.

His entire body is tense, his muscles contracting and relaxing underneath his golden skin. "You should've told me this was your first time. I wouldn't have been a fucking madman thrusting into you." His jaw is tight, the muscle underneath the skin flexing. I can see how he's trying to rein in his control, how he's trying not to break. And even though it's uncomfortable, and the pain is there, I've waited for this moment for too long. I'm not about to stop it.

"I won't break," I finally say, forcing myself to relax. It takes some long seconds before he finally relaxes as well. "Fuck me, Beau." I watch as he shifts, changes. My words have done something to him; have his control slipping. He groans and then starts moving inside of me, back and forth, in and out.

He's slow at first, his motions easy, maybe trying to get me adjusted. But the pleasure increases, the pain diminishing. I arch my back, my breasts thrusting up. I make a long, drawn-out cry. That seems to be his breaking point. He grabs my hands and brings them above my head, holding my wrists, his fingers wrapping gently around my skin. And then he starts really pounding into me, faster and harder, the sound of wet skin slapping together filling the tent.

I'm breathing so hard, sweat starting to blossom over me. I lift my head slightly and look down the length of my body, seeing his six-pack flexing as he thrusts in and out of me. The rain has let up slightly, but I can still hear the patter of droplets on the tent. The light from the lantern glows within the interior, and as he pulls out I can see the glossiness of my arousal coating his shaft. I also see streaks of blood, the product of my virginity taken, given to Beau.

"Lexi, fuck, baby." His eyes are closed, his jaw set tight. He doesn't have a hold on my wrists any longer, but his hands are still by my head, his fingers digging into the sleeping bag. The sound it makes as the nylon crinkles underneath his fingers fills my head.

He pulls out of me before I can even comprehend what's happening. He's on his back, has me over him, my legs on either side of his waist. I feel the stiff length of his erection pressed between my thighs, both of our breathing heavy, hard.

"Grab hold of my cock, Lexi," he says on demand. "Put it inside of you, baby."

I do as he says, reaching between our bodies and wrapping my finger around the thick root of his dick. He's so big, so thick that my fingers don't touch when I hold him. And then I place the tip at my entrance and slowly sink down on his length. We both groan, and tingles race along my arms and legs. He fills me to the brink, making me feel as though I'm going to split into two.

"Now ride me, Lexi. Fuck yourself on me until you

come. I want to watch the pleasure wash over your face."

His words nearly have me climaxing as it is. I start bouncing up and down on him, my breasts shaking from the motion. I force my eyes to stay open so I can stare at Beau and see the pleasure on his face, as well.

Up and down. Faster. Harder. Finally I can't keep my eyes open any longer. I tilt my head back as ecstasy washes through me. I cry as I come, my pussy clenching around his thick cock, needing him deeper inside of me. It's only a second later that I hear Beau groaning out as well. He has his hands on my waist, his fingers digging into my skin. I know there'll be bruises in the morning, but I anticipate them, want to see them covering my flesh.

It'll be a mark of ownership.

He comes inside of me, filling me with his seed.

"That's it," he says in broken words. "Milk my cock; suck all the cum out."

The pleasure is never ending, and I absorb it all. It feels even more incredible because I'm with the man I love, the one person I've wanted for as long as I can remember.

When the pleasure diminishes and I can no longer hold myself up, I collapse on his chest. For a second I wonder if he'll push me off, say this was a mistake, that we should've never done this. But instead he wraps his arms around me and just holds me for long minutes. Then he rolls us so we're facing each other on our sides, lifts his hand, and pushes a strand of my hair away from my face. He looks into my eyes and I can see that he cares for me, that this wasn't a mistake. What we shared was perfect.

"You're mine."

Yes I am.

12

Beau

"What are you doing?" Lexi asks from the zippered opening of the tent.

She looks so fucking good this morning my dick aches, the remembrance of what we did last night like a brand in my fucking marrow. Her hair is all rumpled and she has it pulled up in a messy bun. She doesn't have a stitch of makeup on, but then Lexi never needs makeup. She's naturally beautiful, inside and out. Her lips are bruised from our night of lovemaking, swollen, red and unbelievably sexy. I imagine them sliding down on my cock and the semi-hard-on that I've been sporting all morning instantly turns into a raging erection. I should be fucking worried when a woman's lips can make my dick hard enough to drive nails into concrete. She's not just any woman, though. She's Lexi and she's always owned my heart.

She's always been mine.

"Fixing you some breakfast," I tell her with a smile. "Come over here and give your man a kiss."

I watch as she walks gingerly toward me. She's obviously still sore and tender from our lovemaking last night, which I fucking like—even if that does make me a bastard. Possessiveness slams into me knowing that I claimed her, that my cock is the only one that's ever known how hot and wet, how fucking tight she is. *I'm the only one who will ever know what she feels like.*

"Are you my man?" she asks, her eyes wide, and despite what we shared last night, innocent.

"Definitely, sweetheart and the only one you'll ever have."

"Really?"

"I'm not letting another man have you, Lexi. You're mine now. You gave that to me last night, and I'm not letting you go."

"I like the sound of that," she says softly and wraps her arms around me.

"I do too, baby. I do too."

I hold her close for a few minutes, breathing in her scent, and just let the fact that I have her in my arms soothe me. For so long, I've felt like there has been half of me missing. Now I realize that it's not been the military, or any of that shit. It's been Lexi. She's been mine since that first kiss, I've just been running from it. That's over. Brooks isn't going to like it, but I don't give a fuck. He can get the hell over it.

"That does smell good," she says and I grin.

It's a simple breakfast. Toast, eggs and bacon, but I like that I'm taking care of Lexi. I always want to do that. She deserves a man who will put her first, and I want to be that for her.

"Go back inside the tent, relax and stay warm, and I'll bring you a plate."

"I'd rather eat out here, around the fire," she says, surprising me.

"You aren't cold?"

"I've got my sweater on and besides, it feels good. I love the smell of the fresh air. It's exactly why I came out here."

"If you're sure," I hedge.

"I am, but you don't have to do everything. I can help."

"I want to take care of my girl. Is that a crime?" I ask her with a wink, putting the food on the plates.

"Beau, if you only knew how long I've been dying to hear you call me your girl," she laughs as she sits down. "To be honest, it's kind of surreal to hear you say it now."

"Get used to it, sweetheart. I'll be saying it often," I tell her and hand her a plate of food. I just stare at her, unable to believe that this is reality right now. I feel good, really fucking good.

"If it's a dream, do me a favor and don't wake me."

"I hope it's a good dream at least," I joke, suddenly jealous of the bacon she's eating as it slips between her lips. I reach down and adjust my dick before the bastard bursts through my jeans.

"The best."

I clear my throat and do my best to pull my gaze away from her eating. If I don't I'm going to fuck her right here in front of the tent and I'm not sure her body is ready for that. I tried to be gentle with her last night, but she's way too tender for what my dick is demanding.

"Not everyone will be happy about the two of us," I tell her, tackling the one issue that is worrying me.

"You mean Brooks, don't you?" She doesn't state it like a question.

"Yeah, honey. He doesn't want me with you. He's made that clear over the years."

She shakes her head. "That's crazy. You're his best friend. He has to know the kind of man you are. You'd never hurt me." She scowls. "Besides, I'm an adult, and I know what I want." She looks me in the eyes.

I love that Lexi only sees the best in me. I want to

tell her that Brooks knows I've not always been the best kind of man. I've fucked up a lot in my life. The thing is, I was always running away from Lexi and my love for her, knowing I wasn't what Brooks wanted for his little sister.

I don't tell her that, however. I don't want to dim the picture of me she has in her head. I'm going to fight like hell to live up to that image. I want to be a good man. I want to be a man that Lexi can be proud of.

"You're his little sister, honey," I say instead. "He's just protecting you."

"He'll just have to get happy or get sad," she grumbles and she looks so cute I laugh.

"What does that even mean?" I ask, shaking my head.

"It means that I'm not giving you up, Beau. I don't care what Brooks or anyone else says."

"Is that a fact?" I ask her, feeling more at ease than I've felt in years.

"Damn skippy," she says as she sucks bacon grease from her fingers.

As much as I want to laugh at her use of words, my gaze is drawn to the way her lips suck on her finger. She's not doing it to be sexy; it's completely just Lexi being natural, and maybe that makes it even hotter.

"Sweetheart, if you don't quit sucking on your

fingers like that, we're going to have problems," I warn her, my voice hoarse.

"We are?" she asks, instantly stopping what she's doing and watching me closely. "Like what?"

"Like I'm going to give you something else to suck on," I mutter, adjusting my cock again.

Lexi puts her plate on the ground beside her and comes over to me. I don't say anything; I just wait to see what she does. It doesn't take long. She drops to her knees in front of me.

"Give me something else to suck on, Beau. I dare you," she whispers, her voice thick with desire and fuck, I'm lost to her.

Completely and utterly lost.

13

Lexi

I follow Beau up the trail, beads of sweat dotting between my breasts and the length of my spine. The ground is damp from the storm last night, the leaves sticking to my shoes. I straighten, pushing past the burning in my thighs and the ache in my feet. He looks over his shoulder at me and grins. I know he can see how this seemingly easy hike is a pain in the ass for me by the look on his face. But I keep my mouth shut and trek on.

Apparently this isn't the first time Beau has been camping up here by himself. And when he said he wanted to show me something special, I hadn't even thought of denying him.

"How are you doing back there, baby girl?"

I can't help the blush that no doubt steals over my body at the endearment he calls me. "I'm good." I give him two thumbs up and he grins and gives me a wink.

When he turns back around and starts walking, I brace both of my hands on my thighs and lean forward, huffing and puffing. Sweat is dotting my forehead now, and I realize how out of shape I am. I see him start to turn to look at me again and I straighten and follow him up the path like I'm not dying inside.

"Just a little bit farther," he says and gives me another straight, white-toothed grin.

We only walk for another five minutes or so before I see where he's taking me. I take off my backpack and set it beside me, bracing my hands on my hips as I stare out at the lake. The sun is high in the sky, glistening off the water, making it look like it is sprinkled with glitter. Large pine trees surround the lake, and I can see water lapping at the shore.

"It's beautiful," I look over at Beau and see he's watching me, this longing expression on his face. "Thank you for bringing me here," I say and smile.

"It's almost as beautiful as you are."

Any other time, and from any other guy, I would've thought it was a clichéd saying, but hearing Beau say it to me makes me feel pretty damn special.

He is in front of me a second later, his hands on my

waist, pulling me closer to him. My breasts press against his chest. I feel his body heat through our clothes and instantly become wet. Even though I am sore from last night, I want him.

I lift my arms and wrap them around his neck, rising on my toes and pressing my lips to his. I don't think about anything else except showing Beau how much I care for him, how much I love him.

He gives me a small kiss on the lips, but before anything can become hotter he takes a step back, to my disappointment. And then, surprising me, he starts undressing. Before I know it he is naked, his erection prominent. He gives me a half smirk and I feel my heart flutter.

He is big and strong, with muscles that are defined, and with boyish good looks that make him seem like he's not the bad boy I know he is. It's that rebellious streak that I love.

"Go on, baby. Get undressed so we can see how cold the water is."

Although it stormed last night, the air is surprisingly warm. But I have doubts on if the water matches that. I know that shit is probably ice cold. I look over at the lake, and although it looks beautiful, the truth is I don't care how cold it is. It can be freezing and I'll still want to go in with Beau.

I turn back toward him and smile, quickly undressing myself.

Before I know what he is doing, Beau is in front of me again, his arms wrapped around my body, and he easily lifts me as if I weigh nothing. He has us in the water seconds later. I scream out, the chill so sudden that my entire body tenses.

I can hear him laughing, and I push away from him, scowling. He splashes water at me and I sputter as it hits me in the face. I can't help but laugh in return. For the next ten minutes we do nothing but swim around, occasionally splashing each other, but overall just having a fun time. I can't remember the last time I felt so free, so happy.

Beau is in front of me and pulls me close to his body. His body heat seeps into mine and I sigh, wrapping my arms around his shoulders and my legs around his waist. I can feel how hard he is, his erection pressing right between my legs.

"I'm never letting you go," he says softly right beside my ear. I close my eyes and rest my head on his shoulder.

"I don't want you to."

14

Beau

The ride back home is quiet. Lexi is obviously as lost in her thoughts as I am mine. I'm nervous as fucking hell, to be honest. Everything was perfect on the mountain. Lexi was mine and nothing else mattered.

What happens now?

Will Lexi still be proud to call me hers once we get back to reality? Her family will never think I'm good enough for her. Fuck, it's probably a good thing Brooks is still overseas. If he were here he'd no doubt kill me for just knowing I looked at Lexi the "wrong way." I'm not exactly the high-class type of man her friends mess with either. Will Lexi be ashamed of me?

I need to quit being a damn pussy and just talk to her. You would think I've lost my balls. I pull into Lexi's drive, shut the engine off and just stare at her garage door. I undo my seatbelt and from the sounds, I can hear Lexi doing the same. Still, neither of us talk for long moments. Lexi is finally the first to break the silence.

"I'm sorry about my car. I didn't mean to be a problem for you," she murmurs.

"It's not your fault you had a flat, baby girl. You really do need to always have a spare, though. What if you had been out alone? There's no cellphone signal up there." Shit. I sound grouchy as hell. It's just that the thought of her being stranded in the middle of nowhere scares the hell out of me. She needs to be more careful. "Besides, I wanted to drive you."

"You don't really seem like it, Beau. Has something changed?"

I turn to look at her—*really* look at her. That's when I see the same fear on her face that I'm feeling, and I feel like a chump. I turn into her, pulling her up on my lap—which isn't easy because of the steering wheel, but I manage.

"Absolutely nothing has changed for me, Lexi. I'm actually more worried about you changing your mind. Things might look different for you here than they did on the mountain, when it was just the two of us," I confess. I gently tangle my fingers in her hair, holding her head back so she looks me in the eyes, so she knows I'm fucking serious. Her pulse beats against my palm. That, combined with the feel of her warm skin, seems to center me.

"You're being silly, Beau. I've loved you for years, even when you barely spoke to me. Do you really think that would change now that we're together?" she whispers softly. I wrap my arms around her body, pulling her in closer. I close my eyes, breathing her scent in.

"I've been a fool, a stupid fool," I groan.

She pulls back to look at me, her beautiful face smiling and, as hokey as it sounds, it's like the stars have been captured in her eyes. She's so beautiful... *she's everything.*

"I know how you can make it up to me, Beau," she says with a naughty little smile and a blush that makes my dick push against the zipper of my jeans.

"How's that?"

"Stay with me tonight. Don't leave."

"What about your car?"

"We can go get it tomorrow, or I'll send Triple A. Right now the only thing I want is you in my bed and..."

"Say it, Lexi," I order roughly, my hand palming her breast as her body rocks teasingly against me.

"I want you in my bed, Beau. I want you inside of

me, all night. I want to fall asleep with you inside of me."

"Fuck, baby girl..." I growl, the images of what she's describing enough to drive me to my knees.

"Please, Beau? I've waited so long for you, I don't want to spend any time apart," she says, laying her heart out for me to see. She gave me her body, but this is something else entirely.

I don't know how I manage it. I couldn't begin to explain it, but somehow we make it out of the truck, me kissing her and barely taking time to breathe. We even manage to make it through the front door and down the hall to her bedroom.

I have to have her, all of her.

Now. Hard. Fast. Urgently.

15

Beau

I pull Lexi in closer, her naked body so warm, so soft and feminine against mine. I just got done making love to her, fucking her until she couldn't even breathe. And only when she came three times for me did I finally find my own release.

Now, after the pleasure has diminished, just holding her is perfection. I run my hand over her flat belly, thinking about my child growing inside of her. I want that. I want her as my wife, by my side forever. But I don't want to say any of that yet, don't want to freak her out. I don't want her running from me, from us.

We are meant to be together, and it is just a damn shame it took this long for it to happen. I close my eyes and bury my face against her hair, inhaling deeply. She smells sweet, like flowers and a hint of vanilla.

I feel her stir, her soft, breathy moan causing my cock to come to attention again. The fucker is sore from being buried deep in her these last two days, but hell, I can go all fucking night if she wants me to.

"How about I give you something to put a smile back on your face?" She moans in response, and I rise up to look down at her. She turns and faces me slightly, her sleepy smile making my cock jerk again. "You want me to wake you up, baby?"

She grins now and nods, not saying anything.

I move down her body, pulling the covers up over me. She already has her legs spread, her pussy smelling so fucking sweet. I want to get drunk off of her, off of her flavor. I don't bother waiting, don't even try and control myself. I place my hands on her inner thighs, pushing them open even farther, and devour her. I suck and lick at her folds, take her little clit into my mouth and run my tongue around it. She's panting above me, her hands under the sheets and tangled in my hair.

I feast on her, sucking her clit even harder, needing her to get off for me, to climax against my lip and tongue.

"I'm so close," she breathes out harshly and I renew my efforts. I pull her pussy lips apart with my thumbs and lick her slit from her pussy hole right back up to her little nub.

And then she comes for me. Her thighs close in around my head, holding me there as I eat her out. I'm dry humping the mattress, my cock hard as steel again. When she relaxes on the bed I climb up her body, my cock pressing right at the center of her. I'm about to push in deep, claim her once more, when I hear a door open and close in the house.

We both stare at each other, confusion clear on Lexi's face.

"You expecting someone?"

She shakes her head and I glance at her closed bedroom door.

"Alexandria?"

Oh. Fuck.

Everything in my body tenses, freezes. The sound of Brooks calling out for Lexi shocks me to my core. It's not so much the fact that I'm lying in bed naked with his sister, about to have my cock balls deep inside her, but the fact he was overseas last I heard.

"Oh my God. Is that Brooks?" she whispers.

"Lexi?" Brooks shouts again.

"Lexi, baby, I think we got trouble." I'm not afraid of being honest with Brooks. I am more worried about how he'll handle me telling him I love Lexi and I'm not going anywhere.

"Shit. He'll flip if he sees us like this." I get off of her and she rushes to get dressed. I, on the other hand, take my time. I have my jeans pulled up, the button undone, the zipper down, when Brooks knocks on the door.

"Alexandria? You in there?"

Lexi looks at me with these big eyes, anxiety clear on her face.

"Ugh, yup. Be right out." She hurries and puts her shirt on. "What are you doing here anyway?" Her voice is high-pitched, and I know Brooks can probably sense there's something going on.

"Are you okay?" he asks. "You sound weird."

I stand up, walk over to her, and kiss her on the mouth, hoping to calm her down.

"I'm fine," she finally says, her voice softer. I give her a smile, help her with her shirt, and finish getting dressed. Then I go to her bedroom door, open it, and face Brooks. I know shit's about to hit the fan, but hell, I'm ready. I've been ready for a long fucking time.

16

Beau

"What the hell is going on here?" Brooks asks.

I ignore him for a minute, pulling Lexi to my side as I show her through the door and using my body to keep Brooks away from her. I know he won't hurt her, but I don't give a damn if he is her brother. Lexi is mine and I just made her come. Her pussy is wet with her climax and she's my woman. No one but me gets close to her—especially when she's like that.

"What are you doing here, Brooks? I thought you were overseas. Oh my God! Were you hurt? Are you okay?" Lexi asks, trying to push me to the side to get to her brother.

"I'm fine, little sister. I'm on medical leave for a bit," Brooks says to Lexi, but he's glaring at me. There are a lot of unspoken questions on his face.

"Medical leave? What the hell for?" I ask, knowing full well they don't just pass those out.

"That's not important right now, asshole. What's important is you tell me what the fuck you're doing in my sister's bedroom, half dressed?"

"Brooks, it's not what it looks like," Lexi interjects, trying to move between us. I smirk at her response. I can't help it. I move her behind me. The day I hide behind my woman is the day they need to just go ahead and chop off my balls.

"Really sis? Because it looks like Beau has had his dick in you!"

I hear Lexi's gasp and then her muttered, "I guess it kind of is what it looks like," and any other time I might find that funny—but not right now.

I punch him hard in the face for saying that crude shit to my woman. Sister or not, he needs to watch his mouth. Brooks is a big asshole, but I'm just as big and I'm pissed as hell. He falls back, hard. I hear Lexi cry out, but I keep my eye on Brooks.

"You will not disrespect my woman like that," I

growl, rubbing my fist because fuck, it hurts. I hit him that hard.

"Damn it, Beau. You didn't have to hit him," Lexi chastises me and pushes past me to move down the hall. I hear water running and look over my shoulder to see her wetting a cloth in the kitchen sink. She brings it to Brooks and he takes it from her, still staring at me. To prove I really am an asshole, I reach down and grab Lexi's hand and pull her away from Brooks. He might be her brother, but I don't want her touching another man right now and helping him.

I'm feeling as possessive as hell right now. My woman's hair is still messed up from being in bed. I know she's wet, and I know how her hands feel. Brooks is as safe as any bastard around her. He's her brother, for Christ's sake. I still don't want him near her.

"What is wrong with you?" Lexi growls, swatting at my arm and trying to go to her brother.

"You don't need to help him," I grumble, trying not to tell her the complete reason and sound like the asshole I am.

"Of course I do! You hit him!"

"He deserved it and you're mine. I hurt my hand, you can see to that," I grumble.

"You hurt your hand?" she asks, sounding shocked.

"Your brother's face is hard." I shrug.

"You want me to ignore my brother's bleeding lip,

just to doctor your hand because it's sore from hitting him?" Lexi asks and, put like that, it probably sounds as bad as it is, but I don't care.

"You're my girl. You're supposed to see to me," I mutter.

"Holy shit," Brooks mutters, standing up.

"Shut up," I growl at him, because I can see the understanding in his face.

"You love my sister."

"Brooks, we've just started dating and I really don't think it's your place—"

"Call it like it is, Sis. You've just started fucking."

"Asshole! I told you to keep your tone civil when it came to Lexi," I yell, and I'm getting ready to hit him again when he starts laughing.

"You're completely gone on her. You sad sack. When the hell did this happen?"

"I've loved her for years; you were just too busy demanding I stay away from her to realize it."

"Doesn't look like you've stayed away from her at all from where I'm standing," he replies.

"Because I'm not—not anymore, Brooks. You can get sad or get glad about it. I don't give a fuck, but I'm not letting Lexi go," I tell him, throwing it down. Lexi curls into my side, holding me close.

"Beau," she whispers, pressing a kiss to the side of my neck.

"Well, hell," Brooks says, looking at the two of us.

"I love her, Brooks. I'm going to marry her. I'm going to raise a family with her and I will kill myself every damn day to make sure she never wants for anything."

"Beau, honey. I think I'm the one you're supposed to tell that stuff too," Lexi says softly. I turn my head to look at her. She's smiling and there are tears in her eyes. She's never been more beautiful to me.

"I will tell you, but your brother needs to know this shit, Lexi. I'm not playing here. I'm keeping you, sweetheart. This time, I will not give you up. I want it all with you."

"Even babies," she whispers, proving she heard my speech to her brother.

"Definitely babies," I agree, closing my eyes when she kisses me.

"I can't wait to have your son, Beau."

"It might be a girl, you know—one as beautiful as her mother."

"Jesus. Will you stop getting wood over my sister? At least while I'm here."

I laugh when Lexi's face heats and reach down and adjust myself.

"It might be easier to tell the sun to stop shining, brother," I sigh, giving him the God's honest truth.

"I'm going to need some coffee if I have to handle this crap," Brooks complains.

"Grab a seat at the table and I'll fix us some," Lexi says, giving me a quick kiss on my lips.

"You all right, brother?" I ask Brooks when Lexi leaves and we walk to the table together.

"Fuck off. You always did hit like a girl," he mutters.

"It was strong enough to knock you on your ass," I remind him.

We sit down and stare at each other a moment. I don't see anger on his face anymore. Unless I'm wrong, I think he's good with this. If I knew he was going to take it this well, I never would have run from Lexi like I did.

"You and my kid sister," he says, shaking his head.

"I love her, Brooks. I know I'm not good enough for her, but I meant what I said. I'm going to bust my ass to make sure she never regrets loving me."

"How the hell did this happen?" he asks as the smell of coffee starts to permeate the room. I feel Lexi's arms go around me and loop lazily at my neck. Her breasts push against my head. Happiness fills me. My woman and my best friend and this time... I get to keep Lexi. This time I don't have to rip out my heart and send her away. This time, she is mine. I bring my hand up and lay it over hers, feeling for the first time in my life like everything is exactly the way it is supposed to be.

"That's easy, Brooks," Lexi says.

"Easy?" he asks.

"Definitely. We went camping together and I

impressed him with just how well I could pitch his tent."

"Jesus," Brooks growls, his fist hitting the table.

"I can't believe you just said that, Lexi," I laugh, looking up at her.

"What? Are you saying you don't like the way I handled your tent pole?"

"And I'm out of here," Brooks growls, getting up from the table.

"Wait! Where are you going?" Lexi asks Brooks, laughing.

"Away from here," he answers, opening the door.

"But, I was just about to tell you how much fun Beau and I had when we—"

"La-la-la-la! I can't hear you," Brooks grumbles, slamming the door behind him. Lexi starts laughing, and I stand up and pull her into my arms.

"I can't believe you just did that," I whisper, shaking my head. My hands travel down to her ass, holding her and pressing her against my hard cock.

"I wanted him gone," she confesses, her hands pushing at my pants.

"Why's that, baby girl?" I moan as she wraps her hand around my cock, squeezing it firmly in her hand.

"You told me you were giving me babies. I've decided I want them now."

"Is that a fact?"

"Definitely."

"I guess I better get started, then."

"I couldn't agree more," she says before I take her lips in a kiss.

It's a kiss full of love, of happiness and promise, and everything good. Because that's what Lexi is.

She's everything.

EPILOGUE

Lexi

One year later

I sit on the couch, my shirt pulled up, the bottle of lotion right beside me. I pump a few dollops into my palm and rub my hands together before smoothing lotion over my round belly. I've long since removed my wedding ring, my finger too swollen to have it comfortably on. But I can't help but smile at that fact. Since being with Beau, it seems like everything just fell into place. We dated, got to know each other on a level that wasn't because I was Brooks' little sister, or because we were friends.

And even though we haven't used protection since that night camping, I didn't get pregnant until now. I suppose things just have a way of working out.

We really got to know each other in the way that two people who love each other are supposed to.

He officially proposed a few months after that camping trip, surprising the hell out of me and making me cry big, fat, ugly tears.

I didn't even hesitate in saying yes.

We were married a couple months after that, the wedding intimate. It might have been done fast, but it was beautiful and perfect. It was exactly how I'd always envisioned it.

Beau is the only man I've ever wanted, the only one I've ever loved. After the confrontation with him and my brother, everything was settled. We made it clear that we would do what we wanted, because we were grown-ass adults and we cared about each other. That's all it really took, and Brooks was happy for us. Sure, it was strange for him at first, seeing his best friend and his sister together. But he got used to it, because he didn't have a choice. And when we were married, Brooks was Beau's best man. I loved seeing my brother standing at the altar behind my soon-to-be-husband.

And I love that I am carrying Beau's child. I look down at my belly and smile. I am eight months, huge as a house, but I've never felt prettier. Beau ensures that. Every day he tells me how beautiful I am, rubbing my belly, talking to our child ... little girl. Hell, when we found out the sex of the baby he said he's buying stock in guns and ammunition to ward off any "assholes" who come knocking to date his little girl.

I laughed so hard.

The sound of Beau pulling into the driveway has my heart beating faster. Even after a year of being together I still get the same reaction when he's near, when I know I'm going to see him. He's out of his truck and in the house before I can even get off the couch. But in my defense, at eight months pregnant it's pretty hard doing the latter.

"Baby?" he calls out. I'm sitting on the edge of the couch, staring at the living room entrance when he walks in.

"I'm here, stuck on the couch." I laugh softly.

He grins from ear to ear and is by me a second later, helping me up and pulling me in for an embrace. He leans back and instantly has his hand on my belly, rubbing small circles.

"How you feeling today, baby?" He cups my face with his hands and leans down to kiss me. He holds me close to him, making me feel like I'm the only person in the entire world that matters.

I am.

"Tired, but I'm good," I say, my hand on my lower back, the ache constant. But honestly, all the little twinges and pains that I feel during this pregnancy are worth it. I know the end result will be miraculous.

"Here, sit down and rest, put your feet up. I have something for you." He gets me in the position that he approves of and I can't help but chuckle. But he's gone before I can say anything. A few moments later he returns with a big bundle of roses. I know my face probably lights up. I can feel it.

I'm not surprised he brought me flowers, though, because that is the type of man Beau is. In fact, he gives me flowers seemingly every week. He is a good guy, will fight anyone who tries to hurt me, and I know, without a doubt, he will be an incredible father.

He sets the flowers on the coffee table and sits beside me on the couch. Then he wraps his arm around my shoulder and pulls me in close, kissing the top of my head. For long seconds we don't say anything, the quiet calming, the feeling of sitting next to my husband bringing me more joy than I can even put into words.

"Do you know how much I love you?" he finally says and I shift so I can look up at him. He's already looking at me, his blue eyes so bright, so full of love. "Do you know I would do anything for you?"

I smile and lift my hand to cup his scruff-covered

cheek. I smooth my thumb over his cheekbone, loving this man more every day. "Probably as much as I love you?" I raise an eyebrow and grin. He leans down and kisses the tip of my nose, his hand on my belly again. I tip my head back so our mouths meet, and for long moments we kiss, our tongues moving along each other, our breathing increasing. Just then the baby decides to kick something fierce. I gasp and Beau chuckles. We break apart and both look down at my belly.

"With moves like that she'll be a fighter."

I look up at him and smile. "She'll be able to kick guys' asses so you don't have to."

He sobers and shakes his head. "Hell no. Any little punks come asking her out they have to deal with me."

I close my eyes and rest my head on his shoulder, laughing. "Daddy's girl for sure."

"Damn right she will be."

God, this life is perfection, and it is so damn addicting.

Once long ago I saw Beau and knew in my heart that I wanted him to be mine and I wanted to be his... *forever.*

And now... we are. We are exactly that and I couldn't be happier.

The End.

Want to read more in the Hot-Bites series? **Check out Volume 2,** which contains the next 4 books in this super sexy collection!

ABOUT JORDAN MARIE

Want to read more by Jordan Marie? Find all her titles here:

https://www.jordanmarieromance.com

Newsletter: **http://bit.ly/2XJIXs3**

ABOUT JENIKA SNOW

Want to read more by Jenika Snow? Find all her titles here:

http://jenikasnow.com/bookshelf/

Find the author at:

Newsletter: http://bit.ly/2dkihXD

www.JenikaSnow.com
Jenika_Snow@yahoo.com

Printed in Great Britain
by Amazon

15287648R00271